OTTO PENZL
AMERICAN MYS

T0022223

THE PROBLEM OF
THE WIRE CAGE

JOHN DICKSON CARR (1906-1977) was one of the greatest writers of the American Golden Age mystery and the only American author to be included in England's legendary Detection Club during his lifetime. Though he was born and died in the United States, Carr began his writing career while living in England, where he remained for nearly twenty years. Under his own name and various pseudonyms, he wrote more than seventy novels and numerous short stories, and is best known today for his locked room mysteries.

RIAN JOHNSON is an American filmmaker who made his directorial debut with the neo-noir mystery film *Brick* (2005), then received recognition for writing and directing the science-fiction thriller *Looper* (2012), followed by writing and directing the blockbuster *Star Wars: The Last Jedi* (2017), which grossed over a billion dollars. He returned to the mystery genre with *Knives Out* (2019) and its sequel *Glass Onion* (2022), both of which earned him Academy Award nominations for Best Original Screenplay and Best Adapted Screenplay. Johnson was named one of the 100 most influential people in the world by *Time* magazine in 2023.

THE PROBLEM OF THE WIRE CAGE

JOHN DICKSON CARR

Introduction by
RIAN JOHNSON

AMERICAN MYSTERY CLASSICS

Penzler Publishers
New York

Published in 2024 by Penzler Publishers
58 Warren Street, New York, NY 10007
penzlerpublishers.com

Distributed by W. W. Norton

Cover image: Andy Ross
Cover design: Mauricio Diaz

Paperback ISBN 978-1-61316-487-7
Hardcover ISBN 978-1-61316-486-0
eBook ISBN 978-1-61316-488-4

Library of Congress Control Number: 2023918548

Printed in the United States of America

9 8 7 6 5 4 3 2 1

INTRODUCTION

You HOLD in your hands one of Otto Penzler's American Mystery Classics, a series that resurrects out-of-print gems in handsomely designed new editions. I owe this series a great debt because it introduced me to the work of one of my favorite mystery authors, John Dickson Carr.

Carr was an American but lived and worked in England during the 1930s. Outlandishly prolific, he quickly built a body of work that placed him in the pantheon of what is now known as the "golden age of detective fiction." This isn't the brute poetry of Hammett or the seedy sexual decay of Cain, no Spades or Marlowes or gumshoes packing gats. This is murder as a gentleman's game, the fair play of master puzzle-smiths, or to quote Anthony Shaffer quoting Philip Guedalla, "the normal recreation of noble minds." This is Agatha Christie, Dorothy L. Sayers, Ellery Queen, G.K. Chesterton. Carr is less well known today than those contemporaries, and that deserves to change, because he is one of the very best.

The first quality that blows your hair back in any of Carr's novels is so fundamental that it's easy to take it for granted: beyond the plotting or the puzzling, beyond the mystery itself, first and foremost the man is just hell of a writer. Like walking into a well-put-together room, when you're in the hands of a good writer you can just feel it. His prose is genteel without being fussy, brisk but rich, funny while keeping your feet in the dirt, and all of it woven with that effortless breeze of step that we as readers recognize and happily fall in behind. To quote Sayers, no slouch herself:

> Mr. Carr can lead us away from the small, artificial, brightly-lit stage of the ordinary detective plot into the menace of outer darkness. He can create atmosphere with an adjective, alarm with an allusion, or delight with a rollicking absurdity. In short, he can write.

That menace she mentions is palpable in Carr's work. Tonally his books lilt towards the Gothic horror of Poe, often turning from cozy warmth to chilling terror on a dime. Yes, you'll get the comforting burnished warmth of libraries and club chairs, but it's when the story blows the windows open and the candles out that Carr really shines. *Hag's Nook*, another of my favorites, centers on the events of a dark stormy night in a crumbling ancient prison. What could have been a hoary trope of a setting is in Carr's hands a sensual feast of rotting, rat-infested terror, so effective that, though we know the essential cozy moral compass of the genre will not be betrayed, at moments our sense of security slips away, leaving the thrill of "oh god what if this gets truly nasty?"

The Problem of the Wire Cage has a relatively genteel setting, an English estate with an adjoining tennis court. The clean lines and manicured safety of a gentleman's game. But it has images of unsettling power that have stuck in my mind as much as any Gothic dungeon. Carr begins it with a storm. Violent disruption. The electric smell of lightning in the air and loamy wild petrichor. With a few brush, strokes the blackened clouds frame pastoral green, the driving brutality of the rain and wind cuts the structured idyll, and we feel the invasion of something dangerous and primal, all the more effective for its contrast with the comforting.

In that way, Carr's similarity to Poe goes beyond style. Although the resolution will always solve the crime, turn on the lights and restore order, it's obvious that that is not where Carr's heart lies. In fact, to risk sacrilege here, though Carr is one of the premiere puzzle constructors of his age and his denouements are always surprising and satisfying, those final chapters are consistently my least favorite part of his books. The beating heart of any John Dickson Carr tale is the delicious terror of the unsolvable, the tactile details of the unexplainable and horrific, and the implication that the monster is just outside your window. All your careful structure and cozy comforts will not protect you from the darkness.

But let's talk about puzzles.

Carr is known as a master of a very particular subset of detective fiction, the "locked room mystery." In the most literal sense this is exactly what it sounds like: a corpse is found alone in a locked room, knife in his back, but he is alone and there are no ways in our out, bah dah dum. With such a constrained premise there are only a few real options to work with, usually some combination of ingenious contraption and manipulated timeline. It's the mystery version of a chess puzzle, with just enough pieces on the board and no more, a few predetermined moves at your disposal. If you can stand another metaphor, it's also the mystery equivalent of a margarita pizza—possibly the purest test of a pizza artisan's skill in that its simplicity leaves nothing to hide behind. The most famous of Carr's locked room mysteries is his masterpiece *The Hollow Man*, titled *The Three Coffins* in the United States, which features a little meta mini-lecture from the detective on the solving of locked room crimes. It's creepy and ingenious and delightful and, if you're new to Carr and enjoy what you read here, it should probably be your next book.

But even an author as ingenious as Carr could not work in rooms his whole life and most of his books open up the locked room concept to its (in my opinion) much more fun cousin, the "impossible crime." This brings us back to our present volume, *The Problem of the Wire Cage*. A man is dead, strangled in the center of a sandy tennis court after a rain, with just his own footprints leading to his final resting spot.

It's as clean and beautiful a set-up as you could ask for. Graphic and perfectly clear, it presents the impossible challenge to the reader in one single striking image. This might be why Anthony Shaffer begins his film adaptation of *Sleuth* with fictional mystery writer Andrew Wyke (modeled to some degree on Carr) narrating the denouement of his latest novel with this *exact same premise*. The film opens with Wyke (played by Laurence Olivier) standing in a hedge maze, listening to his dictation recording of this passage:

> "But since you appear to know so much, sir," continued the inspector humbly, "I wonder if you would explain how the murderer managed to leave the body of his victim in the middle of the tennis court and effect his escape without leaving any tracks behind him in the red dust. Frankly, sir, we in the Police Force are just plain baffled."

Sleuth is one of my favorite films. I can recite the rest of this scene verbatim and I put a reference to a case involving a tennis champ into my own film *Knives Out* as a tribute, so I was greatly relieved that Shaffer did not spoil the actual solution to *Wire Cage*. He does, however, take great pleasure in spoiling the idea that cozy detective fiction is the "normal recreation of noble minds."

The locked-room or impossible-crime mystery has its detractors. Some find the solutions by their very nature to be overly theatrical, fussy, and belabored. Very often the crime is impossible in a way that implies some supernatural element must have been involved and, for children of the 1970s, this can have the unfortunate effect of evoking two words every mystery writer dreads: "Scooby Doo."

I wouldn't go that far. But look. I do get it. I can appreciate the fun of an ingenious puzzle, especially when an artist of Carr's caliber is crafting it. But these types of set-ups have much in common with magic tricks and there will inevitably be something slightly anticlimactic and tawdry when the mechanism behind even (or especially) the *best* trick is revealed.

So why is Carr, the foremost practitioner of this method of mystery, one of my favorite authors? To put it simply: his best work never mistakes puzzles for story. And he's a damn good storyteller. His books may be known for their puzzles, but they're powered by the narrative engine and driving pace of a Hitchcock thriller.

The Problem of the Wire Cage is a fantastic example of this. I'll tread lightly here so as not to spoil any of the book's delights, but in the very first pages Carr yanks you right in with a love triangle, complimenting the rising rainstorm with jealous violence. Then, even more crucially, when the mystery of the body in the middle of the tennis court is revealed, Carr does not rely on the detective's investigation to hold the reader's attention. Instead, he takes the two characters we care about the most and snares them into a web of guilt and culpability. Suddenly we are not thinking out a puzzle but flipping pages on the edge of our seats to see how these two could possibly get out of it.

I sincerely hope by this point you've skipped ahead and just started reading the damned book but, for the patient ones still with me, I'd like to end with an appreciation of Dr. Gideon Fell. Carr created several detectives over his vast oeuvre, but the most famous are Sir Henry Merrivale and Dr. Gideon Fell. Fell features in this book, and he deserves to be ranked with Poirot and Holmes, Marple and Wolfe and Wimsey and whoever else you'd put in the pantheon.

A wheezingly massive man who walks with two canes, with an appetite for beer, cigars, and eccentric knowledge, by turns blustery and sly, blunt and humane, he can be a bull in a china shop one moment, then vanish into the shadows the next. Like all great golden age sleuths, you underestimate him at your peril. Carr modeled him on one of his own heroes, G.K. Chesterton, who authored (among many other things) the Father Brown mysteries. Besides the physical resemblance, Fell reflects Chesterton's earthy morality. Father Brown's skill as an amateur detective lies in a loving intimacy, not with the perfectly divine, but the painfully flawed and human. We read the same knowing compassion into Gideon Fell though, if I had to choose one of the two to go out for beers with, Fell would be much more fun.

Enjoy the book! If you're familiar with Carr's work, you're in for some fresh delights. If this is your introduction to the man, I hope it's the first of many, and that you spread the gospel far and wide. Thanks are owed to Otto Penzler for the opportunity to write this introduction, and for publishing the wonderful American Mystery Classics series. I'd highly recommend the previous Carr volumes, in which you will find illuminating introductions from authors and luminaries such as Charles Todd, Michael Dirda, Tom Mead, and Otto himself.

Rian Johnson
Paris
May 2023

I.

LOVE

She sat on a couch at one end of the long, dusky drawing-room. Beside her on the table had been set out a tea-service with tea now cold and biscuits almost untouched.

Hugh Rowland never forgot how she looked at that moment: the thick fair hair, darkish at the edges and bobbed below the ears; the light blue eyes, with a trick of looking up sideways and smiling; the fine lines of the body, which was just slender enough to escape being too well developed, for she was small. She wore a sleeveless white blouse, with white tennis shorts and tennis shoes; her bare legs were curled up under her on the chintz-covered couch. But she was not smiling now. Hugh Rowland felt her looking steadily at him, warning him.

Possibly because the day was sultry, emotions were growing sultry too. Long windows opened out on a garden that was all grass and trees. Despite the dimness of the drawing-room, there was a blaze of sun outside. The late afternoon light looked hot, bright, and yet overshadowed, as though it came through glass. No air stirred, no leaf moved, in that brilliant thickness of heat. Grass was too bright a green; the sudden flutter of a sparrow

I

across it was startling, as though in a dead garden; and down at the end, where the terrace sloped to the trees round the tennis court, each leaf had taken on a glitter against the darkening sky.

Hugh Rowland turned round from the window.

"Look here——" he began abruptly.

She knew what he was going to say. After that long silence, when they had come to the bitter end of talking trivialities, he was bound to say it.

"It's going to storm," said Brenda White quickly. She swung her legs out from under her and sat up straight. There was colour under her eyes, which had acquired a kind of a luminousness like the clear glow of her skin. "More tea?"

"No thanks."

"I'm afraid this is cold. I can ring for fresh, if you like."

"No, thanks. Why are you smiling?"

"I wasn't smiling. I was thinking how you looked. That professional air of yours, of the young solicitor girding himself up——"

Yes, he thought rather bitterly, the young solicitor. The young solicitor with eight hundred a year. The young solicitor who depended on crumbs from his father's legal table. The young solicitor whose only time off was a Saturday afternoon like this one, which he was wasting.

"In spite of my professional air," he said, "there is something we have got to talk about now."

He went over and stood in front of her. As she looked carefully past him, her light voice became clear, rapid, and hurried.

"Can you imagine what's keeping the others?" she demanded, looking at her wrist watch. "I told Frank five o'clock and it's twenty past five already. He was to pick up Kitty at her house and come straight on here. Listen to that! Thunder, wasn't it? If we don't hurry up we shan't even have time for a game, let alone a set."

Hugh did not remove his eyes.

"It's about Frank Dorrance," he said.

"That's the trouble with tennis," complained Brenda, shaking the watch beside her ear. "Whenever you've got time off to play, the other person never has, and—and vice versa. You know? So you never do play. Wouldn't it be wonderful, though, if Nick *can* invent that tennis robot he's been promising, the machine or dummy that will return your strokes so that you can play alone?"

"I don't know. Would it?"

"Yes. Those ordinary 'come-back' things are not much good, are they? I mean the ones with the ball attached to a long rubber string. You hit it, and———"

"I am a persistent swine," said Hugh grimly, and sat down beside her on the couch.

The springs of the couch creaked as he sat down. Despite the thick and thundery weather, he was wearing a tweed sports coat with a silk scarf round his neck. She moved away from him, slightly and with elaborate unconcern, but her arm still touched the sleeve of his coat. The sense of even that slight contact was so strong in him that it jumbled and made difficult what he was going to say.

Yet, even as the matter became vitally personal enough to cloud his judgment, a part of his mind remained awake and analytical. In these evasions she was not coquetting with him. There was no coquetry in her nature; she rather despised coquetry. She must know, too, that he was in love with her. Every gesture, every turn of her eyes, every slip of her speech showed that. But, even if she found the fact uninteresting or repulsive or merely comic, that was no reason for her attitude in this matter of Frank Dorrance; and he meant to understand it.

"I only want to ask you a question," he said. "It should be a very simple one for an engaged girl to answer. Are you going through with this and marry Frank Dorrance?"

"Of course."

"So! Are you in love with him?"

"What a question!"

"I'll go farther. Are you even fond of him?"

She did not answer, except by a slight movement of her shoulder. She was looking away from him, her hands on her knees, towards the blur of sun in the windows.

"To begin with," he went on doggedly, "there's no treason in what I'm going to tell you. Frank knows I hate his insides, and the fact affords him great amusement. I warned him I was going to tell you——"

"Hugh!"

"So it's all square and above-board. Then let us weigh up the pros and cons of this admirable match. Item, I suppose we must admit that Frank is an attractive fellow——"

"Terribly attractive," said Brenda.

That was a lie. A part of his business, was to judge of liars, and he suddenly knew that she felt nothing of the kind. The faint undertone in her voice escaped and was checked instantly; but he had heard it.

Hugh Rowland felt a vast sense of relief, almost a choking sense of relief. That was what had worried him. He had never been quite sure about Brenda. Probably nine out of ten girls would find Dorrance irresistible: in fact, Frank himself admitted as much, with that boyish and open charm of insolence which most people found so attractive. Frank always smiled no matter what he said, which enabled him to get away with saying almost anything. A happy personality, twenty-two-year-old Frank, with no nonsense about him.

Brenda was—what? Twenty-seven? Hugh Rowland supposed so, though he had never thought much about it; two or three years younger than himself, anyway. Twenty-seven. A Nice Girl, whom twenty-two-year-old Frank Dorrance very carefully kept in her place.

And that was what made him decide to attack.

"Then you're marrying him for the same reason he is marrying you: Noakes's money?"

"Perhaps."

"And perhaps not."

What she said was fired back so quickly that he wondered if she had been waiting for it. "Why do you say that?"

"Because I don't believe you."

Brenda began to speak, and then hesitated. "Please. It must be the weather that's got us both into this mood. But don't *you* begin idealizing me; you, of all people."

"It's not a question of idealizing you. So help me, it isn't! But forget that, if you like, and take the thing on its most practical basis. Why should I blame you for marrying for money? It's a perfectly sound reason why a woman should get married—that is, if she at least likes or is fond of the other person."

"Of course." Her head turned a little, and she spoke quickly. "Do you believe that?"

"Yes." And then he could not help being honest with himself. "No, I'm damned if I believe it. I have a quaint old-fashioned notion that there ought to be some decent sign of a grand passion. But never mind that, because it isn't reasonable. I will concede marriage for money as a perfectly sound and legitimate reason, provided you at least like the other person, in which case you can get on well enough. But that's the trouble. I'm beginning to think you don't give two hoots for Frank. In fact, you don't like him at all."

"That's not true! Go on, though."

"Well, you know the terms. If you accept that money on Noakes's terms, there can never be any question of a divorce or even a separate establishment. Be as practical as you like: but what chance do you think you've got for a happy marriage?"

"Almost none," Brenda admitted calmly. "But then I never expected to have a happy marriage, if there is any such thing."

She looked at him over her shoulder. There was no cynicism in her expression. She was simply stating, without affectation, what she believed to be a fact.

"It must be the heat," said Hugh, after a pause during which she returned his look unwaveringly. "Of all the—rubbish, do you hear? *Rubbish!* What's got into you?"

"In nine cases out of ten it might be rubbish. In mine it isn't. Besides, it would upset things terribly if I didn't marry Frank. Nick would be frightfully upset. Even Frank would be upset."

"I still don't understand," said Hugh, after another pause. "You don't get married just to keep the gang in good humour, do you?"

"I wonder."

She turned around to face him fully. She seemed to be fighting in her own mind, struggling to explain something to herself as well as to him. Her head was at about the height of his shoulder, and her expression was far away; but he had never been so conscious of her nearness.

"Yes, I wonder how many people have married just to keep the gang in good humour. But never mind that. You ought to know a few things, Hugh. I know you think I'm talking like a temperamental little fool. Or if you were like Nick"—her eyes wandered round Dr. Nicholas Young's drawing-room, from which Dr. Young himself was absent—"you would begin to talk about complexes and inhibitions and neuroses, and tell me to see a psychoanalyst. The funny thing is that it does amount to something like that by this time. I can't get it out of my system: I can't. Do you know anything about me or my background? Do you?"

"No."

Brenda nodded.

"Thanks," she said with a kind of pounce. "I mean, thanks for not saying, 'All I need to know,' or something just pleasant and meaningless. I hate this bogus gallantry: when it's out of place, anyhow. I've seen too much of it."

"You're talking like a bitter old hag of eighty-five; do you know that?"

"Oh, not out of my own experience! No fear! I've kept clear of that, thank you. I meant that I've seen it in practically every person I've known since I was six years old. So you don't know anything about me?"

The intensity of her expression was beginning to make him uneasy.

"Well, I know that your parents are dead, and that you're living here at Nick's house until the wedding bells ring out."

"My father shot himself in a New York hotel," said Brenda, "and my mother died on thirty shillings a week in a Bournemouth boarding-house. Please wait. That isn't important now, and I don't want you to think I'm making a high tragedy of it. It was their lives I was talking about. And all their friends were exactly like them. You know: Handsome Jack and Graceful Sally."

"Go on."

"Handsome Jack and Graceful Sally," repeated Brenda. "I was

dragged round the world before I was seven. The first thing I can remember is a lot of noise and lights in continental hotels, and faces sticky with paint making a fuss over me. I was either maudlinly pampered or completely ignored. I heard too much, and I thought too much, and I saw too much. What I dreaded most was lying awake in the dark, when they thought I was asleep, and listening to my father making excuses in the next room, and my mother screaming at him like a fishwife.

"Handsome Jack and Graceful Sally. Dozens and dozens of them, all like us. People with little incomes and big tastes, all thinking they had a right to the best things in life without a bean to back them up. People who had to go to the right social places at the right seasons, or die. Running into debt, making airy excuses, being very amused; but false and mean and hypocritical underneath, taking it out on each other when they were alone. All because they were 'charming' on the surface; ugh, how I hate that word! And then the men who were gallant to my mother—learning that 'Uncle' Joe, with the big moustache, was only there to make me a present of a Teddy bear; and wondering what they were saying in the next room, and trying to make sense of it, and only being confused and horribly frightened without knowing why."

Brenda paused.

She caught herself up, tightening her fingers round her knees and giving herself a shake as though determined to stop. When she spoke again it was in her usual cool and noncommittal voice.

"Sorry to go on like that. It *is* the heat, as you say. And if they will leave me alone with a person as easy to talk to as you are," she smiled, "you must expect to have it inflicted on you."

"Brenda, look here——"

"Please don't."

"You are going to get this off your chest. Go on. Let her rip."

"Yes," said Brenda, smiling again. "I've been playing the Jolly Good Pal, haven't I, with nothing much on my mind but tennis? Frank would be surprised. But there isn't anything to tell, really." She hesitated, and her mouth tightened. "There was only one thing that got under my skin so much that I couldn't forget it for years. That was because it went on and on, before I was old enough to understand.

"I called it my Dark Room dream; I told you about it. Only it wasn't a dream, or at least I was never quite sure. I would be half-awake and half-dozing, in that borderline state. I would be lying in my bedroom, with the door open on a lighted room beyond, and all of a sudden I would hear my parents talking. Their voices would wake me up. Night after night I would suddenly hear those thin little ghostly voices begin. Each time I knew it would be something new or terrifying to a child, but always on the same line. Its burden was always, 'What will become of us, what will become of us?' Its burden was always money, money, money, money, money, until I came to hate the very name of money."

Again she checked herself.

"Children hear enough as it is. I heard far too much. Sometimes even now—but never mind that. What's the moral in it, Hugh? You talk about love——"

"I hadn't," said Hugh, "though I was going to."

Colour came into her face.

"Hadn't you? I thought you had. Well, how much of what you call love do you think my parents felt for each other? Or any of the other Handsome Jacks and Graceful Sallys? Not by some of the transactions *I* saw. But even suppose they had been in love? They ended hating each other, and dying in self-pity. And why? Because of money, money, money, money, which I despise like poison but which I daren't disregard. I'm marrying Frank Dorrance for the same reason he is marrying me: to get old Mr. Noakes's money, and be for ever out of danger. Now you know. Do you blame me?"

She slid off the couch, and walked with quick little steps to one of the windows, where she stood looking out into the fiery garden. A faint noise of thunder stirred to the east, over the heights that swept down to Hampstead Heath. She seemed to want to brush away the subject. But she could not let it alone; she kept nagging at herself and it.

"Well? Aren't you going to say anything? Do you blame me?"

"No. But I still think you're being foolish."

"Why?"

Hugh examined his hands, clenching and unclenching the fingers.

"It's like preparing a brief, and trying to get just the right words," he said. "If your parents were as you describe them, money was essential to them. But it isn't essential to you. And you know it."

"Really?"

"Yes. In fact, the question of money hasn't anything to do with it. You've got some sort of mental kink or obsession by which you've somehow convinced yourself that you've got to marry Frank, and I wish I knew why. Don't you realize that if you marry Frank Dorrance you'll only be marrying another 'Handsome Jack'?"

"Perhaps."

"In other words, you'll be letting yourself in for the sort of thing you hate most."

"Perhaps."

"Then why in the name of reason are you doing it? You can't do it, Brenda. By God, it's not good enough!"

He got up from the couch, bumping against the table so that the tea-service rattled. She was still standing with her back to him in the window, with the sun on her hair and on her clear-glowing skin. They were coming nearer to it, approaching the inevitable with every step.

Yet, even as his elbow bumped against the table, it occurred to him to wonder why Dr. Nicholas Young had not come in to tea, and why they had been left alone together at a dangerous time. At any moment he expected to see Old Nick come hobbling in, and to hear Nick's only half-joking torrents of abuse at him for trying to upset the matrimonial apple-cart. A true thing, since Frank Dorrance was the apple of Nick's eye. Old Nick liked to have young people about him; he took pride in a house infested with casual visitors and more food on the table than anybody could possibly eat; but you did as he wished or he had a peculiar cruelty reserved for you. Hurry, was the thought in Hugh Rowland's mind; hurry, hurry, he'd got to hurry . . .

"It's all arranged—" Brenda began.

"Yes, I know. And Kitty Bancroft will be matron of honour, and Nick will dance the saraband, and Noakes's ghost will bless you, and even I will be an usher."

"Well, what would you suggest that I do about it?"

"You could marry me, for instance," said Hugh.

They had stumbled over it like a hurdle. And Hugh waited, the silk scarf feeling tight and hot round his neck.

"I'm not going to make the usual poor man's complaint," he said. "We should at least have quite enough to live on, if that worries you. And I've been in love with you for four months and eighteen days. I suppose you knew that?"

"Yes, I knew it," said Brenda, without turning round.

"If the jury would like to retire to consider its verdict," said Hugh, while the silk scarf grew hotter, "court can be adjourned until then. If, however, there is any possibility of a verdict being returned without leaving the box——"

"Thanks, Hugh. But I can't do it,"

"Well, that's that." In the emotional aftermath, he found himself suddenly angry and as though he had sustained a physical bruise. He had asked for it, he told himself; he had walked up and asked for it, and now he ought to be satisfied when he got the whack. But he could not accept it. "It's just as well to know where we stand. Shall I tell you the truth? What worried me was whether in your heart of hearts you weren't in love with Frank after all——"

"Oh, Hugh, don't be such a fool!"

"Am I being a fool? I suppose so. But is it Frank? I was only—er—suggesting an alternative for your approval, in case——"

The width of the room separated them. She turned round, and he saw that her face was flushed. She walked quickly towards him, to get out of the sunlight.

"You are being the most awful fool imaginable," she told him in a low and rapid voice. She stared at the floor; but he felt the anger round her.

How it happened he was never afterwards sure. In one moment she was standing two or three feet away, with the sunlight silhouetting the edges of her hair and the baffled, insistent set of her shoulders. He saw the expression of her eyes, but he also saw the stubbornness there. A few seconds later (without any apparent interval of time or movement) he was kissing her. Her body was warm; her lips were cool, but violent and responsive.

Again her head was at about the height of his shoulder. And it was perhaps a minute later that he glanced up over it, and saw Frank Dorrance standing in one of the windows, looking at them.

II.

HATE

UNDER ONE arm Frank carried a racket in its press; in his other hand he swung a small network bag of tennis-balls.

"Bit warm for that sort of thing, isn't it, old boy?" he inquired—and whooped with laughter.

Frank Dorrance was young-looking even for his twenty-two years. His fair hair curled closely to his head; he had one of those high-coloured, delicate-featured faces which contrive to be handsome without being effeminate. He was of medium height, slight, and immaculate; his blue-and-white silk scarf was knotted round his neck and thrust into the opening of a brown sports coat; even his white flannels were of an arrogant fashionableness. About him was the polish and gleam of the precocious young man: the absolute assurance of manner, the tendency to speak out exactly what was in his mind, the mannerisms of one twice his age. He had one particular look, a sort of bored and amused scepticism, which roused the ire of many men.

But he was whooping with laughter now. He went over, tumbled into a chair, and regarded them frankly.

"You find," Hugh managed to say, "you find something funny?"

"Yes. I do, rather."

"What?"

"You, old boy," said Frank critically. "Making such an ass of yourself with old Brenda. I say, you did look silly."

He was, in fact, the only unruffled person present, swinging the net of tennis-balls over his hand, and swinging it back again idly. His clear, high voice carried his amusement to the garden and seemed to carry it to the world.

"Oh, *I* don't mind," he added coolly. "Only—don't let it happen too often, old boy, or I should be compelled to take offence. And you wouldn't like that."

"Many thanks."

"That's supposed to be sarcasm, isn't it, old boy? Only I'm afraid it never goes down with me. And you mustn't try to come the heavy lawyer over me. You see, you've put yourself at a great disadvantage with me, and I mean to use it. Besides, you were carrying on rather, weren't you?"

And he whooped with laughter again.

Hugh Rowland tried to be casual. You must keep your head with this clever young man, or you put yourself at even more of a disadvantage and he had you.

"We'd better have this out. I've just been asking Brenda——"

"To marry you. Yes, I know."

"You were listening?"

"Stuff! Why heat about the bush?" asked Frank, unperturbed. "Of course I was taking in what I could. But, you see, you can't have her."

"Why not?"

"Because *I* want her," said Frank agreeably.

"That seems to you to be a good enough reason, does it?"

"Well, ask old Brenda herself. You popped the question (and between ourselves, Rowland, a jolly rotten pop it was). What did she say?"

"I said no," interposed Brenda, and went across to sit down on the arm of Frank's chair.

Inside Hugh Rowland crept a small sickish feeling which gradually spread until he wondered whether he could face this out.

"I see," he said. "Right!"—But the emotional temperature of the room went up several degrees.

"Sorry, Hugh," murmured Brenda, smiling.

He could make nothing of her expression, nor of anything else. There was still colour under her eyes, but little sign of disturbance or embarrassment, and certainly no further interest in him. It was as though nothing had happened. Probably nothing had.

"Hold on," he said, so abruptly that Brenda jumped. "I know I ought to say, 'Right,' and let it go at that. But I'm not going to do it. You can't chop off a person's arm and then go on your way rejoicing without any explanation. We've got to have this out."

"I'm afraid I can't discuss it any further, you know," said Frank.

"I'm afraid you've got to."

"Look here, old boy." Frank assumed an air of reasonableness. "You've already made ever such an ass of yourself over this, and you'll only make it worse if you go on. *I* don't hold any malice, though some fellows would. But if you're thinking of trying to take Brenda away from me, that would be plain silly."

"Would it?"

"Yes. In the first place, Brenda is rather gone on me. (Aren't you, old girl?) In the second place, even if she weren't, it's a plain matter of business."

"Oh, definitely," murmured Brenda.

"Yes. And I hope you don't think I mean to let anything get in the way of that. As I say, I don't hold any malice, old boy; but don't push it too far and compel me to take offence. I can make myself ever so unpleasant when I take offence."

For a time Hugh studied him curiously. A sharp, angry ache had got into his chest; it did not grow, but it would not be still; and yet it was better than the sickish feeling of not knowing where he stood.

"You agree with that, Brenda?" he asked.

"I agree with that, Hugh."

"Then that's all right," declared Frank, not unkindly. He grew brisk and affable again. "So, while we all know where we stand, let's go down to the court and get in a set before the storm comes on. Brenda and I will play you and . . . Here, I say! I was forgetting! Kitty." Sitting up straight, he craned round towards the windows. "It's all right, Kitty. You can come in now."

"Oh, really?" cried Brenda, and jumped up from the arm of the chair.

To Hugh it seemed that half the neighbourhood must have been outside those windows. But he minded Kitty Bancroft less than most, for he liked Kitty. Someone had once said that you were always aware of Kitty as a sort of pleasant dark shadow in the background. She was a widow in her early thirties; a lively, bustling, sympathetic sort whose manners contrasted with her rather sombre Spanish looks. She, was a little too tall, and had little pretension to beauty except a good figure and a pair of fine dark eyes, restless and expressive; but her attractiveness grew in your acquaintance with her. In addition to the tennis costume, her sweater and eye-shade gave her a Wimbledon air which was not misleading, for she was a first-rate player.

Kitty almost plunged in through the window. In her evident desire to make things smooth and easy for everybody, she over-did it.

"Hello, everybody," said Kitty, flashing white teeth. "Frank, you young imp, you went away without that book after all. I expressly put it out on my hall table for you, and you forgot it. Hello, Brenda. Hello, Hugh. Having a good time?"

Frank guffawed again.

"He's a young villain," observed Kitty, covering what she might have felt by looking indulgently at Frank. "Don't pay any attention to him. I'd just bought that book myself, and he begged it off me, and then went away and forgot it. Did you ever? What glorious tennis weather, anyway! Ready to give us a trouncing, Hugh?"

Frank's mirth grew more delighted. Hugh went over to get his racket from the table. Removing the racket from its press, he hammered the heel of his hand against it until the hum and twang of the strings sang in the room.

"Tell me one thing," Hugh said abruptly, and turned to Frank. "Do you always get your own way, whatever you happen to want?"

Frank grinned.

"I do, rather. Nearly always."

"As a matter of academic interest, would you mind telling me how you do it?"

"I use my natural charm, old boy. Why should I deny that I have natural charm? I have, and there it is. But I'll tell you. When I was a kid, I tried my natural charm. If that failed, I used to lie on the floor and kick and yell until I got what I wanted. I could usually hold out longer than the other person, so I usually got it. Now that I'm of more mature years, the technique is a little different; more subtle, you know; but the principle's the same, really."

"I see. Didn't you ever get walloped?"

"Oh, yes. But that only made me worse, so they gave it up— Don't you like the idea?"

"The idea," said Hugh, "makes me sick."

"Stuff! Why pretend?" grinned Frank. "The fact is, you're not clever enough to manage it. You're one of those people who like a quiet life. You would do nearly anything to avoid trouble and embarrassment. Now, I love trouble and embarrassment; I thrive on 'em. So I can still hold out longer than anybody else, and I still get my own way. Simple, isn't? As Nick would say—" His eyes narrowed. "By the way, where is Nick? Why didn't he come down to tea?"

It was Brenda who spoke.

"He couldn't, Frank. A police-officer came to see him, and they're still in Nick's study."

A puff of warmer wind shook the foliage in the garden, making it rustle, and crept in round their ankles. If Hugh had been less preoccupied, he would have noticed the slight raising of Frank's eyebrows.

"A police-officer, old girl?" he repeated. "Oh! About Nick's motor-smash, I suppose?"

"I don't think so."

"Why don't you think so, old girl?"

"Because I saw his card when Maria took it in," answered Brenda. "He's a Superintendent of the Criminal Investigation Department."

Kitty Bancroft opened her eyes. "Do you mean it, Brenda?

How thrilling! You mean from Scotland Yard? You know, I never really thought that place existed outside books. Having a real detective under your own roof! Why, it's like entertaining Father Christmas or Hitler or somebody. Are you sure?"

"I only know what I saw."

"But what does he want?" Kitty laughed a little. "I mean, he isn't after anybody, is he?"

"Stuff! Who would he be after?" inquired Frank coolly. "You must have a guilty conscience, my girl. It's probably something about income tax or some such rot. Anyway, Nick can deal with him; Nick will toss him out of the house if he doesn't behave. If you like, we'll come back and have a look at him when he goes, but just now I want some tennis and I mean to have it. Are you all coming along before it starts to rain?"

"Oh, I hope it rains!" cried Brenda, with such abrupt savagery that they all looked at her. "I hope it rains and rains and rains!"

And, just as abruptly, she ran out into the garden.

Hugh followed her, leaving Frank to bring Kitty. But he did not catch up with her until she had reached the tennis court. From the house along the garden to the edge of the terrace was about a hundred yards in a straight line. Here a dozen steps in crazy-paving led down the terrace to flat ground below, and to the court enclosed in trees and hedges.

It was Old Nick's idea. Old Nick, ingenious as usual, had tried to plan a tennis court which should be protected from having the sun in the players' eyes at any time of the day. It was a hard court, surrounded by high wire netting. But some dozen feet outside the netting, beyond smooth grass walks, lines of dwarf poplar trees had been planted so close together that they made an oblong round the oblong of the court. Even the dwarf poplars were twenty feet high, catching the sun in their pointed tops. And outside everything ran a thick yew hedge taller than a man, with a wicket-gate, making another enclosure within an enclosure.

Entering first through the gate in the hedge, and then through the opening in the wall of poplars, was like entering a secret garden shut away from the world. The middle of the court baked in fierce heat, its white lines glimmering against the brown. But all its edges were dim with long shadows. It was cooler here, despite the midges and the thick stagnant smell of greenery.

Brenda was there. Hugh found her leaning one hand against the wire round the court, and breathing hard.

"I needed that run," she said, giving him a quick look. "This weather is frightful— You're furious with me, aren't you?"

So it was beginning again.

"Oh, Lord, Brenda, haven't we had all that out?"

"But you ran after me down here. Why did you run after me?"

"I don't know. Because I'm fated to, I suppose. But I'm not going to run any farther: is that clear?"

Round the court was a smooth, clipped border of grass a dozen feet wide. And towards the east, near a wire door in the netting, stood a tiny shed or pavilion painted bright red and green according to Old Nick's artistic taste. It was small enough to fit into the border between the tennis court and the wall of poplars; but it was equipped with glass windows, lockers and benches inside, and even a miniature porch. He kept his eyes on it.

"Why did you run after me?" persisted Brenda.

"Do you want me to tell you all over again? I've had my answer already, thanks. All the same, I'd like to know what's got into all of us today. We're none of us quite in our right minds: if we're not careful, there'll be murder done before the day's over——"

"I know."

"*You* know?"

He had tried to speak lightly, but Brenda made no pretence of doing so.

"Yes, I know," she insisted. "Anyway, that's not what I wanted to tell you. You think you understand, but you don't understand at all. I mean, it's about—about the other thing."

Danger again.

She was looking at the ground, scuffing the toe of her white tennis shoe in the grass. "I meant what I did, Hugh. I meant what I *did,* no matter what I said, do you see? Only there are reasons why I've got to marry Frank and please everybody. I wasn't going to tell you what the reasons were, and I certainly couldn't tell you when there was anybody else about, but I can't help it: I'm going to tell you now. Hugh, the reason——"

"Well, well, well, well!" interrupted a light, far-carrying amused voice, bursting through the opening in the poplars.

"Brenda and I against you and Kitty," pursued Frank, and spun his racket into the air. "What'll you have, rough or smooth? Rough. You lose, old boy. We'll take the south side. You can serve first, if you like."

And again he chortled with laughter.

"Come along, partner!" said Kitty Bancroft cheerfully.

When Hugh dropped his coat on the steps of the little red-and-green shed, and pushed through the wire door into the court, he was in a state of mind that startled and disquieted him. It is a mistake to play any competitive game in this state of mind; but he did not think of that now.

Ahead of him the court stretched large and blank and dusty, a cage with a white net inviting bad shots. Frank opened the bag of tennis-balls, which promptly rolled all over the court, and the sweat stung Hugh's eyes as he retrieved them. There were midges in the shady corners of the court, which stung still more.

If possible, he was not going to let Frank Dorrance win a point that afternoon.

It had become a kind of symbol. And it occurred to him, as he toed the base line to serve, that there were other symbols as well. He saw the persons on the other side of the net through a slight haze: Brenda's white blouse and white shorts, Frank's creamlike flannels and pleasant smile. Frank was the perfect machine-player. You could not make him run. No matter where you put a shot, he was already there in front of it. He could not or did not hit hard, but every shot was placed, with unhurried machine-like regularity, exactly where he wanted it. To Hugh—whose only virtue was speed—it seemed that Frank walked about the tennis court as he walked through life. As the thick air darkened towards storm, and the sun died behind the poplars, Kitty Bancroft took up her position at the net.

"*Ready?*"

"Serve."

Hugh tossed the ball high.

He felt the power of the shot through his arm and shoulder as his body came over. Curving, the ball whistled across the net, stung white dust from the corner of the line—and was back at him before he had time to move a foot. Frank, a formless white blob, returned an effortless cross-court shot which sent him diving, his heels sliding on gritty sand. But he had time to set himself. He drove, hard and low, deep to the base line. Frank was again in front of it, again keeping the ball out of Kitty's reach on his return. Again Hugh drove, the *thung* of the racket whacking out in that enclosed space, and whitewash flakes flew from the corner of the base line. Frank walked over and inspected the result. His clear, pleasant voice rose up.

"Sorry, old boy. Just out."

Brenda was staring at him.

"But, Frank——"

"Just out," said Frank. "Bad luck, old boy. Love-fifteen."

III.

INDULGENCE

As THAT set of definitely mixed doubles began, Dr. Nicholas Young sat in his study with Superintendent Hadley of the Criminal Investigation Department.

The study was on the first floor at the back of the house, a long low room with two windows overlooking the garden, and two more overlooking the shaded drive that led down to the garage. It was cooler here, for an electric fan hummed on one of the long low bookcases. On Dr. Young's desk stood a small clock whose hands indicated ten minutes to six, with a calendar attachment set at the date of Saturday, August 10th.

Superintendent Hadley, who was tall and heavy and looked like a Guards colonel, had not finished the good cigar he had been offered.

He said: "May I speak frankly, Dr. Young?"

"That means it's a kick in the eye," grumbled the gentle man known as Nick. "All right, all right, all right! Get on with it."

"I've now delivered the message Sir Herbert sent. I'm tempted to add something on my own. Would you believe evidence, if you heard it, that this paragon of yours, this Mr. Frank Dorrance, is little more than an infernal young blackguard?"

Nick's under-lip came out. "That's taking a bit on yourself, isn't it?"

"I know. But you certainly don't seem impressed by anything I've already told you."

Nick grew fretful.

"Well, what do you expect me to do?" he demanded querulously. "Lecture the boy? All right; I don't mind. But what else can I do? You can't tell me he's done anything actionable."

At the moment Nick neither looked nor felt his best. Since his sight was defective in one eye—one of the lenses of his spectacles was frosted, which gave a sinister and misleading cast to his face—he should not have tried to drive a sports car as fast as Frank Dorrance. Only a week ago he had managed to squash a new Daimler as flat as an opera-hat against a tree in Highgate village, breaking such necessities as his right arm, his right collar-bone, and his left leg. This afternoon, propped up like an unwieldy idol in his desk chair, he seemed all splints and bandages.

A great dandy was Old Nick, still impressive, if a trifle short and squat. His broad face, with the bullfrog jowls pushed down into the collar, showed defiance. Inactivity maddened him. He could not dance. He could not ride or play tennis. He could not even strike a match or mix a drink. His grim determination never to grow old might have seemed rather ghoulish, if his incessant activity had not been mental as well as physical.

At a time when psychoanalysis had been almost unknown in England, he had taken it up as a profession and made a fortune out of it. Now he was active even when cracked up; devising cross-word puzzles, inventing games that were too complicated for anybody to play, and outlining all the best medical ways of murdering people. With the aid of a crutch under his good shoulder, or in a wheel chair, he managed to get about fairly well. But it would be over a month before the bones mended; and in the meantime the cocoon of bandages merely hurt and itched and made him fretful.

So he took a firm line.

"See here," he said. "Don't think I'm not grateful——"

"There is no question of gratitude about it," said the tall and hard-jawed man on the other side of the desk. "That was my message for you. I'm sorry if I have wasted your time."

"Wait, wait, wait! Let's get this straight. Frank has been seen about with a shady bottle-party crowd who'll get into trouble as sure as guns. And because Sir Herbert Armstrong is a friend of mine, he sends a full-fledged superintendent to warn me about it. All right. That's a mark of respect; and I appreciate it. But as for Frank getting into trouble—pfaa!"

Hadley looked at him curiously.

"I suppose you know everything he does?"

"Just between ourselves, I don't care two hoots *what* he does, so long as he behaves himself in public. I'll tell you something. That boy's got character."

"Evidently."

"That—boy's—got—character," repeated Nick, sitting back to survey his guest, and nodding impressively at every word.

"I wasn't doubting it, Doctor."

"Guts," said Nick. "Plenty of it. Takes after me. And I'll tell you something else. Just a month and three days from today, he is marrying one of the finest girls you'll ever meet: Bob White's daughter. And when they marry, they jointly inherit a cool fifty thousand pounds.

"A cool fifty thousand," repeated Nick, stressing the temperature popularly attributed to banknotes. "With any sort of luck, their first child will be born within a year. That child will be named Nicholas Young Dorrance. He will be educated at good preparatory and public schools, and then go to Sandhurst or Dartmouth; I don't care which; but Army or Navy it's to be. Definitely. Old Jerry Noakes had the bringing-up of Frank; and I won't say, mind you, that there aren't things in Frank's character I'd have made different; but this boy will be the one *I* bring up. And no mistake."

Hadley was curt.

"I have no doubt," he said, "that the child will be a credit both to you and to his prospective father. By the way, what relation is young Dorrance to you?"

"Frank? No relation at all."

"But you keep on saying he takes after you."

"So he does. I don't want to bore you with the details," said Nick, glowing with a dream of grandfatherhood, "but it goes back a good many years. There were three of us at college—blood-brothers: you know? Bob White, Jerry Noakes, and myself."

"Well, sir?"

"Well, Bob White was the only one of us who had any children, and also the only one who didn't get on in the world. He married one of the Bedfordshire Stantons, a girl I was rather sweet on myself once, and they had one daughter: Brenda. We all made a lot of her. But old Bob was such a damned liar that we never knew how he stood: he lied and bragged for years about how well he was getting on, and we thought he was a little Rockefeller. He was mostly abroad, you see.

"I had got on pretty well, if I do say it myself. And Jerry Noakes was doing uncommonly well in the City. He adopted a nephew of his: Frank. Mind, I'll say this for Jerry; he did everything for that boy, and didn't do such a bad job of it. But I helped a good deal. Well, the next thing we heard—out of a clear sky—was that Bob White had shot himself after going the pace in New York, and the wife and kid were supposed to be in Bournemouth. I traced 'em there. I felt pretty sick, I can tell you. Nelly was too full of gin to last much longer, and she didn't. I took the girl, of course.

"It was too late to do much about forming her character, worse luck. This was only five years ago. I found she hadn't had much formal schooling. I put her for nearly four years at the best school in England, which irked her like the devil because she was older than the other girls; but what could I do? Then I brought her here to live. Nothing improper to that," said Nick with a somewhat self-conscious chuckle, though it had not occurred to Hadley to see anything improper in it. "Meantime, Jerry Noakes and I were laying plans. He took to Brenda as much as I did. He was going to get Brenda and Frank married.

"I hope he's drinking beer in Valhalla," added Nick fervently, "for he did it. He caught flu during this business last November—you remember?—and when his fever was up he altered his will. He was leaving Frank and Brenda his money anyway, but now he left it to 'em on condition that they got married. The lawyer said he was loony in the head to make a will like that, but I stuck by Jerry. I have a simple sentimental soul," said Nick, with the light on the one frosted lens of his spectacles, "and I liked the idea. He was a lonely old man, that was *his* trouble. He pegged out two days before Christmas. He wanted to put in a clause that the first child should be named after him, but I washed that out. No fear! Hah!"

In the pause after this energetic speech, the humming of the electric fan rose loudly. Throughout the room, throughout the house, throughout the grounds was the deathly quiet which precedes storm. It was so still that Hadley even imagined he could hear faint voices from the direction of the tennis court. The sky had grown darker. Nick was sweating under his muffle of bandages, though their irritation had half gone.

The pause was broken by a sharp noise as Hadley struck a match.

"That's very interesting, Dr. Young," he said, and lit his dead cigar. "Excuse me: I've got reasons why I'd like to ask you a question about it."

"Question? What question?"

"What do the young people think about this arrangement? Do they think it's all right?"

"All right?" repeated Nick, bridling instantly. "Of course they think it's all right. They're in love with each other: or as much in love as they need be. What exactly do you mean?"

"Nothing at all. I was only asking."

"You had a funny kind of look on your face," persisted Nick, turning a sinister spectacle-lens. "What are you getting at? Do you know anything to the contrary?" He reflected. "There's a young fellow called Rowland. Hugh Rowland. He's been making calf's eyes at Brenda, unless I'm much mistaken. I don't anticipate any trouble there. By God, though, if I thought——"

"There's no need to get excited, Dr. Young. Rowland? Rowland, Rowland. Hold on: is that the son of the solicitor? Rowland and Gardesleeve?"

"Yes, he is," said Nick suspiciously. "What about it?"

Hadley's tone was dry. "Well, sir, it's no business of mine, but if you're up against him in the way of business, I shouldn't take things too much for granted. He's a very clever young man."

Nick made an incredulous noise like compressed air coming out of a tube.

"*Young* Rowland? Clever? Bosh! Clever!"

"Well, he's beaten us, whatever that amounts to," said Hadley. "You probably remember Mrs. Jewell, the poisoner. I still think she was a poisoner, in spite of the verdict. We had a practical certainty of a case against her, but she was acquitted. That was due to the efforts of Rowlands senior and junior—principally junior."

"Nonsense!" said Nick. "I know the case. Gordon-Bates got her off."

"Yes: it's customary to give all the credit to the barrister. But don't. The barrister only goes by his brief. Your young friend prepared this brief; and even the pathologist took a licking. However! What happens if either Miss White or Mr. Dorrance refuses to marry according to this agreement?"

Nick sat back. There was an almost senile note in his voice.

"See here," he said. "What do you mean by coming here and worrying me like this? What do you mean by sitting in my chair, and smoking my cigars, and playing the heavy policeman as though you'd got a pair of handcuffs up your sleeve? What business is it of yours, anyway? Clever! Why, Frank can argue rings round that boy! Frank can make him look foolish; and does it, too. We had a debate up here only the other night: on crime, it was: and Frank made him look foolish. Of course Brenda and Frank are going to marry. If they don't, every penny of Jerry's money goes to charity. They wouldn't let that happen, you can bet!"

"I don't imagine they would. What happens, Dr. Young, if young Dorrance should die before the marriage?"

There was a silence.

Outside the windows, the thick dark air stirred with faint

lightning. There was no thunder except a faint vibration as though the air itself were being shaken; but a warm breeze began to thrash the curtains at the windows. Even at that distance they clearly heard the thud of tennis rackets.

Nick suddenly chuckled. He was himself again.

"Oh, I don't think that's very likely. Frank's a pretty healthy specimen, you know. If either of 'em dies, the survivor inherits the lot. But I think Lloyd's would give you pretty long odds on Frank's continued health."

"*I* wouldn't," said Hadley.

Again the electric fan hummed loudly.

"Come on: cards on the table," snapped Nick. "You've been beating about the bush with something for the past ten minutes. What is it?"

"It's this. Did you ever hear of a girl called Madge Sturgess?"

Nick whooped with relief.

"Oh, Lord, is *that* all? By the look of you I thought you were going to say he'd robbed the Bank of England and murdered the watchman. So he's got tied up with a girl called Madge Sturgess, has he? What is it? Breach of promise?"

"No."

"Then that's all right," said Nick, still more relieved.

"Just a moment, Dr. Young. You've told me a little story, now let me tell you one. Listen to the facts in the case of Madge Sturgess. About two months ago, your young paragon Mr. Dorrance met Madge Sturgess at the Orpheum Music-Hall——"

"A pick-up," said Nick.

"You could call it that, yes. At this time she had a job as a clerk at a dress shop, or whatever they call it, in Kensington. She went out with Dorrance five or six times, and fell for him. But that's only incidental. To keep her end up, she used to sneak evening gowns, and once a fur, out of the shop; and return them before anybody got wise to it. Unfortunately, she was found out. Dorrance managed to tip half a bottle of claret down the front of a white satin evening thing that cost fifteen guineas. The stain wouldn't come out, and she had to own up. There was a flaming row, with the shop, but they were decent about it. They said she could keep her job if she paid for the dress."

Superintendent Hadley was noncommittal. He did not raise his voice; he did not move in the chair; but the expression of his eye brought out on his host as clammy a feeling as the heat and bandages.

"The girl was half-crazy. She couldn't stump up anything like that; not on two quid a week. So she went to young Dorrance. I think he has a flat in the West End. Yes. Well, he said he was sorry. He said it was no concern of his. He said that if she was fool enough to try to swank it by using dresses that weren't hers, she must expect what she got. He said that in his opinion she was only trying to gold-dig him for a new gown."

Nick shifted in his chair.

"That boy's got character," he insisted, with a snap of, discomfort. "Anyway, she should have come to me."

"Oh, he was very level-headed, no doubt. But I was telling you. Madge Sturgess didn't get another job. She put her head in the gas-oven last night."

"Whew!" muttered Nick. He was now sharp, alert, and serious. "I see. An inquest. That's really bad. You mean there'll be an inquest at which Frank's name may be——"

"No. She didn't die. By quick work on the part of her landlady and the hospital, she's getting over it. That's how I happen to know these details: D Division sent in a report this morning."

Hadley got up. He dropped his still-dead cigar in the ashtray, dusted the knees of his trousers, and picked up his bowler hat from the desk. The heat of the room, now in a semi-darkness of blowing curtains, was making his own head swim. Above a flapping and thrashing of trees in the garden, the electric fan sang like a wasp.

"That's all I wanted to tell you, Dr. Young," he concluded politely. "It's no business of mine or of the police. There'll be no inquest; and we're not so hard up for cases that we want to prosecute poor devils like that for attempted suicide. You needn't worry. As you say, Mr. Dorrance has done nothing actionable; and, also as you say, he's not likely to. That young gentleman is far, far too clever. But what do you think of it, between ourselves?"

Nick shifted again, flapping his good arm.

"I don't mean," Hadley went on, "that he's in any danger of dying. But it's only fair to warn you: he is likely to get a hiding that will keep him in bed for a month."

"It's unfortunate," Nick fretted. "Of course I agree with you: it's unfortunate. By the way, leave me the girl's address and I'll send her round a little cheque. We must also see if we can't find a job for her. But, after all, you know, Frank was quite right. It might just as well have been a racket that——"

Hadley studied him.

"You still wouldn't like to take that young gentleman aside and instil the fear of the Lord into him?" Hadley suggested with powerful restraint. He added hopefully: "You wouldn't like *me* to do it, for instance?"

Nick chuckled.

"I doubt if you could, Superintendent. That boy doesn't take easily to bullying. He's got the gift of repartee, Frank has."

"So!"

"Now, now, you just trust me!" urged the host, soothing and persuasive. "It's all right. I'll make it up to her. Nobody ever appealed to Old Nick in vain. Must you go?" He picked up a large handbell from the table, and made it clatter in a way that jangled every nerve in Hadley's teeth. "Maria! Maria! Damn that woman; she's never about when you want her, and the other servants are out. Do you mind letting yourself out? Thanks. Good-bye, Mr. Hadley. Give my regards to Sir Herbert, and thank him for the tip; but tell him I think Frank can manage his own affairs. Er—there wasn't anything else, was there?"

Hadley contemplated his hat.

"Only the warning I wanted to give you," he answered. "It seems that Madge Sturgess has a boy-friend."

The bell gave a violent clang and stopped.

"Boy-friend?"

"Yes. She didn't dare go to him for the money she needed, because she didn't dare admit she'd been out with another man. This fellow had no idea of what was going on until he read about her attempted suicide in this morning's paper. I wonder if Mr. Dorrance saw that item, by the way?"

Nick was almost screaming at him. "Never mind what Frank saw. What are you getting at? Who is this man?"

"His name is Chandler. He's a music-hall artist; gives a very unusual and spectacular show, which you ought to see." Hadley paused. "He streaked round to D Division for details. And got them. The divisional inspector says Chandler isn't in any state of mind to be met safely on a dark night. He passed on the warning, which I pass on to you. If you should happen to want us, the number is Whitehall 1212. Good afternoon, Dr. Young. Good afternoon."

What Nick might have said in reply was lost under the

ear-splitting assault of the thunder. Nerves and heat had been strung to too high a pitch on the earth. A balance tilted; a decision was made. Hadley was just getting into his car outside the house, and the hands of Nick's clock stood at a quarter past six, when the sky burst across and the storm tore down.

It was all nonsense.

For several minutes after the first deluge struck the house, Dr. Nicholas Young sat motionless. It was almost dark in the study; the clock went unheard, but, under that uproar, the electric fan kept up a small spiteful core of noise.

If anybody had asked him, Nick would have replied that he was not disturbed. But his vivid mind ran on. After some minutes he awoke to the fact that the rain was sluicing down on the carpet, soaking the curtains, and stinging his face from many feet away. His crutch lay against his chair. Propping himself up, he swung across the room in awkward jerks like a mechanical toy, fell against each window in turn, and stood on one leg while he closed them. The storm roared at him. It blinded him and lifted his hair: a darkness through which only its own movement could be seen or heard or felt.

For the preceding half-hour he had been able to hear, even at that distance, the faint pick-pock noise of tennis rackets. It was always there, always in the background, as a reminder that the young people were enjoying themselves. His west windows looked out over the garden and toward the tree-enclosed tennis court, though nobody could see the court itself from any position. And now he could not even see the trees, except when a lift of lightning showed sodden foliage. Towards the left of the garden, a banked driveway lined with tall trees sloped down to the garage, which was on the same level as the tennis court. Between the garage and the tennis court, a gravel path went on still further to a gate in the rear wall round the grounds. By that gate you went out to Kitty Bancroft's trim little house not far away; and beyond it, dim and tumultuous under the rain, fell the slopes of Hampstead Heath.

Nick shut the last window.

He switched off the electric fan, blundered across to a couch by the bookshelves, switched on a bridge lamp over it, and managed to lie down amid twitches of pain that turned him dizzy. But he would not acknowledge pain: he cursed any one who came near or tried to help him.

Though it was long past time for his after-tea nap, he knew that he could not sleep. Beside the couch ran the "crime" bookshelves, a storehouse of murder filling one side of the study, and dominated by the tall blue volumes of the Notable British Trials Series. He looked at the latest addition to the set, *The Trial of Mrs. Jewell.* That was the case in which Hugh Rowland had prepared, or was said to have prepared, the defence.

Under the close light of the bridge lamp, Dr. Young's face showed rough-skinned and pitted. The one frosted lens of his spectacles gleamed; the other eye, sharp and dark, moved angrily. He turned down the corners of his mouth, flattening the broad jowl; his nose twitched as though he were going to sneeze; and he sneered at the book. After studying it for a moment, he reached out and took it off the shelf. He began to read.

Until nearly seven o'clock the rain roared steadily, preventing sleep. Dr. Young read just as steadily, the book propped up at a distance on his stomach, and his head up at a neck-breaking angle. He sneered much; he admired little. By ten minutes to seven the rain slackened, and at seven it ceased. Dr. Young crawled up to open the windows and admit fresh, healing air. Before seven-thirty he was sleeping peacefully, *The Trial of Mrs. Jewell* open across his chest.

The next thing he knew, someone was screaming, and he kept hearing endless repetitions of the same word.

Then, shatteringly, distinct words.

"For God's sake, sir, get up. Miss Brenda says——"

He opened his eyes.

The face of Maria, the maid, was bending over him as close as a vampire come to take his blood. He knew a second of pure superstitious terror; he kicked out by instinct, as though to kick away fancies; then pain burnt him through his broken limbs, and shocked him awake.

"It's Mr. Frank, sir. He's lying in the middle of the tennis court."

Then, gabbing on, words still more wild.

"I can't hardly believe it, sir, but I seen him there. He's been strangled with that silk scarf of his, and Miss Brenda says he's dead."

IV.

CRAFT

At a quarter past six o'clock—just before the later-celebrated thunderstorm began—the mixed doubles composed of Brenda White and Frank Dorrance v. Kitty Bancroft and Hugh Rowland were finding it almost impossible to continue.

In the first place, it had grown too dark to see the ball. Hugh found it suddenly appearing under his nose from nowhere, a startling shape; it was never quite there when you swiped at it. But he had given up any idea of playing good tennis. All he wanted to do was slam it, and slam it hard, whenever it came within reach.

With the score at five-two in favour of Brenda and Frank, Frank was nagging for match-point. They had changed sides of the net after the fourth game; Hugh and Kitty were now on the south side, with their backs to the gate-opening in the wall of poplars. A convulsion of wind shook the poplars; it swept the court, loosening Kitty's eye-shade and stinging their faces with dust. The next flash of lightning, followed by a shock of thunder striking close, showed even the net tugging at its moorings. Brenda, a ghost on the other side of the net, cried out.

39

"Frank, let's give it up! Come on. Please!"

"Nonsense, old girl."

"Frank, please! I don't care—I'm afraid of thunder. Let's run for the house; or the shed, anyway. Won't you?"

"I certainly think—" began Kitty uncertainly.

"Nonsense, old girl. The thunder can't hurt you. It's the lightning that does the damage. But we're all right. Come on! We only want one game to win, and we've got fifteen of that. It's your service to Kitty. Come on! Be a sport!"

This was the certain way to appeal to Brenda. As lightning winked again over the tops of poplars, Hugh saw her set herself, and Frank dancing close to the net. Her service was sharp to Kitty's backhand; Kitty returned a cross-court drive which Brenda dropped at Hugh's feet; and Hugh, who only wished the whole thing were over, stepped back and smashed blindly. Darkness drowned sight and thunder blotted out sound, so that he could not tell what happened; but Frank's triumphant voice rose up.

"Got you that time! Thirty-love!" Then the voice went higher. "But I wouldn't try that sort of thing too often if I were you, Rowland."

"Try what?"

"Driving straight at my face from ten feet away."

"I can't see your face. Sorry."

"You didn't do it on purpose, of course. No, of course not. Go on, Brenda; pick up the ball and stop jittering. I rather thought Rowland would lose his temper. Two more points and we've got 'em."

As a matter of fact, Hugh had lost his temper completely. He knew this himself, but he still tried to be casual as he left his position and walked up to the net.

"Like every other time today," he said, "you're right. For the past half-hour I have been considering the advisability of plugging you in the eye. Now I think I'll do it. Frankly, I would like to kill you."

The other was not impressed.

"No, you don't, old boy. You're three inches taller and nearly three stone heavier than I am. I don't funk it at anything like my own weight, and you know it perfectly well. Furthermore, I'm not at all afraid of you. But mixing it with you would be plain foolish; and I don't do foolish things."

Studying that indomitable figure across the net, the high-coloured face looking waxy and the eyes glistening under the lightning, Hugh had a change of feeling. He could not help it. In the midst of everything he detested, there was something he could not help admiring. Some of the anger washed out of him, to be replaced by a bitter honesty. He realized that the main reason why he found Frank insufferable was merely because Frank was eight or nine years younger than himself, and sure of himself in a way that few people beyond the twenties can be. Yet inside all that, inside Frank, there was a hard core, a kind of viciousness, which might in time put Frank in a class by himself.

Yes, he thought, it might really be a good thing if Frank were to die.

"I should simply, and rightly, refuse," Frank was explaining. "And you can't hit a man who won't hit back, can you? You'd look an awful cad if you did."

From the background Brenda spoke. Her tone was curious.

"*He* can't," she said. "But suppose you met somebody who could?"

"Then I'd take care of him in another way," Frank told her coolly. In the windy darkness he turned to Hugh, and spoke in a friendly, kindly way. "Look here, old chap. Twice today you've made an awful ass of yourself, which is remarkable for a fellow who's supposed to be so hot at his job as Brenda says you are. I think myself you were only swinging the lead to impress Brenda, because you certainly didn't seem so hot in the discussion we had the other night. However, let's have no more of this, shall we? Get back to your place and let's finish this set before the rain comes."

There are limits to human patience. What might have happened just then—instead of happening a little later—it would be impossible to decide, for at that moment the storm broke.

"Pick up the balls, somebody!" yelled Frank, taking Brenda's arm and hurrying with her. "Get 'em, Rowland, will you? They're mostly on your side of the net. Come *on!*"

The first drops hissed in the dust of the court. Then they thickened and swept it black. Round the edge of the court, inside the wire netting, ran a foot-wide strip of humped grass; most of the balls had rolled up on it and nestled away under corners of the wire, where they were difficult to find. Hugh was half soaked by the time he raced after the others to the miniature pavilion.

They were gathered together under the overhang of the miniature porch, which gave no protection at all. Brenda was trying to open the door, but the door appeared to be stuck.

"Give me a hand with this, won't you?" she urged, raising her voice above the uproar. "I don't think it's locked, but it won't open. Ugh! That was a bad one." She looked up at the sky. "If you people aren't interested in getting inside, I am."

"You certainly don't like thunderstorms, do you, old girl?" said Frank, who was leisurely putting on his coat and scarf.

"I don't, and I may as well admit it."

With difficulty Frank continued to fold the scarf. It was of thick, voluminous silk, dark blue and white in colour, and it flapped like a flag in the wind. He folded it over twice longways, slipped it round his neck, and knotted it over.

"The door's only warped," said Kitty. "Frank and I looked in here on our way to the house. Here, let me try." She put a sinewy bare shoulder to the door, and it screeched under the pressure. "There; that's got it. Phew! It's stuffy enough in here!"

It was. The hammering of rain on the roof was like a physical pressure against the brain, for the pavilion was little more than an oversized children's playhouse. The unstained walls had turned brown. An oil lantern hung from a nail in the roof, very convenient for running your face into; there were wooden lockers along one wall, and two short benches cramped into the middle. Many childhood memories returned in that musty atmosphere, and from the intimacy of being crowded close together in a confined space.

"Come in and shut the door," said Brenda. "That's better, but it's not over yet by a long chalk. Ugh!"

Kitty's voice spoke on a note of faint surprise. "I say, Frank. That's odd. Somebody's been in here since we were here last."

"In here? Nonsense. Who'd be in here?"

"I don't know, but somebody has. Look here: on the bench where Brenda's sitting. Somebody's been here and left a newspaper. Strike a match."

Frank complied. The match-flame, which looked large in that little space, showed a copy of that morning's *Daily Floodlight,* a tabloid of the sensational variety.

"It certainly wasn't here three quarters of an hour ago," said Kitty, who loved worrying about such small points. "Frank will tell you that. Do you think there are tramps or thieves about?"

Nothing interested Brenda less at the moment. Hugh saw

with sudden concern that her face was white and waxy; at inter-vals, as though fascinated, she would glance towards the light-ning-whitened windows, and glance back again. But she was evidently determined not to give in to what she felt. She half laughed.

"Thieves? I shouldn't think so," she answered, showing a sort of desperate interest in the new topic. "There's nothing to steal. I've got a spare pair of tennis shoes and a few odds and ends in one of the lockers, that's all. And then there's that, of course. But it wouldn't interest a thief."

She nodded towards a battered object in one corner, which they saw just before the match went out. It was a picnic hamper in leather, a once-expensive affair like a very large and very heavy suitcase; now neglected and beginning to be spotted with mould. Frank kicked at it, and it gave out a rattle of china. Kitty uttered a cry of dismay.

"Brenda, you ought to be ashamed of yourself! That love-ly hamper, and all the wonderful china inside. And those ther-mos-flasks! It's been here since that picnic of ours last year, and it's *rotting* to pieces. Why don't you take it up to the house?"

"I will, I will, I will," said Brenda. "Today. Maria's been after me about that china, too. I solemnly promise,"—her voice was going up—"to take it to the house today. There! Will that satisfy you?"

Kitty's tone changed.

"Sorry to be such a nuisance, Brenda. But it is a worrying thing about that newspaper, isn't it? How could it have got here? Strike another match, Frank." She read the headline aloud idly. "PRETTY SHOP-GIRL GASSED IN FLAT. Why do they print such things, I wonder?"

"Because people like 'em, old girl," said Frank coolly. "That is, if they put a bit of ginger into it. You know the sort of rot. Every typist or shop-girl is pretty, every bedsitting-room is a flat——"

"But she is pretty," argued Kitty. "Look at the picture here. 'Madge Sturgess.' Don't you think so, Frank?"

Frank glanced at the picture before the match went out. "Not bad. Silly little fool, though. She didn't die. Attempting suicide is a felony—I looked that up—and now she'll be in trouble with the police, and serve her right."

Without knowing why, Hugh Roland felt that a new turn had come into the conversation. There had been an edge in Frank's voice, a kind of subdued triumph. Hugh had shut the door. In spite of themselves, they were all closed into this musty little shed and crowded into intimacy. Frank had sat down on the bench beside Brenda, and even in the gloom Hugh could see that he had put his arm round her. Hugh and Kitty sat down on the bench facing them. Even under the uproar of the storm they had no difficulty in hearing each other speak; they were so close that they could hear each other breathe.

"You looked it up?" asked Kitty out of the dark. "Why should you do that?"

"Oh, I'm interested in things," said Frank promptly. "Murders and suicides and whatnot. Murder is more interesting anyway." (Hugh had a feeling that even in the dark his eyes were gleaming with amusement.) "I say, here's a game for a rainy afternoon! We'll put it up to everybody in turn, including our criminological expert——"

"Our criminological expert?" inquired Kitty.

"Rowland. Didn't you know?"

Hugh was conscious of Kitty as an apologetic weight close beside him, flashing white teeth. "I'm afraid I didn't."

"Oh, yes. Ask Brenda. Though he's always been very modest

in front of me, and I won't say it was because he didn't want to get the raspberry. However, here's the problem. No rotting, now. Suppose you actually *were* going to commit a murder—how would you do it?"

He held up one finger.

"Wait! Stop a bit. This is to be the real thing and no rot. I mean, it's for home consumption and not one of these mathematical 'perfect crime' things. I asked Nick the same question once. He got all excited and worked out something that may have been an absolutely wizard scheme: all about a perfect alibi: only it was so complicated that no murderer would ever be able to remember half of what he was supposed to do. When I told him so, he got very shirty and said I had no artistic sense. Well, so I haven't. This isn't to be some eyewash out of books. This is to be real. And practical. You're really going to murder somebody— how do you do it? You first, Rowland."

"Do you honestly want to know that?" said Hugh.

Frank appeared to grin. "I don't give a hang, old boy," he admitted with candour. "Nothing interests me less, really. Only it's one way of passing a rainy afternoon, and I'd rather like to hear how you'd deal with it."

(He had now only a comparatively short time to live.)

"I suppose it's morbid to talk about it," put in Kitty, with a sort of hesitant relish and in a low voice which added a greater feeling of intimacy to the proceedings. "But it *is* interesting, isn't it?"

"Very," said Hugh.

"I should use carbon monoxide gas," Kitty went on, as though musing. "You know: the gas in a motor-exhaust. You get the victim drunk, and shut him up in the garage with the motor running, and the gas from the exhaust does it like winking. It's pain-less, and not messy, and seems more sporting, somehow."

"I say, Kitty," observed Frank. "How did your husband die? The late lamented Mr. Bancroft, I mean?"

The ensuing pause could not be called a silence, due to the din of rain on the roof. But it came close to that. Frank continued with his usual engaging charm and candour:

"I mean, we don't really know anything about you, do we? We know you came here, and keep a house round the corner, and keep wire-haired terriers, and make yourself pleasant to every-body, and seem to be well off. But that's all. You never speak of your late governor, or anything else. How did he die?"

"He died in the way I've been describing," answered Kitty. "As a matter of fact, I was accused of having killed him. But they never proved anything. When I heard a little while ago that there was a Scotland Yard detective here, I was secretly horribly worried for fear they'd found new evidence after three years."

The utter and appalled shock caused by those words seemed to be felt most of all by Frank himself.

They heard his tweed coat rustle on the bench. But, when lightning lit the inside of the shed with fiery intensity, they were all looking at Kitty. She had drawn her sweater across her shoulders, and was pushing back her hair; the slim, hard neck was arched, head up, and she was staring hard at what had been darkness.

Then, delightedly, she burst out laughing.

"You know, you *are* young," Kitty said. "That's how you show it— For a second I think you almost believed me."

Frank sat up.

"You mean it's not——?"

"Of course it's not true, you young imp. My husband was a

very worthy Canadian, twice my age, who died of flu in Winnipeg. I've never said much about him because he was rather a rough diamond who wouldn't have interested you, though I was very fond of him. But I couldn't resist puncturing you."

"Dash it all, I'm not so sure! There was something in the way you looked—just for a second——"

Again Kitty laughed.

"Well, if you must read secrets into my dark past," she said, "that will do to start with. And if you really think I'm a murderess, you must be very careful about walking home with me. Though I'm going to insist you do that, you young villain, and you know why. But you don't think I'm a murderess, do you?"

"No; but you oughtn't to talk like that, old girl."

"Frank, you're worried about something."

"Rot!"

"Yes, you are," said Kitty very quietly. "You've been worried about something ever since we came in here and started this nice eerie chat. What is it? Come on: tell Aunt Kitty."

"Stop talking such utter bilge!"

Kitty was still quiet. "If you won't, you won't. Anyhow, this is interesting: about the murders, I mean. You've been very quiet up to now, Brenda. You haven't said a word. What's your contribution to the game? How would you commit a murder, if you'd made up your mind to do it?"

"Oh, I've got it all worked out," said Brenda. "I know the perfect method."

V.

MURDER

With the four of them in that confined space, the thick air had grown difficult to breathe. Also, the roof was beginning to leak; pressed in by dampness, Hugh felt a raindrop strike the back of his neck, and heard another hit the leather of the picnic-hamper beside him.

"Well, well, well!" said Frank, withdrawing his arm from round Brenda's waist. He tried to achieve a satiric note. "So the little lady knows all about it, does she?"

"Yes. Kitty will remember. Nick told us."

"*Nick* told you? I hadn't heard anything about it."

"You must remember," said Brenda without moving, "that you don't live here, Frank. You have your flat in town. So you aren't here all the time. It was the other night. There was Kitty and myself and two or three others, and the very same subject came up."

"What about it?"

"Nick told us what was, medically speaking, the smoothest and easiest way of committing murder without a slip-up. He

49

said most people wouldn't think of it, because they wouldn't believe it was so easy. Remember, Kitty?"

"Yes."

"It's not fair," said Frank, "if you didn't think of it yourself. Anyway, what is this triple-dyed foolproof method?"

Kitty's mood seemed to change. "That would be telling," she laughed. "We don't want too many people knowing about it, do we, Brenda? No, seriously: this talk has gone far enough. I am beginning to get all sorts of queer and guilty feelings inside. Have you seen any good shows recently? They say *Pandora* is awfully good."

"My God, these women!" said Frank. A yelp of irritation escaped him; pure temper made him half get up from the bench. "I ask you, Rowland: I appeal to you: did you ever hear anything like it? You start a topic of conversation. You do your best to amuse 'em. Then they take it right out of your hands, and first go all serious on you, and then shut up like oysters. Rotten bad form, that's what I'd call it. I ask you, man to man: what do you think?"

Hugh had been staring out of one window. He could hear the ticking of Brenda's wrist watch.

"I think you'd better drop it," he said.

"So you side with them, do you? Why?"

"I'll give you some advice," said Hugh. "Murder's an interesting subject, if you keep it to the theoretical like Dr. Young. Leave it there. Stick to your perfect alibis, and your ingenious ways of bamboozling the police, and your problems and puzzles on paper. But don't ask for advice about practical ways of killing people."

"No? Why?"

"Because you've never seen anybody who has died of violence," said Hugh. "I have."

The ticking of the wrist watch sounded inordinately loud.

"It's something about the expression of their eyes. Or their open mouths. Anyway, it's the ugliest sight in the world, and you dream about it. Keep off."

"This place is unbearably stuffy," said Kitty. "A little rain won't hurt us. Can't you open that door, Hugh?"

He dragged it open.

The subject was killed, as dead as the images that had floated in front of Hugh Rowland's eyes. For a long time they sat silent, looking out into a solid downpour that was turning the tennis court to mud-mire and breaking the back of the sodden net. It whipped the door-step and stung up into their eyes; round Hugh at least it stirred cold and healing. He relaxed, listening drowsily. After an aeon in space the noise began to diminish. At seven o'clock, incredibly, there was a great silence in the world.

Frank, waking up, was the first to run out into it.

"That's over!" said Frank, in a startlingly clear voice. "I feel a whole lot better. Millions better. I say, the court's in pretty rotten shape, though, isn't it?"

(At this time he had less than twenty minutes to live.)

"Hardest rain in ten years, I'll bet," said Frank. "And now a bath, and a Martini, and dinner. Sorry you can't stay to dinner, Rowland. It'd be inconvenient anyway. Brenda and Maria are getting the dinner; the other servants are out. But you won't be too long about it, will you, old girl? I could eat a horse."

"No. I won't be too long about it."

"Well, *I* must run," Kitty informed them, flashing a smile on them all. "I dine early and I've got a temperamental cook.

Thanks for a *grand* game of tennis, everybody. We'll get our own back soon, Hugh. Frank, you're walking over home with me, aren't you?"

Frank hesitated.

"Cigarette case," insisted Kitty, holding up her racket. "And that book, which I'm not going to allow you to forget."

"All right. Yes, I suppose I'd better." All four were walking towards the gate, and Frank considered. "But—over there and back in less than five minutes, Brenda. So no funny business while I'm gone, old girl. Good-bye, Rowland. I don't think we'll be seeing each other again."

Hugh stopped short.

They had gone through the opening in the line of poplars, and then through the gate in the hedge. At their left was the terrace, with the crazy-paving steps. Ahead of them, beyond and beside the terrace, was the driveway leading down to the garage; and by it the little gravel path leading to the rear wall of the grounds, by which Frank would take Kitty home. Frank had also stopped in the wet grass.

"You don't think—?" Hugh began.

"Well, you could hardly expect anything else after what happened here today, could you?" asked Frank coolly. But for the first time Hugh noticed that his eyes were shining curiously. "If you think I've forgotten anything, you're very much mistaken. And after what I have to tell Nick about it, I hardly think your presence will be very welcome hereabouts in the future."

"I see."

"'You see,'" mimicked Frank.

"So you've been saving all this up, have you?"

"That's neither here nor there, old boy. You needn't think you can try to draw me like that. But there is one thing I should rather like to tell you before you go. Don't think you have roused any great interest in Brenda. Don't flatter yourself. Brenda's mother was no better than she should have been, as Brenda herself will tell you; and since she's beginning to follow——"

He stopped, for Hugh was laughing.

Hugh could not help himself. Whether the storm had cleared the air, or what dull cloud had lifted off his wits, he did not know. But, for the first time in the five or six months he had known Frank, the spell was lifted. He suddenly saw Frank for what Frank was. And he saw that Frank was not worth bothering about. So he stood in the wet grass and roared with laughter.

"Oh, hop it," Hugh said. "Get out. You've done your last bit of damage, my lad. Coming this way, Brenda?"

And he strolled up the drive, with Brenda's arm through his. It was a long drive, but he was still chuckling when they reached the top of it, and Brenda was shaking his arm.

"Stop it!" she urged, rather anxiously. "What did you mean by saying that?"

"Just what I said. Due to being in love with you, and over-ir-ritated with him, I have been sub-normal. The young snipe had me under a kind of mental and spiritual hypnosis. That has gone. I rather like him now."

"Hugh, listen to me. Where is your car?"

"Out front. Over there somewhere. These infernal hedges——"

"I want you to do something for me. I want you to leave now: now, do you hear? You can come back a little later, if you like, but you must go now." She hesitated. "I—I want to tell Frank and Nick that the White-Dorrance marriage is off."

"*Wow!*" said Hugh, swinging round towards her. "And the White-Rowland nuptials?"

"That's on," said Brenda rather lamely, and looked at the ground. "That is, if you still want it to be."

"If I still want it to be? My dear, the subject is too vast and comprehensive to be commented on at once. As a matter of fact, I had just decided to force you into it. Kidnap you, if necessary. If I want it to be!—And you're right about telling Cousin Frank and Uncle Nick. I'll go and tell them at once."

"No," said Brenda very quietly.

Her tone checked him.

"I'm going into the house now," she went on, raising her eyes. "If you won't promise anything else, promise that you'll go away now. I'm not going to tell them now. I'm going to wait until after dinner, because I want to think. Unless I get everything I want to say all arranged and in order, they'll argue me round."

"If there's any chance of that———"

"There isn't. Only it's more complicated than you think."

"I know, blast it. I'm asking you to give up———"

She almost laughed. They had come out into the street, the dim tree-lined road known as The Arbor, where his (very) old Morris two-seater waited half in the ditch. The sky was still dark except for a strip of silver to the west, between the houses; and she looked up and laughed at him in the dusk.

"You're not asking me to give up anything, Hugh. Only it's not all black and white. Frank really does like me, in his way. And Nick keeps me in cotton wool because I'm supposed to be Nelly White all over again and because I'm to be the mother of Nicholas Young Dorrance, who (in case you didn't know it) is to go to Sandhurst. Do come back. I'll need your support rather badly. Besides, you may have to take me away with you, if Nick is on his high horse."

"Good. Come back when?"

"Nine-thirty?"

"Nine-thirty it is." He stopped on the step of the car, and his throat hurt him. "Look here, Brenda. You're sure you know what you want? You're sure you're doing the right thing for yourself?"

"You can kiss me here in the street, if you like," said Brenda.

Then she was gone.

Hugh, in a soaked driving-seat, was not in a mood to observe trifles. He had driven twenty yards along a soaked road before he realized that the offside front tire was flat.

He got out and inspected the damage caused by a nail with a head as big as sixpence. After staring at it for a long time, his mind full of plans about Brenda, he realized that he had better do something about the tire. So he bumped out the tool-kit and set about exchanging the front wheel for the spare on the back of the car. It was a job which his thoughts made longer: they moved to each click of the jack or fierce twist of the spanner. By the time he had finished the dashboard-clock showed that it was nearly twenty-five minutes past seven. And he remembered that his tool-kit contained no pump.

He glanced back along the street. There was a pump in Dr. Young's garage. He could remember seeing it, hung on brackets to the wall.

It would be no violation of the agreement if he went back after that pump.

After all, they would all be indoors. It was true that Frank—in returning from Kitty's—would have to pass the garage and come up by way of the drive or the terrace steps. But Frank would have returned long ago. Perhaps, subconsciously, he half-hoped to meet Frank. Now that he held no animus against Frank, now that he regarded Frank almost as a good fellow, he wondered what Frank really looked like. It is certain that the pump was beginning to assume an importance out of all relation to its value.

He went back after the pump.

The sky had lightened. All things swam in that clear, watery, after-storm glow which is as kindly as the air. As Hugh Rowland went down the drive, he was genuinely happy. He realized, almost with a start, that he now had everything he wanted in this life. It was amazing. It was incredible.

Life had picked up again; clocks resumed their ticking, and there were no more wasp stings in Frank Dorrance. As for the future, a future with Brenda was something to dream about. If she wanted money, she should have it. He would work his heart out to——

Hugh stopped.

With his hand almost on the garage doors, he glanced to the right. He saw that the gate in the hedge round the tennis court enclosure, which he remembered closing, was now wide open. He went to investigate; and so he determined, by his first free act of will, the fate of a person who was carried, fighting and hysterical, to the execution shed on a morning three months later.

It was darkish inside the enclosure of poplars, and thick with the smell of wet foliage. As you entered, the narrow side of the tennis court was towards you. He studied it inside its tall cage of wire: a brownish-grey rectangle, smooth as mud except for a few humps where rain-water pools glittered faintly. The net, looking half-squashed, was a muddy white. At the other side of the net, far away from him, he thought he saw something like old clothes lying in the middle of the court.

But something else moved.

A figure in white, with bare arms and bare legs under shorts, jumped out through the wire door. This also was some distance away from him, on the side towards the pavilion. The figure seemed to be staggering under a weight. It deposited on the ground something like a suitcase, which rattled. Then it turned round to close the wire door.

Hugh began to run.

He found Brenda standing between the wire door and the pavilion; bent forward a little, her hand pressed to her side. Her bobbed hair hung forward, and there was a smear of mud down her cheek. Beside her was the decayed leather picnic-hamper, over which she stumbled.

"Hugh!" she said.

He caught her shoulders; his own hands were grease-stained.

"Hugh," she said, "I'm in awful trouble."

Frank Dorrance had been strangled to death. His face was swollen blue and there was froth on his lips, for the silk scarf had been knotted so tightly as to be embedded in the flesh of the neck.

But this was not at first apparent. Hugh could see only one eye: which told him the fact of death, because it was like the eye of a fish on a slab. Frank lay on his back not far from the middle of the court, his head towards the net. His legs were tangled, and one shoulder was partly hunched. By the muddy state of his white flannels, his coat, even his face and hair, he had rolled (or been rolled), in the attack that finished him.

That was all. He was dead: just dead.

"I didn't mean to do it," said Brenda. "Oh, God, I didn't mean to do it."

"Steady."

"This is the end of me, Hugh."

"No. Take it easy, now."

He looked at the scene coldly and clearly, assessing it as evidence. The surface of the court, with much clay in its composition, took clear footprints. Beginning at the little wire door, one set of footprints—Frank's—went straight out to the place where he lay. Beside them were two other sets—Brenda's—going out and returning. In all that brownish-grey expanse of court there was no other footprint.

Brenda had walked out there with Frank. But only one of them had come back.

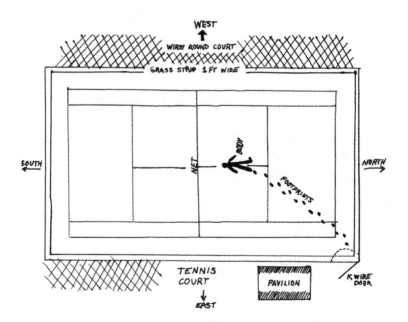

VI.

INCREDULITY

"Listen to me," said Hugh. "You didn't do this. That's the first point. Got it?"

"Yes, of course."

"Good. The next point——"

"Wait, Hugh. I don't think you understand. I mean I *really* didn't do it."

Dim colours were changing and darkening in the sky. "No, no, I swear I didn't! That's the horrible part of it. I didn't"—she could not complete the sentence; she made the gesture of one pulling tight the ends of a scarf—"do that. You didn't think I meant that, did you?"

"Steady."

"When I said I shouldn't have done it, I meant I shouldn't have run out there to where he was. I did it without thinking. And all of a sudden, as soon as I was out there, I knew what it would look like. As soon as I do a thing, I can always see how I'll get the blame for it. I left my tracks. Look. But I didn't do it."

She was telling the truth.

He believed that by what he saw in her face, and more: he

knew it. In that afternoon they had reached a state of mind, a kind of emotional intimacy, where they could read each other's feelings like plain print. He did not show his sick feeling of relief, but she knew it too.

"You do believe that, don't you?"

"Yes, you know I do. So that's all right."

"No, it's not all right, Hugh. It's very far from all right. He was lying just like that when I got here. His—his poor old face was all over dirt and that thing was round his neck. He was a beast and I hated him; I even thought of killing him in just that way; but when I tried to pick him up all I could think of was that he was the pitifulest-looking thing I'd ever seen."

"Wait. That's right; turn your back to him. Now tell me exactly what happened."

Brenda gave a jerky sort of nod towards the big picnic hamper.

"That was my excuse."

"Excuse?"

"To get away so that I could be alone. On Saturday evenings, when all the servants are away except Maria, I always help Maria prepare a cold dinner. But she's old and pampered, and very difficult sometimes. She was in one of her worst moods tonight. After I left you at the car I went back to the kitchen with her, but I couldn't stick it."

"Go on."

"Well, then I remembered the hamper. I told you Maria had been going on about the china in it. Kitty went on about it this afternoon. So I mentioned the hamper to Maria, and she flew off about it again. I said if she felt like that I'd go down and bring it back straightway. I came down here——"

"What was the time then? Do you remember?"

This was better. She was still speaking very rapidly, but she was much steadier.

"Yes, it was about twenty minutes past seven by my wrist watch. It wasn't quite ten past seven when I left you. I'm sure of that, because I kept looking at the watch and wondering how long it would be before you came back for me toni—oh, Hugh, tonight! Tonight!"

He stopped her.

"So Maria knew you were coming here. What time is it now? Just seven-thirty. Right. Go on."

"Hugh, why are you talking to me like that? As though you were prosecuting me?"

"I want you to have your story straight. This is murder, Brenda; and we're not going to let you get mixed up in it."

"Oh, as though I weren't mixed up in it! Darling, it's no *good*. You don't know the whole story, or you'd realize. They'll have me for this, Hugh. They will."

"No. They're not going to have you for anything: just remember that. Now. Go on."

(She was catching his mood.)

"Well, I—I came down here. I didn't hurry. In fact, I took a long time about it. I didn't see him when I first came in. It was darkish, and he was over at this side of the net, and anyway I was thinking about other things. But I thought that since I was here I might as well get the picnic-hamper after all. So I went round to the pavilion and lugged the hamper out. Just as I was coming out of the pavilion, I looked up and saw him lying there. Then I ran out to him."

"Not carrying that heavy hamper?"

"Yes."

"Why?"

"I don't know. I didn't think about it. I was carting it ahead of me with both hands, and I just ran."

"Was the wire door open or shut?"

"Open."

"Good! Go on."

"You can see him. He was lying just like that. The knot in the scarf was loose, because it was only folded over once, and I tried to pull it out to see if there was any life in him; but it had been pulled too tight and it was stuck in his neck, Hugh—I broke the top of the nail off my middle finger. It caught in that fuzzy tweed stuff on his coat collar, and it's stuck in between the collar and the scarf as though I'd left it there when I had my hands on the ends of the scarf."

"Go on."

"That's all. I suddenly remembered about my own footprints, so I ran."

"Yes. About those footprints: the tracks running out to him and back again. You made those?"

"Of course I did."

"*But there must have been some footprints besides yours and Frank's?*"

"There weren't, though."

"No marks of any kind?"

"None at all."

He spoke gently. "Listen, Brenda. That's impossible. Look at him. Yes, turn round and look. He's lying in the middle of a kind of gigantic cage made out of wire, with a soft floor like sand. I know you didn't kill him; but somebody did. So somebody had to get at him in order to kill him. You see that?

"Well, a tennis court is seventy-eight feet long by thirty-six feet wide. But that's only the extent of the white lines. Outside the lines there's a six-foot clearance on every side, to allow for runway, which makes the whole of the sand floor ninety feet long by forty-eight feet wide. Frank's in the middle of that. And there's at least twenty-four feet of completely unmarked sand round him in every direction!"

"Of course. Only it's true."

It was growing chilly in the dim enclosure.

The shock of the Fact of death had ceased to stun. They had not grown accustomed, and never would grow accustomed, to the picture of Frank lying squashed in a wet glimmering court. The realization of how this would affect Dr. Nicholas Young struck at them both at once. But it was now possible to think, and to ask questions. Hugh found a whole series of such questions forming in his mind. What was Frank doing there, anyway?

Presumably Frank had come back from Kitty Bancroft's house. In coming back, he would have to pass close to the gate of the enclosure. Somebody could have been waiting there, and could have persuaded him to come in. But there the picture vanished in smoke. What was he doing on the tennis court? Why does anybody walk out on a surface like that? Where, for instance, was his racket and the little net of tennis-balls, both of which he had been carrying when they saw him last?

Brenda passed the back of her hand across her forehead.

"That's not all," she said. "We were talking about it, weren't we? I've condemned myself out of my own mouth. Do you remember that very easy method of murder I was telling you all about—the one I said I'd got all worked out?"

"Yes?"

"It's strangulation, Hugh."

"*Strangulation?*"

She gritted her teeth. "And of course Kitty will remember, so I can't lie about it. So easy. So very, very easy. I wouldn't believe it when Nick told us, until I looked it up myself in the medical books. Come to think of it, Maria found me looking it up; she has the most intense horror of girls reading medical books, and she treats me as though I were twelve years old. Listen, Hugh. You can make a person unconscious in three or four seconds just pressing on what they call the carotid arteries and the vagus nerve . . . Look! Suppose I put the palms of my hands on your cheeks, and my thumbs on the corresponding carotid arteries in your neck. And I press. Three or four seconds! It doesn't require any great strength. And you're losing your senses before you know what's happening, you see?"

Hugh yanked away her hands.

"Stop that," he said sharply.

"But——"

"Do you want to scare yourself to death? Stop it, do you hear?"

"Let me finish. I must finish. It's far easier when the person is wearing a scarf with loose ends. All you do is catch hold of the loose ends from behind, and pull. Like the thugs. It closes the arteries automatically. The victim can't cry out or defend himself. He's unconscious in a few seconds, and you finish him. I was thinking about it this afternoon, when I saw Frank's scarf. Oh, I don't mean I would really have done it; but that storm upset me and I *thought* about it. You see how easy it is? Nick says that's why people kill other people accidentally, when they don't mean to. Nick says——"

"So the good Dr. Young is responsible for this," said Hugh through his teeth. "God, I hope he's proud of himself now."

Brenda grew very quiet.

"It'll be the end of him. You know, I can't realize it." She paused. "There'll be no marriage now." She paused again. "And I'm a rich woman."

"What do you mean, you're a rich woman?"

"Uncle Jerry Noakes's orders. If either Frank or I die before the marriage, the survivor inherits the lot." Once more there was a vast pause, while wind stirred in the trees. She added: "That's what you call motive, isn't it?

"I know exactly what they'll say," she went on. "They'll say I waylaid Frank on his way back from Kitty's, to tell him the marriage was off. They'll say he got into one of his rages; and Frank's rages are a thing to remember, I can tell you. They'll say I lost my head, and—it might have happened like that! And my fingernail is torn off in his collar. And only my footprints go out to him and come back. I'm caught, Hugh."

"No."

"You mean there's a way out?"

"Yes. This is a frame-up. Why was that tabloid newspaper left in the pavilion today? Why did Frank know so much about the attempted suicide of a girl called Madge Sturgess? Why did a superintendent of police come here—" He stopped. "Good God, I've forgotten all about him! He's not still at the house, is he?"

"No, that's all right. Maria told me he left just before the storm. She didn't know what he wanted. Something about a car, she thought."

"It still looks queer," Hugh said thoughtfully. "But if it's a frame-up—well, we've got to meet it with a frame-up."

"You mean—fake a defence?"

"Yes. Now tell me. Do you think you can lie convincingly, if I tell you exactly what to say? No, don't jump at it. Think before you answer. If you can't, we'll have to try something else."

"I can!"

"Sure of that?"

"I know it! But oh, Hugh—I mean, won't we get into trouble?"

"Quite possible. But it's certain trouble as things stand now."

"I'm with you," said Brenda, with a fierce joy in her voice. "*How* I'm with you! What do you want me to do? Just tell me."

"First, forget everything you've told me except the fact that you came down here, which Maria knows and we can't deny. Second, we'll forget all that case you built up against yourself: that's rubbish: there are a dozen objections to it: except for one thing—the footprints. They're a Fact, the only thing juries understand. So the footprints must go. Have you got any gardening tools here?"

"There's the tennis court things, behind the pavilion. Roller, wooden rake to smooth the court with——"

"That'll do." He looked down at her shoes, which were gritty-brown and caked almost to the ankles. "Didn't you tell me you had a pair of spare tennis shoes here?"

"Yes. In the locker."

"Go and put them on."

"Why?"

"Go and put them on. Bring the other shoes to me. Hurry!"

Brenda hurried.

Without knowing it, they had been speaking in urgent whispers. The place was very quiet. That watery half-light, in which details are blurred but outlines stand out distinctly, showed that the twelve-foot grass borders outside the tennis court would hold no footprints. The little pavilion looked squat and ugly. Above it the poplars whispered gently; a sparrow protested against sleep; and footfalls swished with startling loudness in the grass. To Hugh, rounding the side of the pavilion, it seemed that only time was now important. Hurry, hurry, he'd got to hurry.

A snap-decision had to be made. The firm of Rowland & Gardesleeve might not have approved. He could imagine his father and old Mr. Edwin Gardesleeve, not moralists and not over-scrupulous, shaking their heads and pursing their lips over this. "Hasty, Hugh. Ve-ry hasty." They would have preferred something more subtle. Subtlety be hanged. There was only one sort of evidence the police understood. And rightly. If they found those footprints, that was the end of it. Once all the footprints had been messed up beyond recognition with a rake, so that a herd of elephants could have walked out and back without identification, then was the time to talk about subtleties. Meantime, hurry, hurry, he'd got to——

Watch out!

Behind the shed had been pushed a huge iron garden roller, two rakes, a spade, and a whitewash roller for the lines. They were in the middle of a broad patch of mud, in which Hugh had been just about to set his foot.

He jerked back, and felt the sweat come out on his forehead. Here, this was bad. He was beginning to feel like a criminal already; and that must be conquered or he would be of no use to Brenda. How was the real murderer feeling now, for instance? The thought made him cool again. In addition to the flat wooden rake for smoothing the court, there was an ordinary garden rake with spikes: that was a bit of luck. Fingerprints? No: the rough surface of the wood would not hold them. He plucked out the rake and hurried round to the front of the pavilion, where Brenda, her colour up, met him at the door.

Their words sounded sharp and quick in the dim garden.

"Hugh, that newspaper. It's gone."

(So there had been an outsider here.)

"Bit of luck for us; not much, but a bit."

"I've changed my shoes. What do we do now?"

"Put that hamper inside."

He unlatched the wire door to the tennis court. Every moment those footprints burned with more obvious danger; they were growing to huge proportions. Once they were gone, he could remove a broken fingernail stuck in Frank's collar. Once they were gone, he could himself "find" Frank while Brenda remained behind with clean shoes on the grass. Once they were gone, once they were gone, once they were gone. He manoeuvred the rake through the wire door, and, as he swung it, a voice spoke from darkness at the other end of the enclosure.

"Mr. Rowland!"

The voice rose shrilly, thin and fussed and querulous.

"Mr. Rowland, sir, what do you mean keeping Miss Brenda from dinner? What are you doing with that rake?"

VII.

DOUBT

OLD NICK, Dr. Nicholas Young, who had decided never to grow old, awoke on his couch to find Maria the maid bending over him and shouting at him.

The dream was gone. He was in the long, low, cool study, with the Epstein bronzes on the low bookshelves, the rich-bound books gleaming by the light of the bridge lamp at his head, the etchings on the walls and the picture of Nelly White over the mantelpiece. The windows were open. The clock on his desk, at which he blinked automatically, showed that it was just twenty minutes to eight. He relaxed, closing his eyes to shut out Maria's face and soothe the pain of his first movement.

But his voice was petulant.

"Dead? What's dead?"

"Mr. Frank, sir. I'm a-telling you."

"Nonsense. He's playing tennis," said Nick.

Maria, a stout laundry-bag of a woman, went down on one knee by the couch. Never a beauty even in her young days, she had nowadays a face which (as Frank had frequently pointed out) would stop a clock; and emotion did not improve it. For she

69

was frightened, too frightened to be anything but natural. And she whispered at him.

"Listen to me, Nickie," she whispered. "I'll go off my chump if you don't listen. I tell you it's him. He's dead. Somebody murdered him. I seen him myself, looking like our old Mr. Watson that put his head in the gas-oven. Your Brenda, she wanted to go down and get a picnic hamper out of that shack where you play tennis. I said, All right, go, and to get me some clothes-pegs too. That was twenty minutes ago. And she didn't come back, and she didn't come back, and I was waiting for her to mix that salad-dressing I don't know how to make, so down I went to see what was what. And there she was with that Rowland, and there Mr. Frank was as stone-dead as I hope to live and breathe."

Now she was frightened for fear she had said too much.

Nick did not move; *The Trial of Mrs. Jewell* remained open across his chest. His eyes remained closed, but with an ugly squeezed-up look. It was the sound of his breathing she could not endure. The silence went on too long. Whether out of grief, or hysteria at what he might say, or mere sympathy with his feelings, a large tear blotted the corner of Maria's eye and splashed on his hand. Hers was proper grief, in which she luxuriated.

Nick shook his head.

"No," he said.

"But I'm a-telling you!"

"Sure?"

"I only wish I wasn't, dearie."

"How?"

Maria did not trust her speech: she made illustrative gestures on her own neck, which he watched dully.

"Who?"

By this time she was glad of any excuse for an outburst, any relief from monosyllables. She bawled at him.

"They wouldn't tell me. They ordered me straight up here to ring up the police. But it was that young Rowland, if you want to know what *I* think. Even after poor Mr. Frank was dead, he was trying to hit him and beat at him with a rake. Yes, he was. I seen him. Only the rake wasn't long enough."

Nick tried to push himself up on one elbow.

"May heaven strike me dead if it ain't as true as I'm here this minute," cried Maria, now in such a welter of emotion that she could not see him. "They've been carrying on, Nickie Young, and you might as well know it soon as late. That Rowland and Miss Brenda. There they was standing guilty as ghosts, him with the rake in his hand and her standing on the porch of that shed hiding something behind her back. I don't say she had anything to do with it, mind you; but if they weren't her foot-marks going out to where poor Mr. Frank was, in the tennis court where it was wet, then I'd like to know whose they were. *I* saw 'em, and they know I saw 'em."

"Quiet, you vixen," shouted Nick. Now she saw that she had gone too far in earnest. His sick eyes terrified her. *The Trial of Mrs. Jewell* slid to the floor with a thump.

"But what was she doing down there? Why did you let her go?"

"Holy Mary, did I know what she was going to do?"

"I don't believe it," said Nick. "Tell me what you saw. Tell me. Go on."

She told him what she saw, or thought she saw. "Then this Rowland spoke up sharp and quick, before I could think, and he says, 'There's been an accident here,' he says; 'you'd better telephone for the police.' I said, 'I'll go to Dr. Young, that's what I'll do,' giving him as good as he sent."

"And this is true—what you say about the Rowland boy?"

Maria, at a wild loss for words, merely raised her right arm as though she were taking an oath.

"Help me up," said Nick.

"Yes, dearie. There's another thing, too. That police-officer's back again."

Nick, propped to tousle-haired uprightness, looked so sick that she held him still and repeated the statement.

"Police-officer? What police-officer?"

"That Superintendent Whatshisname, that was here before."

"Eh?"

"Hadley, he says his name is."

"But how did he get here so soon?"

"He didn't come about that," said Maria, weeping again. "He come to see you again, and said it was important. I said you'd skin me if I ever woke you up between tea and dinner. This was before ha' past seven, just before I went down to them others. I told the Superintendent I'd wake you up at ha' past seven if he'd wait. I put him in the library, and forgot all about him. I bet," she added, with a gleam of savage joy, "he's still there, and mad as fury. But you don't want to see him, do you, dearie? You needn't, if you don't want to."

"Oh, don't I want to see him? On the contrary, my dear vixen. That is the thing I want most in this world."

"But don't you want to lie down?"

"Lie down!—Give me my crutch." He nodded towards the telephone. "Ring the police-station; no, wait; I'll do that. Go downstairs and send Superintendent Hadley up here immediately. And don't let me hear you calling me 'Nickie' and 'dearie' again; in public, anyway. Understand?"

He crawled up, supporting himself on the crutch. His eyes were hot and still dizzy. He hopped across the room, propped himself against one of the west windows, and stared and blinked down towards the tennis court.

It was just as well that he could not see into that place. By the tennis court, feeling every minute more the weight and menace of that dead body, two figures stood amid the ruin of a plan. Hugh Rowland still held the garden rake. Brenda was too cool not to be very near collapse.

"It's no good now," she pointed out. "Maria saw the tracks, and she'll tell. We can't destroy them. Hugh, what were we thinking of? We must have been mad!"

"No. It was the only possible way out, only it didn't work." He shut his teeth. "Well, that's that. If it can't be done in one way, it must be done in another."

"Hugh, we can't. Not again!"

"I don't mean any more fakes. I'm afraid"—he grinned sourly—"I'm afraid we'll be reduced to the simple and unpalatable course of telling the truth. We've got to find some interpretation of the facts that they'll believe. Some interpretation."

He flung away the rake, and strode up and down on the broad strip of grass.

"Curse it, I can't explain how the fellow should have been strangled in the middle of a trackless desert of sand with no footprints coming near him except yours. I can't explain miracles. There's only one man I know who can. His name is Gideon Fell, and he's not available. If only *you* hadn't made those tracks! If only somebody else had walked out there in your shoes, to throw the blame on you, and killed him!" Hugh stopped short, regarding the new white pair of tennis shoes she was now wearing. "By the way, where are those other shoes—the muddy ones you just took off?"

She jerked her thoughts back.

"They're in the picnic-hamper."

"The picnic-hamper?"

"Yes. When I saw Maria coming, I nearly fell through the ground. I was standing on the porch of the pavilion with the hamper behind me, and I was afraid she'd see the shoes. So I stuffed them inside the hamper while she was looking at Frank. There wasn't much room for them, because it's full of china; but I got the clasps snapped together again, and put back the hamper where it was in the first place."

"H'm. What size shoes do you wear?"

"Fours. But——"

"That's pretty small, isn't it?"

"Yes, rather. The average size is five. What are you thinking about?"

Hugh's mind toyed with the idea, and discarded it.

"No!" he decided with some violence. "Even as a fake defence, that won't do. A woman might have worn those shoes, but no man could have. And, in spite of what you say about the 'case' of strangling, it was a man who did this. Strangulation has never been a woman's method and never will be. Besides, we're ruddy well not going to play the murderer's game for him and keep him laughing at us. That's out. We'll stick to the truth; but we'll beat them yet."

"I suppose you're right," Brenda observed in a colourless voice. She drew her fingers through the thick dark-gold hair, which had fallen low on her forehead, and pushed it back. Even her eyes seemed colourless. "Hugh, I'm going up to the house. I can't stay down here any longer." How—how soon will the police get here?"

"Fifteen or twenty minutes. Why?"

"Because I can't face anybody just yet." She clenched her hands. "I want to get into a hot bath; I want to get the grime off me in every way. If I had to face anybody this minute, I don't know what lies I'd tell. Ugh!"

"Yes, that's the best thing. Go up to your room, lock your door, and lie down. I want to stay down here for a few minutes more——"

She spoke on a faint note of alarm. "Why do you want to stay down here? What are you going to do?"

"Nothing. Nothing at all! Just a few little things I want to look at."

The alarm deepened. She moved closer.

"Hugh, you're up to something. I can tell. What have you got up your sleeve now?"

"Speaking of sleeves," he interposed, "you're cold, and you're shivering. No wonder, with no sleeves on you. Here, have my coat round you. Come on, have it. It's a bit grease-stained from messing with that wheel, but it's warm." Disregarding her protests, he wrapped it round her. When her insistence would not be disregarded, he faced it out. "Brenda, on my solemn word of honour, I am not up to any funny business. The truth will serve us best, and it's truth from now on. I won't say I'm not going to find that piece of fingernail you broke off in Frank's collar, and get rid of it; because that's just exactly what I'm going to do, so you can stop worrying about it. But, for the rest of it, truth. There may be some bit of evidence out there, some indication, something to explain the miracle; and that's what I'm looking for. Off you go, now. Keep your chin up."

"All right," said Brenda; and gripped his arm hard before she ran.

For a time Hugh stood and studied the tennis court. The evening was turning colder; there would be less than an hour of daylight left. In his trousers' pockets he found a petrol lighter and a loose, flattened cigarette. He lit it, inhaling deeply and gratefully, while his head sang with plans.

This murder was a very definite frame-up. The frame-up could not be directed against Brenda, since nobody knew in advance that she would suddenly make up her mind to come down to the pavilion after the picnic-hamper. But she had been caught in a well-greased trap. What infuriated him was feeling that the real murderer was laughing at them; that the real murderer had all the luck, while they made fools of themselves; that the real murderer had wormed away from them as neatly as he had wormed over a wet tennis court without leaving a trace.

Who this real murderer might be he had no idea. He knew nothing of Frank's affairs, except as they touched Brenda. He refused to think about that now, for there were certain practical things he had to do. After a few deep pulls at the cigarette, Hugh dropped it in the grass. Opening the wire door, he walked straight out across the tennis court.

It was a queer sensation—like being on a tight-rope over a big open space.

The court was beginning to dry and harden. Though he left clear footprints of his own, they were very shallow ones. He was careful not to tread on or cross any of the other prints, and he approached Frank's body in a wide swerve. Then he studied the facts.

Frank's footprints came straight out in an oblique line from the wire door to the middle of the court at a point some ten feet back from the net. Here Frank had fallen. There had been a struggle, or else someone had attempted to mess up the ground round the body by scuffling and trampling on the sand. The surface of the court had been churned up in a wide circle, tracks obliterated with heels drawn over and over again: to such an extent that there was not even an identifiable patch where Brenda must later have set down the heavy picnic-hamper.

Frank lay now with his head towards the net, one arm outstretched, one shoulder humped, legs twisted together. But it was impossible to tell what direction he might have been facing when he was attacked, for he had been rolled over at least once. His head and shoulders had left marks in the soft surface. One of the ends of the silk scarf with which he had been strangled was torn and scratched by his own fingernails, where he had tried to tear the murderer's grip away from his throat.

Fingernails.

It was that thought which turned Hugh cold.

He flicked on the flame of the petrol lighter and held it close to Frank: not a pleasant business. After a close examination he found, stuck and entangled in the fuzzy tweed collar of the coat, a little ragged half-moon of varnished nail where Brenda had broken it off.

*Ha*d she done it after all?

He didn't believe she had; but, all the same, had she? It was a sick-minded thought, a disloyal thought, a ratty contemptible kind of thought, but it flashed through his mind and it was all the more disquieting in her absence. If she were here, if he could see her, he would be reassured. But the whispering suggestion persisted. For until he came out here to see Frank's body for himself, he had not quite realized the hopelessness of this "miracle" murder.

"I told her," he said to himself, and stared round him. "From here to solid ground—at the sides of the court—is fully twenty-four feet in the shortest direction. From here to the back of the court must be nearer thirty-five feet." All round him, vast and impressive, stretched that unmarked area of soft sand which a murderer would have had to cross; and which, obviously, a murderer had crossed. But how?

It was unbelievable. Round the sand surface ran the foot-wide grass border, and then the tall wire netting supported at intervals by iron poles. Could a murderer have stood on the grass border and *jumped* as far as this scuffed patch? Nonsense! Jump twenty-four feet? Hugh found his mind playing with all sorts of wild and fantastic ideas. For instance, could the murderer have walked out here on the top of the net, like a tight-rope walker?—and then jumped the ten feet to the scuffed patch where Frank lay?

That notion was madder still; it made him want to laugh. He would have laughed, if the situation had not been too ugly for that. Yet—it came to him with swift, sure conviction—Frank could (and would) have been lured to the middle of the court by just some such stunt as that. Suppose the murderer had said, "Look here, I'll bet you ten bob I can walk across the court on top of the net." Such bets or challenges were the meat of life to Frank; Hugh remembered, with a twitch of repulsion, the fierce argument he had had with Frank only a fortnight ago, in the presence of Brenda and Kitty, over a certain feat of gymnastics. But—to walk out on that weak-supported net; to jump back up on it again, balancing, and walk back? Incredible, and worse than incredible!

Yet the only alternative to any of these insane fancies was Brenda's guilt.

He didn't believe it. He shook his fist in the air and wouldn't believe it. Besides, nobody could have attacked Frank here, clinging in that merciless bulldog grip to the ends of the scarf, without getting all over mud. Had there been mud on Brenda's legs or knees, or on her white frock? For the life of him he could not remember. He remembered the smudge across her cheek, and that was all.

Nonsense. That air of innocence, the fierce clarity of the eyes, the despair and hope intermingled, could not have been counterfeited. An inner voice said: "Don't fool yourself; you know it can be counterfeited; you have seen it counterfeited." He cursed that voice and shut his ears to its buzzing. Carefully detaching the fragment of fingernail from Frank's collar, he put it into his pocket.

He did not act too soon. So abnormally alert were his senses that he heard someone approaching even though the person was many yards away: the faint swishing in the wet grass, as of someone running. A dim gleam of silver—of a long silver evening gown—appeared in the opening of the poplars to the south.

It was Kitty Bancroft. She was holding the trailing evening gown up round her ankles while she hurried with short, quick strides. She was made-up for an evening out: mouth painted dark red, sleek black hair drawn behind her ears, pearl ear-rings, jumping and dancing as she ran. Hugh went to meet her. Even from a distance her bearing told him that she already knew. Her eyes were open and set with an almost lunatic concern; she stopped, stared, and let the ends of the silver gown fall.

"So it's true," she said.

"Yes, it's true."

Kitty could not seem to leave off staring. "I didn't believe it," she panted, "even when I knew it was true. Even when Brenda told me——"

The fear inside Hugh deepened to a definite chill.

"You've talked to Brenda? Where?"

"Up at the house. I've just come from there. The last thing Frank said to me, he asked me to go out dancing with him and Brenda tonight. He wanted to use my car. I drove up a few minutes ago and found the whole place in an uproar, with Maria weeping, and Nick saying he'll see you hanged for this and telling the police you did it——"

He yelled at her. "The police? But the police can't be here yet!"

"Well, they are. There was a detective in Nick's study. Brenda tried to sneak up the stairs, and ran straight into him."

"Did she talk to him?"

"Of course. She had to."

"What did she say?"

"I don't know. They wouldn't let me stay in the room. But her nerve seemed to break right in two when she saw this man and Nick told her who it was. She was crying, and wanted to see you. Whatever she said, she apparently didn't make a very good story of it. Maria was trying to listen at the keyhole, and she says it's practically certain they're going to arrest Brenda and maybe you too."

VIII.

FEAR

A DRY, hard flame of rage seemed to burn in Kitty. She lifted her hands to her ears and pressed them as though to ease the pain of a headache.

"It's that Scotland Yard man," she went on. "The one who was here before. He came back about something, and there he was. If you want to do anything for Brenda, you'd better get up there in a hurry."

"But he has no authority here! He's Metropolitan C.I.D. This has got to be handled by the divisional station. If they want to call Scotland Yard later they can, but in the meantime he's got no more authority to butt in than I have!"

"I don't know anything about that," observed Kitty coldly and practically. "All I know is that he's asking questions twenty to the dozen, and unpleasant ones at that."

"I'd forgotten all about the fellow," muttered Hugh. "He slipped straight through my mind——"

Kitty spoke with a certain bitterness. "Yes. You were much too concerned with making love to Brenda at the time, weren't you?"

"Now I suppose the whole thing is *my* fault?"

"If you hadn't done it, this mightn't have happened, Hugh. Did you try to beat Frank's face in with a rake after he was dead? Did you?"

"Great Scott, no!"

"Well, Maria says you did. She says she saw you. What were you doing with the rake, then? There's the damned thing," she burst out. "I can see it for myself. What were you doing with it? That's what the police want to know."

"I can explain about the rake in good time. Steady, Kitty! Listen to me. Admitted that I wasn't listening very carefully when Brenda mentioned him before, just who is this fellow? She said he was a superintendent. Which superintendent: do you know?"

"His name is Hadley. . . . Why are you looking like that? Do you know him?"

"Yes. I've met him in court."

"Is he—is he——?"

"Yes. He's what is humourously known as a gentleman, but he's about twenty times tougher inside than the copper with the walrus moustache. Kitty: be honest, now. You don't actually think either Brenda or I had anything to do with this?"

The anger seemed to die out of Kitty. She lifted her shoulders. Again she hitched up the ends of the silver gown, so that it should not trail in the grass. She had become like a hard, tall, over-decorated statue, hollow inside and bedecked for nothing.

"I'm sorry, Hugh. I don't suppose I do, if you pin me down to it. But the whole thing is so horrible and so—well, so disgusting! Look at him there. One moment he was so full of life, and making jokes, and planning the future; and now they'll put him down under the ground, and it can rain on him all night and he won't feel it." She shivered, closing her long, sinewy fingers. Her voice grew harder.

"Besides, I knew there was going to be an explosion of some kind after what happened this afternoon. To be quite frank, Hugh, there was a time when you frightened me. That was just before you left us, when you laughed in that queer way and said, 'You've done your last bit of damage, my lad.' I think you scared Frank a little, too. And then Brenda—talking about strangling, and saying she'd got it all worked out."

This was the sort of suggestion which must be cut off at the root.

Hugh spoke dryly. "I see. First she would carefully explain to us what she was going to do, and then go and do it."

"I don't know." Kitty hesitated; her forehead was pitted with wrinkles of concentration. "Brenda is a delightful person; nobody knows that better than I do; but, you know, I've sometimes thought she wasn't quite *normal,* somehow. I mean, she doesn't seem to like the things most normal girls like, with the exception of—well, we won't go into that. But she positively hates small-talk and all things social. If you simply tell her a person is charming, she's got a chip on her shoulder at once. It wouldn't thrill her a bit to go to Buckingham Palace or Ascot. And then she reads too much; she reads and reads and reads: it's not natural."

"Highly sinister. Highly."

"You needn't sneer at me, Hugh Rowland."

"I wasn't sneering. On the contrary, I was hoping you could help."

"I? How?"

"Well, since you were the last person to be with Frank before the murderer got him——"

Kitty's arms stiffened at her sides; her head was raised, her neck arched, in the same position he had seen it once before that day, against a flash of lightning.

"I know, poor old boy," she said. "But he wasn't with me two minutes. You remember, he said he was going to dash over and dash straight back again? He'd left his cigarette case on the mantelpiece: that valuable one with the watch set in it: and that book I was going to lend him. He simply took them and left. It wasn't five minutes past seven when he left. I remember, he said, 'I've got to hurry back, in case those two go into a corner and start canoodling again.'"

"Very appropriate last words."

"Don't you dare talk like that about him," snapped Kitty, whirling round in a white fury. "He's dead."

"I know he's dead, and I'm sorry; but what am I to say? I had no animus against him in spite of what you think. But I still believe that despite all this charm you talk about he was a vicious, cold-blooded slug."

"I suppose you'll tell that to the police?"

"Yes; why not?"

"No doubt you're the best judge of that. But they'll be rather curious to know what you were doing at the time he was killed."

"As a matter of fact I was changing a wheel on my car in the middle of a public street. Not that it matters."

"Oh, doesn't it?" inquired Kitty, raising her eyebrows. "After the obvious pack of lies Brenda told that detective: denying that she'd been out on the tennis court at all: saying the footprints there weren't hers, when anybody can see with half an eye——"

Hugh had a feeling as though he had been physically struck across the back of the neck with the sharp edge of a hand: the rabbit-punch, which explodes the brain and distorts eyesight. He waited a moment until vision steadied. He asked quietly:

"She—said—what?"

"She denied she had been out on the court at all," repeated

Kitty. "She said somebody must have been walking in her shoes. Her shoes! Fours! It's true I didn't hear all of it; I wasn't in the room; but Maria heard part of it, and that's the gist."

"Excuse me," said Hugh. "I've got to go up there at once."

"I should," advised Kitty. Again her mood changed. "Wait. Don't let's quarrel. Believe me when I say this: nobody wants to see Brenda in trouble less than I do. Nobody likes Brenda more than I do. The shock of this has upset all of us. But—if she's said anything foolish get her to retract it before it's too late."

He spoke coolly. "How do you know she's said anything foolish? She'll tell the truth, you know. Did you hear anything else?"

"No. I'll give you another tip, though. Watch out for Nick. He's dangerous."

"Thanks, Kitty. I'll remember."

Once outside the now stifling enclosure, Hugh took the terrace steps three at a time.

So again the real murderer was having all the luck. On the other hand, Hugh told himself, it was his own accursed fault. He had put the idea into Brenda's mind; he had suggested it to her himself, and apparently it was the first thing that had come bubbling out. Never mind. He must find out what Brenda had really said. Emerging into the garden at the top of the terrace, he heard the words, "Look out!" from somewhere below him and towards his right; he stopped abruptly, and moved into the shadow of a tree just in time.

Superintendent David Hadley and Dr. Nicholas Young were coming down the driveway. The latter sat hunched in a wheel chair which he was impelling, powerfully, with his left hand, at such a speed that it skidded on the concrete, slipped out of control, and lurched for the bank.

From the bank just above, under trees dim against redembered sky, Hugh saw Hadley plunge forward to keep the chair upright. Then he lost sight of them both. But he heard mutterings, a thump, a pause of hard breathing, and Hadley's cold voice.

"If you want to break your own neck, Dr. Young, that's your business. But, next time, look out for my ankles. Give it a spin backwards."

"An oversight," snarled Nick's voice, above whistling breath. "I had forgotten a policeman's feet were the most valuable part of him. To lose them would be a major tragedy. No, no, I beg your pardon—stop; I'm winded."

"Don't mention it."

"I want you to be reasonable," said Nick, in the tone of one who is reasonable himself. "Do me the courtesy of answering me. Don't stride along there like a Chancellor of the Exchequer with a budget box. Tell me if you don't agree with me."

Again there was a pause, as though the Superintendent were looking at him.

"My dear sir," Hadley said, "I don't know how you think I stand here. I don't even know what's happened here. That is what we're going to see. If you can pull that wheel out of the mud, we'll get on with it and stand guard until Inspector Gates arrives. But I hope you don't think I'm going to begin by calling the Black Maria for somebody you think is a murderer, just because you happen to be a friend of one of the Assistant Commissioners."

"I don't ask that."

"Then what do you want?"

Nick was cool. "I want fair play. Come on. To begin with, you know Brenda wasn't concerned in this. Don't you?"

Hesitation.

"Don't you, now?"

"I can't tell you that. It's too soon to say. But if you want my opinion now———"

"I do want your opinion now."

"No, I don't think she was concerned in it," replied Hadley. "She seemed to me to tell a quite straightforward and reasonable story. Besides, she doesn't strike me as the sort who would lie."

(Up on the bank above, Hugh leaned the palm of his hand against the nearest tree, blinked his eyes, and drew a deep breath.)

"The evidence," said Hadley, "will probably confirm her. Her story was straight enough, except"—there was a very brief, colourless pause—"except for one very small point which she'll probably be able to explain later."

"What point?" asked Nick quickly.

"That will be seen later."

"I'm going to suggest something to you, Superintendent," pursued Nick, in a comfortable voice. "Brenda, of all people, never killed that boy. Good: that's established. But I'm going to suggest to you that Brenda was mistaken about one thing. Brenda says the murderer must have put on a pair of her shoes and walked out across the tennis court. Now, I'm going to suggest she was mistaken about the size of the shoes—or something else in the business. The real murderer never wore a pair of her shoes."

"Why not?"

"Because young Rowland is the murderer, of course," said Nick. "I've put that to you as a matter of plain evidence."

"You seem pretty sure of that, sir."

"Naturally," said Nick. "I'm going to hang him. I'm going to devote every minute of the rest of my time, every penny I've got in the bank, and every cell of the not-inconsiderable brains I've got in my head, to make that gentleman wish he'd never been born. There won't be a move he makes that I don't know. There won't be a word he says that I don't write down and study. And if he makes just one little slip—just *one,* Superintendent, in the smallest word he says—as he will, mind you—then I'll have his neck between your fingers before you can say twopence. Why, I'll make you a bet. When we go down to that court, I'll bet you I can find twenty things he's overlooked, twenty things that'll prove he's guilty. And I'll donate twenty pounds to police charities for every one of those twenty things I can't find."

This was the point at which Hugh almost made his second mistake.

Even though he had been prepared for it, the concentration of hatred in Nick's voice startled him. It even shocked him. Dimly, for months, he had been aware that Nick was very much like Frank; Nick had been Frank's tutor, his guide, his counsellor. Hearing this was like hearing a ghost of Frank, or like hearing a Frank Dorrance grown old and wise and subtle as the serpent.

Hugh's foot was on the grass only a yard or so over their heads. His movement was instinctive. He was going to jump down and have this out with the old swine here and now. With his hand on the tree to steady himself, he stopped. If he jumped down there now, Brenda was done for. His story of the murder must tally with Brenda's. But, with the exception of one fact, he had no idea what Brenda had said.

Steady!

He heard Nick's voice again.

"Got it, Superintendent?"

"Yes. I think I have."

"Oh, come off the official manner," said Nick. "Hell of a pukka sahib, aren't you? Don't like it." He was not annoyed; he was cheerful. "Well, I don't ask you to go by anything but evidence.

You heard what Mrs. Bancroft said. He threatened Frank's life, didn't he?"

"Apparently he did," agreed Hadley. "So did Arthur Chandler."

"Ar—what are you talking about? Who's Arthur Chandler?"

"He's Madge Sturgess's boy-friend," said Hadley. "I told you about him. When your telephone wouldn't work, I made a special trip back here this evening on my way back from the local police-station to warn you that Chandler has been seen in the district, and he's out for trouble."

There was a silence, broken by a noise as of someone impatiently yanking at a wheel chair.

Hadley's voice sharpened a little. He added:

"But that doesn't seem to bother you."

"I don't understand you."

"You asked me," said Hadley smoothly, "what I thought about this case. I don't know anything about it yet. If we don't stop this wayside chatter and get on with the business we may never know anything about it. But that's one of the things I *have* noticed. It doesn't seem to trouble you that Chandler made threats. It doesn't even seem to trouble you beyond a decent show of shock, in which of course we all sympathize with you—that Frank Dorrance is dead. What does seem to trouble you is that Rowland goes and falls in love with Miss White." He twisted the knife. "And Miss White with Rowland." He twisted it again. "At least that's what I judge, from what she told me, though it's no affair of mine. But why are you so anxious to get Rowland out of the way?"

A gurgling kind of cry came from Nick.

"Superintendent, are you raving mad?"

"No."

"Then what are you getting at? Are you suggesting that *I* have any interest in Brenda? That kind of interest, I mean? At my age?"

"Not at all—though it did strike me this afternoon that you were rather self-conscious about explaining how very proper it was for her to live in your house. It never occurred to me to think it was anything else."

"Will you kindly explain what you're driving at?"

Hadley spoke with sudden mildness.

"Just a word of warning, that's all. This marriage was a cherished project of yours: very well. It was broken off by Dorrance's death: very well. But don't let your dislike of Rowland lead you into mixing things up for us."

"Oh, you mean manufacturing evidence," said Nick cheerfully. "No, I won't do that. I don't need to. Eh?"

"That's all right, then. I don't say Rowland isn't guilty. He may be. But if he's lying, we'll find it out soon enough. Now can you pull that chair out of there before it gets too dark to see anything on the tennis court, or shall I give you a hand?"

"Can I get it out of here!" said Nick.

Below the bank there was a hiss and whir in mud. Out into Hugh's sight the wheel chair shot backwards, lurching, across the sloping driveway. Nick steadied it. His face was distinct in the reddish afterglow. Squat as an idol, endlessly patient in his mind, he turned up a ruddy face and a frosted spectacle-lens to the sky.

"You don't need to worry about it being dark," he said. "Floodlights. In the trees. I rigged 'em up in case they should want to play after dark. We can go on all night if we like. Now listen to me, my friend. The first thing we do——"

His voice moved on, lowered so that it could not be heard, and faded.

Hugh went quietly up to the house under the shadow of the trees.

So that was two opponents to begin with. He had felt a little sick when he saw Nick's expression. Of the two opponents, Nick and Hadley, he was not sure which might be the most dangerous. And Brenda had already committed herself to a lie. That did not matter in Nick's case, but it mattered very much in the case of the police.

What was the extent of that lie? What were the details of it? It had better, he told himself, be good. She might retract it. But if Brenda's manner had once convinced the far-from-gullible Superintendent Hadley of her truthfulness, and she with equal innocence now assured him it was all lies, he would make himself a very unpleasant customer in the future.

"Hugh!" whispered a voice softly.

The rear of the house, long, low, and white-painted brick, was dark except for a light in the basement kitchen. He looked up and saw Brenda at an upstairs window, motioning him towards the drawing-room. He went in through the open glass doors, and she joined him a moment later.

"You didn't meet them, did you?" she whispered across the gloom. "I wanted to warn you, but there wasn't any way. Did you talk to them?"

"No. I got rid of that broken bit of fingernail, by the way."

"I knew you would," said Brenda tensely. "You said you would. But—listen! Didn't you leave more footprints in the court?"

"Yes, but they don't matter. The court is almost dry. My footprints are so shallow that it'll be easy to show they were made long after what happened there."

"Speak low," she urged. "Maria's downstairs. Hugh—I—want to warn you about something. I told them——"

"Yes, I know. Your version of it. You showed them a pair of clean shoes you were wearing, and said you had never been out on the court at all. You said somebody must have taken another pair of your shoes, to throw the blame on you, and walked out on the court and killed Frank. That doesn't matter now. The question is, what sort of story did you make out of it? What else did you say?"

IX.

DETERMINATION

"I know," he went on, "you got rattled and blurted out the first thing that came into your head. I don't blame you. But——"

"Oh, no," said Brenda with a certain grimness. "Oh, no, I didn't. I mean, I was rattled right enough, darling; but I told that story deliberately, and I mean to stick to it."

She was no longer the frightened girl of the tennis court. He could sense that in the gloom even before she spoke. As though to emphasize how she felt about it, she disregarded her own instructions and spoke in a normal voice. She had changed her clothes; she was fresh from tub and scent-spray; and with it she seemed to have regained her fighting quality.

"I had to tell them that," she said. "Do you know why? I suddenly found they were all trying to throw the blame on you. And I wasn't having any of that, thank you."

"But——"

"Swine," said Brenda, "*I'll* show them. Listen, here's the story quick. Then we can turn on the lights and hoist the flag and dare them to take the fort. I said I went down there at twenty minutes past seven; which was true. I said I went to get the picnic-hamper; which was also true. But I didn't tell them I'd actually got the hamper. I couldn't admit I'd been walking about carrying it, in case they opened it and found that pair of muddy tennis shoes inside."

"Yes."

"There wasn't any trouble about saying that. I told you I'd put the hamper exactly where it was to begin with, so there's nothing to show it's been moved. I simply said I hadn't gone as far as the pavilion to pick up the hamper. I said that just as I was going round the side of the court towards the pavilion, I looked across the court and saw Frank. . . . Did you say anything?"

"No; go on."

Her eyes were shining curiously.

"And there," she continued, reaching out for his arm and shaking it, "was where I got my inspiration. I did, Hugh. There was nothing to show I'd ever been near the hamper. Well, do you know how heavy that hamper is? It's full of china and it weighs a ton. To be exact, it weighs about forty pounds. And I suddenly remembered I'd carried it clear out on the tennis court and clear back. . . ."

Hugh put his hand to his forehead.

He said with careful articulation: "So you told Superintendent Hadley to look at the depth of the footprints in the sand. You said they were much too deep for you to have made. You pointed out that you yourself weigh about seven stone; whereas the person who made those tracks must have weighed about ten stone. Is that it?"

"How on earth did you know?"

"There is thought-transference in this," declared Hugh. "We are what the old romancers called soul-mates. I know it because I thought of exactly the same thing as a possible line of attack.

But it seemed too barefaced even for me to use. Holy cats, trust a woman to come out flat with a flat brazen-nosed lie like that and stick to it even if she's fainting under it!"

"They believe me. I'll swear that police-officer believed me."

"So he may, until he has a look at the evidence. Still, why not? Why not? The truth is obvious to me, because we know it. It seems to stick out a mile, because our guilty consciences are all over us. But is it so obvious to them? I wonder. No; wait; go on: what's the rest of your story?"

"That's all there is, really. I said I didn't go out on the court myself, because I could see Frank was dead and I knew you weren't supposed to mess up anything until the police arrived——"

"Ah."

"But that I could tell there was something awfully queer about those tracks, because I put my foot in the edge of one and it was exactly the same size as mine. Also, it was a Grey Goose shoe, with a goose pattern in the rubber solemark. I said I remembered I had a spare pair of shoes in the pavilion, that anybody might have stolen. So I said I ran and looked in the pavilion, and the spare pair had gone out of the locker." She paused. "That's about all. I said I was frightened and didn't know what to do. Then, at close on seven-thirty (which is true) you came along. There you are. Is it all right? What do you think?"

Hugh considered. His own scarf, still tied round his neck despite the absence of a coat, had begun to feel hot again. He took two steps forward, and two steps back.

"Frankly, I'm not whooping with enthusiasm about it."

"But I've already *said* it! Why not? What's wrong with it?"

"Well, the main difficulty is that if they ever spot the connection between you and that hamper—as it's three to one they'll do, since you admit you went down there after it—then we're done for. As a matter of routine they'll search the pavilion, open the hamper, and find the shoes. Now about practical considerations. When you lugged the hamper out to where Frank was lying, you must have set it down? Yes. Didn't it leave a mark?"

(Even as he asked this, he remembered that it had not left a mark. He had looked for that mark himself.)

"No, Hugh, I don't think so. I scuffed the place about a bit, without meaning to."

"But there must still be sand-stains on the bottom of the hamper?"

"No. There were, but the wet grass rubbed them off. I noticed."

"Your fingerprints on the handle?"

"Rough leather won't take fingerprints. You told me that once yourself."

Hugh took several more strides back and forth. "The celebrated Dr. Frankenstein," he said, "had nothing on me. Well, let's see. The *advantage* of the plan is psychological. Nobody will ever believe—whether you went out there to kill Frank, or whether you only went to look at his dead body—that you ever went out on that court lugging a forty-pound picnic-hamper. Yes, I know that's precisely what you did do; but nobody would think it reasonable. So their minds may not connect the hamper with the too-deep footprints. And there's another strong argument I can think of, which is psychological too. And then Hadley appears to believe you. Yes, on the whole we might have a fighting chance, but——"

"Wait a minute, Hugh. You say we 'might' have a fighting chance?"

"Something like that."

"In other words, you mean you're not going to back me up."

He threw up his hands.

"Brenda, it's not a question of backing you up. If you insist on sticking to your story, I'm with you, of course. But you don't seem to realize how serious this is. You're not back in that school you hated so much, spinning yarns to a form-mistress. This is murder. You're up against Scotland Yard. Let's know where we stand before——"

"*I* don't realize how serious it is?" said Brenda. "*You* don't, you mean. And whoever I'm up against, they're not going to arrest you if I can help it."

"Look here: I may be very dense, but I still don't see how telling this string of whoppers is going to help me. Besides, they're not going to arrest me."

His tactics had been blundering. Under the cool face she presented, he saw that she was angry; furiously angry and hurt. She blazed at him.

"Oh, aren't they? Do you know Maria swears she saw you standing over Frank's body and hitting him with that rake?"

"But that's hysterical nonsense. It's got nothing to do with the case."

"No, and neither have my footprints; but they landed me in the middle of it just the same."

There was a pause, after which Brenda spoke in a hard, tight, repressed voice.

"You don't know what happened to me up here. At least, you haven't bothered to ask. When I came up to the house, I—I loved you so much I couldn't see straight. I mean, the way you pitched straight in to help me, without asking any questions or ever even thinking for a second I might have done it. And do you know what I found when I got here? I found Nick and Maria and that man Hadley waiting for me at the top of the stairs. The first thing I heard was that you had done it: Nick and Maria had got that all worked out between them.

"I was already worried about that. I knew Maria would tell some horrible story or other. What was I to say? If I told the truth, and said there hadn't been any footprints at all until I made them, they just simply wouldn't have believed me. You didn't believe me yourself. But if I said the real murderer must have made the footprints in my shoes, then they couldn't possibly accuse you. You could no more have worn a pair of my shoes than the Man in the Moon. That's all."

Brenda's voice grew even harder and more repressed.

"I'm sorry if what I said seems foolish to you. I'm sorry if it doesn't satisfy your legal mind. Perhaps I didn't stop to 'weigh all the factors.' If you had seen Nick's face, and heard what he was saying, maybe you wouldn't have either. After all you'd done for me, I just felt I'd die if I didn't clear you. When you came up here, I expected you to understand. Perhaps I even expected a word of t-thanks. But all you can do now is pick holes in it and carry on as though I'd betrayed you somehow. You weren't so scrupulous about faking beforehand. Very well. You can do or say what you like; but that's my story and I'm sticking to it."

The silence went on unendurably. She was wearing high-heeled shoes; he heard them rap on the polished floor as she went across to the window.

"Brenda, I beg your pardon. I didn't understand."

"Never mind. It doesn't matter."

"Of course it matters. Speaking of a person being too much in love to see straight——"

"Why bother?"

There was only one thing to be done, and he did it. In the

revulsion of feeling she was clinging to him, her arms pressed round his neck, when brakes screeched on motorcars pulling into the driveway, when the twilight grew loud with voices, and dim figures crowded into the garden.

"Brace up," Hugh said. "Here come the cops. That's our story, and we're sticking to it."

"Shall I put on the lights?"

"Yes, you'd better."

She went across swiftly and touched a switch. Wall-candles, glowing behind parchment shades, were reflected in pale green walls down the long room. They showed silver of age and grace; the bowl of white carnations on the grand piano; the deep chairs covered in white chintz. They also showed a dishevelled young man in his shirt sleeves, and Brenda in a brown skirt and jumper smiling at him with hard, anxious eyes.

At the same time—almost as though controlled by the same switch—a white glow sprang up far down at the end of the garden. Someone had turned on the floodlights in the trees over the tennis court. They made a smoky nimbus; they picked out each leaf with a theatrical green; they glimmered through chinks in the poplars. Across this illumination, figures were moving. There were six of them, mostly carrying bags or cameras. But the appearance of one of them, an enormously large and stout man in a black cloak as big as a tent, with a shovel-hat fastened firmly to a great mop of grey-streaked hair, was so arresting that Hugh pointed.

"Look there," he said grimly.

"Well? What about him? Who is it?"

"The worst person who could possibly have turned up here," said Hugh. "That's Gideon Fell."

As though he had heard his name, Dr. Fell turned round like

a galleon and blinked towards the lighted house. They saw eye-glasses on a broad black ribbon; a vast pink face beaming like that of Father Christmas; and a bandit's moustache. He had stepped up into the garden, wearing an expression of such ami-ability and absent-mindedness that he was walking straight into a tree, until a uniformed constable touched his arm and steered him round towards the drive. Dr. Fell politely raised his shovel-hat—whether to the constable, or to the figures in the window, it was not quite clear—and allowed himself to be steered.

Brenda's nerves were such that her laugh sounded more like a giggle.

"He doesn't look very dangerous. He looks too amiable."

"Yes. Quite a number of murderers have thought that."

There was a silence.

"What do you mean by that, Hugh?"

"Only that there's going to be a battle-royal now. With that fellow, of all people——"

"Is he sharper than the other one?"

"No, but he's got more imagination. He's a great friend of Hadley's, and he's a terror for funny business. A trick like this will be straight up his street. Just keep your fingers crossed and pray he won't spot the connexion between too-deep footprints and a picnic-hamper full of china. Brenda, we've got to find the flaw."

"What flaw?"

"*Good evening, sir,*" interrupted a voice from the window, and they both jumped. (This would have to stop, Hugh decided.) "Gates is my name, Inspector Gates," pursued the new comer. "I'm looking for Dr. Young and Superintendent Hadley."

"They're down at the tennis court. Where you see the flood-lights."

"Ah, good," said Inspector Gates pleasantly. "And what might your name be, sir?"

Hugh introduced himself and Brenda. The new comer added, "I see. You're Mr. Rowland, eh? Well, we shall probably be wanting to see both of you soon. Don't go away."

He nodded and left them, leaving the atmosphere disturbed in a highly sinister way.

"Brr!" said Brenda.

"Yes. This means business."

"You don't think he could hear us talking?"

"No, of course not. We don't want to get to the point where we see ghosts every time the furniture creaks. These people are only human like ourselves. But we've got to find the weak point in the story and correct it now." He told her rapidly of the conversation he had overheard. "Hadley said you told a straightforward and reasonable story, except for one point that you would probably explain later. What point? Where did you slip up? What's the flaw?"

"I can't think of any."

Hugh reflected.

"Stop a bit," he muttered. "That second pair of shoes you wore wasn't *too* clean, was it? Your story is that you were wearing the same pair of shoes all afternoon. But remember: you played tennis on a very dusty court. Was the second pair too clean to have been used?"

"No, that's all right. I've played tennis in them at least twice before since they were cleaned last."

"What about a difference in the shoes? Would anybody (Kitty, for instance) be able to say you were wearing one pair at six o'clock and another at eight?"

"No. They were just the same pattern— Why do you mention Kitty?"

If his own fingernails had been longer, he would have gnawed at them. "Because I don't see why Kitty, on a mere snap judgment, is so certain you weren't telling the truth. She accosted me at the tennis court and said your story was nonsense. After all, the story is reasonable. It took me off-guard at first, but it *is* reasonable. The more I think about it, the more reasonable it seems. Why did she say that?"

"Kitty has been very helpful," said Brenda in a colourless voice. "Very, very helpful. She completed the damage to my morale. Of course she would say I was lying whatever I said. She was in love with Frank."

Hugh stared at her.

"In love with Frank?"

"If you could call it love. Didn't you ever notice that? She's been coddling him for some time now. So naturally it would make a difference in what she thought when she found him dead. For such a big woman——"

"I've got the flaw," said Hugh, stopping dead.

"Well?"

"A big woman," he repeated. "You pointed out to Hadley that the person who walked in those shoes of yours must have weighed ten stone. But ten stone is a fairly strapping weight. And a person who weighed ten stone couldn't have worn size four shoes."

Again she corrected him. "Oh, yes. Lots of women who put on weight can still wear a size four. In fact, they do. And there are tall and compact people who take a small size. Kitty, for instance: Kitty wears five-and-a-half for comfort, but she could manage to get into a four——"

"But, hang it all, we can't throw the blame on Kitty!" he protested. "It's no good getting one innocent person out of trouble on fake evidence if you only get another innocent person into trouble on the same evidence." He spoke slowly. "Which is exactly what is wrong with this whole crazy scheme. We're making this a woman's crime when we know ruddy well it must have been a man's. We're playing the murderer's game again."

Or were they?

Hugh's reason said to him: Don't be a fool. Drop it while there's still time. And yet he knew at the back of his mind that he would not drop it, and he knew why. Emerging from the depths of his consciousness was the real reason.

It was a mental picture of the sneer on Old Nick's face.

Nothing would please Nick better than to have him rat on Brenda. Nothing would please Nick better than to have him go to the police (how very virtuously!) and accuse Brenda of trumping up evidence. He could hear Nick's comment: "So that is the man you are thinking of marrying, is it?" To tell the real truth now would land Brenda in even worse trouble. Nobody would believe her then. This frame-up was the only way out. So Nick wanted a battle, did he? All right: he should have it. So Nick thought it would be easy to trip him up, did he? All right: Nick could try.

Hugh felt a great depression lifted from him. He saw Brenda looking at him in a curious way, and he chuckled.

"Have you found that flaw yet?" he inquired.

"Then I *did* say the right thing?"

"Of course you did. And we're going to tell this story and get away with it, that's all."

From the terrace at the end of the garden, a dark figure appeared against the glow of the tennis court. The figure walked slowly, but with an obvious mission. It approached the windows, growing larger and more weighty, and put its head inside.

"Superintendent Hadley would like to see you both at once, sir," said Inspector Gates. "He has some questions he wants to ask you."

X.

ERROR

AT THE tennis court, under a light of flood lamps so white that it looked bluish, Superintendent Hadley was giving Dr. Fell his real opinion about the case.

"—then," he concluded, "Gates 'phoned the Yard and I've been asked to take over. So I told him to stop by and pick you up. Since you're in this neighbourhood, you may as well start right. Now I don't like this cursed business one little bit. I wish I'd never got tangled up in it to begin with. But what happened is pretty clear, don't you think?"

He lowered his voice.

They were standing by the tiny pavilion. Up over theatrical green was a fine night of stars. But the vast tennis court, with grass all around, was full of a bleak Arctic limelight like the glow over an arena; and the hats and coats of the police looked drab as they hustled with activity on the court. A dozen photographs of Frank Dorrance had been taken, enough to satisfy his vanity had he been able to appreciate them; and the police-surgeon was just bending over his body.

Two more men were taking plaster casts of the footprints.

The plaster had taken on a bluish tint under flood lamp rays, which slanted down from the poplars so that flat shadows of the poles supporting the tall wire netting met in the middle, striping the court and filling it with a vague biscuit-pattern of wire. The whitewashed lines had blurred out, and the net hung in a crumpled arc. A subdued mutter of voices—including that of someone absent-mindedly whistling 'Jeepers Creepers'—might have got on the nerves of a watcher unused to it.

In the miniature pavilion, the old lantern had been lighted. Its windows glowed yellow; and its door was open. On the porch lay three objects which a close examination of the grass round the court had disclosed: Frank Dorrance's tennis racket, a small net of tennis-balls, and a bright-jacketed book entitled, *One Hundred Ways of Being a Perfect Husband*.

Hadley lowered his voice still more.

"I've already got statements," he went on, "from Mrs. Bancroft, from the woman Maria Marten—yes, so help me, her name really is Maria Marten!—and from this fellow 'Nick.' I'm now going to have a whack at the two chief witnesses, the White girl and young Rowland. I haven't had a proper talk with the girl. I only saw her for about five minutes at eight o'clock, when she was too hysterical to talk straight. But—" He turned round. "Inspector Gates!"

"Sir?"

"Didn't I send you up to the house after Miss White and Mr. Rowland?"

"Yes, sir. They're here. Shall I send 'em in?"

Hadley hesitated.

"No. Keep them outside for just a minute more." He turned back to Dr. Fell. "But, as I say, the girl seems to be telling a straight story. Don't you think so?"

"We-el . . ." said Dr. Fell.

"Oh? Got some doubts of it, have you?"

Dr. Fell made a gesture of perplexity. He was a vast bandit-figure in cloak and shovel hat, towering beside the pavilion. The light glinted against his eyeglasses on the broad black ribbon; it showed his out-thrust under-lip, and the expression of distress with which he peered from side to side.

"I do not say I have any doubts," he began. His big voice boomed in that enclosed space; then he checked himself, guiltily. "I have not yet had the pleasure of meeting the lady, and so an estimate of her character would be out of place. That was not what bothered me— Hadley, I've been imagining things."

"No! No, by George, you don't! That's exactly what I want to avoid. The facts——"

"Well, but I was just imagining things," argued Dr. Fell, rolling back his head and screwing up his eyes.

"Now look here," said Hadley. "The issue is simple. So are the facts. It all hinges on the question of who made a certain set of footprints. Look out there." He pointed. "As you can see, there are three sets of footprints in the court.

"There are (one) those made by the victim, going out. There are (two) those made by a pair of Brenda White's shoes, going out and coming back. There are (three) those presumably made by young Rowland, going out and coming back. Now the tracks made by the dead man and also by Rowland needn't worry us. I'm going to give Rowland holy hell for walking out there; but his tracks are very shallow ones that were obviously made long after the murder.

"So the only question is this: Did Brenda White make that middle set of tracks herself, or did somebody else make 'em in her shoes? If she did make those tracks, she's guilty of murder.

If she didn't make them, somebody else is guilty. That's what it boils down to. There's no other alternative."

"Not necessarily," said Dr. Fell.

Hadley's eyes narrowed.

"What do you mean, not necessarily? The girl is either guilty or else she isn't?"

"Allow me for one moment," said Dr. Fell, "to keep on soaring all over the place like Icarus. Just how do you read the situation?"

"That the girl isn't guilty. Just go over there and take a look at those tracks! They're much too deep for her to have made, for one thing. This is my idea of what happened:

"Now, Dorrance was last seen alive at five minutes past seven o'clock. Up to the time it stopped raining, the four of them had been sitting in this shack." (Hadley reached out and knocked his knuckles against it.) "I'll tell you in a minute about something queer that happened in there, which doesn't point to any one here as the murderer. When the rain stopped, the four of them separated. Rowland and the White girl walked up the drive; Rowland was going home. Dorrance went back with Mrs. Bancroft to her house—it's only a step away—to get a book and a cigarette case he'd left behind earlier. He left Mrs. Bancroft's house at five minutes past seven. He was then carrying that stuff you see on the porch: tennis, racket, tennis-balls, and the book. He walked back here by way of the path between the garage and the tennis court.

"Next comes conjecture. My guess is that somebody, evidently wearing Brenda White's tennis shoes, was waiting for him here. The murderer used some pretext to get him out on the court, strangle him there, and left a trail of footprints to incriminate the White girl. What the murderer didn't realize was that the surface of the court was much softer than anybody could have foreseen, after that cloudburst of the year; and the footprints were much too deep for Brenda White to have made.

"All right!" continued Hadley, raising one finger for emphasis. "At twenty minutes past seven, the girl herself came down here. She saw Dorrance's body, and had the sense to realize she was being framed. Along came Rowland. They talked it over; they got the wind up for fear of what we might think; and Rowland decided to mess up those tracks beyond recognition with a rake."

Hadley paused.

He had begun to stride back and forth in the grass, occasionally glancing through a side window into the pavilion. His sharp, sceptical eye turned again towards Dr. Fell.

"Of course that's what he was going to do! Destroy the tracks. This sinister episode of the rake—made so much of by Nick and that she-dog Maria—is all my eye. They've been working like blazes to make Rowland out the murderer; but that won't wash. He's supposed to have made threats against Dorrance's life. What threats? According to Mrs. Bancroft, he was overheard to say, 'If we're not careful, there'll be murder done before the day's over,' to which the girl agreed. Later he threatened to plug Dorrance in the eye; and still later he said, 'You've done your last bit of damage, my lad.'

"All that sounds suspicious, I admit, until you know the circumstances. I haven't questioned him yet, so I won't judge. He may be an accomplice of the girl, *if* she's guilty; he probably is. But he didn't kill Dorrance himself—see tracks. So it all comes back to the question, did Brenda White make those footprints or didn't she? I say she didn't. What do you say?"

Dr. Fell sniffed, a long rumbling sniff like a challenge.

He lumbered over and peered at the porch, cutting at the grass with his ivory-headed crutch-stick. He blinked out at the court, where the police-surgeon was just raising Frank Dorrance's body to a sitting position. He turned back to Hadley.

"I say," he repeated, "that I'm still imagining things."

"Then come off it. The facts——"

"And, as a matter of fact," said Dr. Fell, lifting the ivory-headed stick and pointing it at Hadley as though he were laying a spell, "so are you."

"So am I what?"

"Imagining things. You want to believe what you say; you almost do believe what you say; but inside you you are filled with horned and devilish doubts. Now, why?"

"Nonsense!"

"Oh, tut, tut," said Dr. Fell. "My boy, I have known you for twenty-five years. I know when you are on the point of an explosion, and this is one of the times. Why was I sent for in the first place? My scope in police work, I cheerfully admit, is limited. I could not tell you whether it was One-Eyed Ike or Louie the Lizard who cracked Isaac Goldbaum's safe. If I were to attempt shadowing anybody, the shadowee would find himself about as inconspicuous as though he were to walk down Piccadilly pursued by the Albert Memorial. Nor can I take one look at a footprint and tell who made it. No. I am—h'mf—merely your consultant on the *outré;* or, to put it more popularly, the old guy who enjoys funny business. If the issue is so simple, why am I here? Where is the funny business? Or is there any?"

For a moment Hadley was silent: a rigid, upright, brushed figure with a hard jaw and hair and moustache the colour of dull steel. The colour of his eyes went from grey to black when he was disturbed, and had a very black look now. For a moment he stood stiffly, brushing his fingers together. Then he settled his bowler hat more firmly on his head.

"Yes, there is," he admitted. "The White girl couldn't have made those tracks. But, unfortunately, neither could anybody else."

"Ah, that's better. Who are the other suspects?"

"A fellow by the name of Arthur Chandler," Hadley almost shouted. "He's not only a suspect: he's *the* suspect. Due to a mix-up over a girl called Madge Sturgess, he's the ideal man for our money. He had motive, opportunity, and, above all, temperament." Hadley gave a short sketch of the Madge Sturgess affair. "Now, Chandler's a queer card. The motive, which wouldn't be so strong in most cases, with him would be overwhelming. He's what you might call a cold hothead. I know him, because he's seen trouble before. When he went for one of the other people on the bill at the Orpheum——"

Dr. Fell blinked.

"At the Orpheum Music-Hall, you mean? What does he do there?"

"He's an acrobat. Sensational stuff on the high wire and trapeze; also hand-stands, twirls, and tossings-about in a group. He's not very eminent: only one of a turn called the Flying Mephistos. Chandler is an educated chap who's come down on his luck, with rather a wolfish sense of humour. Likable sort of fellow, too. But he worships this Sturgess girl, and he'd kill Dorrance for a trick like that."

Hadley hitched up his shoulders. A part of his real grievance began to come out.

"I suppose it's partly my own damned fault. I warned the old man—Dr. Young—about him. If he hadn't been so ha-ha about the whole thing, I was going to suggest police protection. But, oh, no. I lost my temper and walked out. When I learned that Chandler had been seen in this neighbourhood this afternoon, I was back here in a hurry. Only to find this."

He pointed.

"Now, Fell, I'm practically certain Chandler was here at this tennis court too. Mrs. Bancroft tells me that somebody got into the shed and left a newspaper, conspicuously head-lining Madge Sturgess's case. If anybody would think of a trick like that, you can bet it would be Chandler. The newspaper isn't there now, by the way. If anybody would think of a trick like killing Dorrance in someone else's shoes, it would be Chandler. I'm certain he was in this very shed. When I first heard about the murder, I plumped for him immediately. I still think he's the likeliest person. Only . . ."

"Only?"

"That," said Hadley, and nodded with emphasis towards the line of footprints. "He could no more have made those tracks in number four shoes than young Rowland. Chandler is a tallish, lanky fellow with feet like canal-barges. It's impossible.

"Then again, as a possibility, there's Madge Sturgess herself. I don't consider her very seriously. I don't think it's very likely that any woman would attempt suicide one night and murder the next. But she must have felt pretty sick when her suicide didn't come off; and the 'farewell' note she left shows enough bitterness against Dorrance to sound capable of anything. But back we come with a bang to the same infernal snag! She is not very tall. She could (I imagine) have worn number four shoes. But her weight can't be more than eight stone, and she could no more have made those deep tracks than Brenda White."

Again Hadley paused.

Leaning forward with some intensity, he tapped the finger of his right hand into the palm of his left.

"Are you beginning to see," he asked, "why this case is a simple issue and a nightmare at the same time?"

"Yes," said Dr. Fell.

"Good. On the one hand"—Hadley upturned his left palm—"we have Brenda White and Hugh Rowland. Either might have done the murder. But neither could have. Brenda White could have worn the small shoes, but couldn't have left the deep track. Hugh Rowland could have left the deep tracks, but couldn't have worn the small shoes. On the other hand"—he held up his right palm—"we have Arthur Chandler and Madge Sturgess. Exactly the same thing applies there. Deep tracks versus small shoes. Consequently . . ."

He broke off.

The police-surgeon, a Highgate G.P. who shared this work with other doctors as a part-time job, had come off the tennis court. He was carrying the scarf with which Frank Dorrance had been strangled: folded over twice, it made a thick, soft band some inch-and-a-half wide, broadening to full width at the loose ends where it had been tied.

"Well, Doctor?" inquired Hadley.

"I suppose," said the police-surgeon, "I've got to do a post-mortem as a matter of form. But I can tell you now what killed him. This did." He shook the scarf. "I'm taking him away now, if you'll give me a receipt for him. I thought you might want this scarf, though. There are some fingernail-tears in the end of it."

Hadley grunted. "I'd noticed that. Yes, you can take him. I've got the stuff out of his pockets." He raised his voice. *"All right, boys!"*

They waited in silence while the body was carried past them. The police-surgeon hesitated.

"I can tell you something else," he offered. "Somebody's been monkeying with your evidence."

Both Hadley and Dr. Fell turned round sharply.

"Somebody," the police-surgeon continued, "tried to untie that scarf and pull it loose after the boy was dead. It's none of my business, but I thought I'd mention it."

"The murderer, you mean?"

"Couldn't tell you that. Might have been. Stranglers don't though, as a rule. Usually, when they find out what they've done, they lose their heads and bolt. That's all, Superintendent. Good-night."

Hadley stared after him. "They lose their heads and bolt," he said, staring at the scarf. "I don't think this murderer lost his head, though. Now look here, Fell. I've told you what the difficulties are. I've told you what . . . *Hoy!* Fell! Wake up!"

For several minutes, in fact, Dr. Fell did not seem to have been listening. First he had peered from one end of the tennis court to the other; then up over its high wire and down to the narrow strip of grass inside. Hadley's mention of the acrobat seemed to fascinate him. On his vast red face there was a hollow, incredulous expression which became half a chuckle. Finally, with concentrated absent-mindedness, he took out a cigar and put it in one corner of his mouth as though he were trying to impersonate a news-editor in a particularly tough film.

"I'm awake," he answered. "I was thinking—well, to tell you the truth, I was thinking about somebody's presence of mind."

"Oh? Whose?"

"Brenda White's."

"Go on," said Hadley very quietly.

Dr. Fell chewed at the cigar. "Let us," he said with an air of Gargantuan distress, "let us for the moment reconstruct the finding of the body by Miss White. Let us suppose that she is telling the truth. At twenty minutes past seven, then, she starts down here to . . ." He stopped. "By the way, I don't think I heard that. Why *did* she come down here?"

Hadley was impatient.

"Oh. I don't know. To get a picnic-basket or something."

"A picnic-basket? What did she want with a picnic-basket?"

"Maria sent her for it," explained the Superintendent. "It sounds like a useless errand, but then you don't know Maria. There was also a question of getting some clothes-pegs; Maria uses the tennis court to dry the wash. Which reminds me—I can't quite make out Maria's position in this household. She gets excited and calls the boss by his first name; but she does all their washing and ironing. She gives orders even to the White girl; but takes 'em from the other servants. What's she doing in the business anyhow?"

Dr. Fell did not seem to hear.

"A picnic-basket," he ruminated. He glanced in through the window of the shed. His gaze wandered incuriously over two benches, a row of lockers, and a dilapidated object like a large suitcase. "I don't see any basket there. Did she get it?"

"No. She saw Dorrance's body, and——"

"And *didn't* run out on the court to see what was wrong," said Dr. Fell.

They looked at each other squarely.

"Hadley," the doctor continued, with thunderous earnestness, "I say nothing against the young lady. You have obviously been impressed by her *beaux yeux*. She may be (for all I know) a combination of Florence Nightingale and Dame Alice Lisle. But aren't you a bit staggered by her inhuman presence of mind?"

"Yes, but——"

"One moment. Put yourself in her place. She comes down here after a picnic-basket. It is still darkish after the storm, and even more dark here inside these trees. Unexpectedly, she comes on the body of the man she has intended to marry. All that flashes out at her, all she can see, is the sudden horrifying view of a man lying strangled at the end of a blur of tracks in the sand. You know what most people would have done. The natural impulse—in anybody—would have been to rush out and see what was wrong. Hey?"

"I know; but——"

"Now what restrains her, even from going just a little bit closer than the door of the court? Shock? Fear? Repulsion? We could understand that. But she says not. If I understand you correctly, even at a time like that she noted the tracks in the court. She observed something queer about them. She noted that they were the same size as her own shoes. She compared them with her own, and remembered a pair of spare shoes she had left in this shed. And, realizing it was all a frame-up against her, she stopped on dry land."

Again Dr. Fell screwed up his eyes behind the glasses on the broad black ribbon. He added more mildly:

"It is not impossible. It is only incredible."

Hadley nodded with a certain grimness.

"Yes, yes, I know all that," he snapped. "It occurred to me, too. The first question I want to ask her is how she took one look at the court and recognized a print made by her own shoe. But (don't you see?) it's not evidence. Show me any evidence of how a girl weighing seven stone was heavy enough to make——"

His uncertain gaze wandered through the side window of the pavilion. He stopped for a moment, and then said abruptly:

"Look here, Fell. I wonder what's in that thing?"

"What thing?"

"That old suitcase. Over there in the corner."

"I don't know. Have you looked?"

"No, but——"

"Superintendent!" called a sharp voice from the tennis court.

One of the men who were taking casts of the footprints, a plain-clothes sergeant, got up hastily from his knees.

"I've got something here that may interest you, sir," he went on. He stepped gingerly over the now-hard court, opened the door, and came round to the pavilion holding out the palm of his hand in front of him.

"It's a piece of fingernail, sir," he said. "Broken off or torn off. Looks like a woman's: at least, it's got that pink varnishy stuff on it. It caught the light off these flood lamps."

"Where did you find this? Near the body?"

"No, sir. Between two of the set of tracks. We've called the set of tracks *A* for the dead man's, *B* for the woman's, and *C* for the other man's. This was on the ground between *B* and *C,* nearer to *C,* about a dozen feet from the wire door."

Hadley examined it. He looked at Dr. Fell, who muttered to himself and did not look back.

"Put this in a cellophane envelope," said Hadley curtly. "Mark it. Also mark its position on that plan you're drawing." He glowered at Dr. Fell; he had a hard, almost colourless face, with a greyish cropped moustache and greyish-black eyebrows, but the blood seemed to come up under his eyes. "I don't know whether the White girl had a part of a fingernail torn off. I didn't notice, though I remember her nails were that colour. But we'll soon have an opportunity to see. And, by the Lord Harry, if that young lady has been telling me a pack of lies——"

"Steady, now."

"If I thought, I repeat——"

"Look here," protested Dr. Fell mildly. "For twenty-five years I have been attempting to instil into you the principles of spiritual calm. And you won't have 'em. You always incline strongly, not to say violently, in one direction. But if by any chance you find your original idea rocking a little, you always go just as violently in the other direction. There may be some quite innocent explanation of that bit of fingernail."

"There had better be."

"You are furthermore," pursued Dr. Fell, beginning to fire up on his own part, "allowing an elementary flaw in your reasoning. I was about to point this out to you when you complained about my imagination. But let that go, for the moment. What are you to do?"

"Do?" snorted Hadley. "Do?" He took his notebook out of his breast pocket and put it on the porch of the pavilion. He placed the blue-and-white scarf beside it. Taking out a pencil and a pen-knife, he opened the blade of the knife. "A piece of fingernail torn off! Fingernail scratches in that scarf! Do? I'm going to have that young couple in here straight away, that's what I'm going to do. And if they don't tell me an absolutely straight story . . . ! All right, Inspector. Send 'em along."

He began to sharpen the pencil. The knife was still scraping against the lead, with sharp, ugly little rasps, when Hugh and Brenda came in.

"Watch me," said Hadley.

XI.

BEWILDERMENT

THAT TIME of waiting just outside the gate had not improved Hugh's nerves. But he believed Hadley had done it deliberately, and steeled himself. He and Brenda waited in the presence of a constable who would not be drawn into conversation. They stared up at the stars; they talked very little; the worst moment was when Frank's body was carried past them, very distinct in the light of motor-car lamps up in the drive.

"This way, sir," said the constable.

"Do we—do we go in together?" asked Brenda, as though they were outside a dentist's office.

"Yes, ma'am. This way."

Entering under the vast and bluish glare of the floodlights, Hugh thought less of a dentist's office than of a stadium or a prize ring: say the ring at the National Sporting Club. He told himself again that he was not nervous, but there was a hollow in his chest and his legs felt light and shaky.

Eyes followed them all the way round the side of the court to the pavilion. Eyes noted every move they made. Superintendent Hadley, with one foot on the low porch, was sharpening a pencil against his knee. He straightened up with an air of great politeness and suavity; much too great suavity, Hugh thought. Hugh, whose nerves were strung up to an abnormal pitch of sensitiveness, sniffed trouble. Hadley had black-looking eyes which fixed you and seemed to swallow up everything else roundabout. He greeted them with a friendly smile, and shook hands with Hugh.

"Good evening, Mr. Rowland. I haven't had the pleasure of meeting you since—let's see, when was it? It must have been at the Jewell trial, wasn't it?"

"That's right, Superintendent. The Jewell trial. I was at the solicitors' table."

(Did his own voice really sound as far-away as this?)

"Yes, of course. You were at the solicitors' table," said Hadley with a certain inflection. "Sorry to have to trouble you again, Miss White." (Brenda nodded composedly.) "But there are a few little points we should like to clear up, and then we'll not have to bother you again. I don't think either of you have met Dr. Fell?"

At any other time, Hugh knew, there would have been a twinkle in the doctor's eye. His face would have glowed like Old King Cole's; chuckles would have animated his several chins and travelled down the ridges of his waistcoat; he would have swept off his shovel-hat and given Brenda a great bow. At the moment he merely removed the hat, showing a mop of grey-streaked hair tumbling over one ear. He studied, rather uneasily, the unlighted cigar in his hand. And Hugh's abnormally alert senses registered something else.

Both Hadley and Dr. Fell had glanced, with brief casualness, at Brenda's right hand.

"I wish I could ask you to sit down," pursued Hadley, "but I'm afraid—here, I've got an idea. We'll just haul out one of these benches." He ducked his head through the little door of the pavilion. "There we are," he concluded, pushing a bench across the porch with a long scrape and rasp of wood. "No, ho, no; sit there, both of you. I'll stand."

They sat down. Again Hadley glanced at Brenda's right hand.

Well, that was all right, Hugh told himself. He had that infernal bit of fingernail tucked away safely in his right-hand trousers' pocket. But did they suspect anything?

"First of all," continued Hadley, holding the point of the pencil up against the light and studying it, "I may tell you that I've taken a statement from Mrs. Bancroft. So what I want from you is mostly—corroboration, shall we say?" He smiled agreeably, looking down from the pencil.

"Whatever you want to call it," said Brenda.

"Good! Now, I understand that earlier this afternoon"— again Hadley inspected the pencil—"Mr. Rowland asked you to break off your engagement to Mr. Dorrance. This was in the hearing of Mr. Dorrance and Mrs. Bancroft. And you refused. Is that correct?"

Brenda had not anticipated this line of attack. Her face grew slowly pink.

"Yes, I did—then."

"I see. You mean you had occasion to change your mind later?"

"I suppose I always intended to change my mind, really."

"Still, you did change your mind a little later?"

"Yes."

"Why, Miss White?"

Brenda turned slightly and gave Hugh a glance of appeal. But, for the moment, Hugh was not listening. Very casually he had thrust his right hand into his trouser's pocket, to make sure the bit of fingernail was safe. And the bit of fingernail was not there.

He sat rigid, filled with a rush of panic. It was not there. His scraping finger found the petrol lighter, found the tobacco-dust with which the seams of the pocket were lined, but they found nothing else.

He had dropped it. Where in God's name had he dropped it? On the court, when Kitty surprised him? Dislodged from his pocket when he put the lighter back in? Where on the court? Because they knew; they knew, right enough. His eyes moved slightly, to take in the court, and Hadley's black, swallowing gaze returned to him.

"I see you're feeling in your pocket, Mr. Rowland. Do you want a cigarette?" Hadley took out a packet. "Have one of these."

"No, thanks."

"You, Miss White?"

"No, thanks; not now," said Brenda, and cleared her throat.

"Just as you like. Going back to this question of changing your mind——"

Hugh interposed. "If you don't mind my suggesting it, Superintendent," he said, and was surprised at the coolness of his voice, "we can't help you much by going over that ground. Miss White didn't dislike him; she just didn't want to marry him. As for myself, I freely confess I thought he was a swine." He added, drawing a bow at a venture: "I wonder what a brother of Madge Sturgess would have thought of him."

The shaft whacked straight to the centre of the target. He saw that. But Hadley was not to be drawn.

"You couldn't have liked him very much, Miss White? You wouldn't have married him even for your share of fifty thousand pounds?"

"No, I wouldn't. Besides, I shouldn't have got it anyway."

(*Look out,* Hugh's inner voice cried out to her. *Watch your step! Watch your*——)

"You wouldn't have got it anyway?" Hadley repeated. "What do you mean by that, Miss White?"

"The money was all in Frank's name."

"But I understood it was a joint inheritance?"

"No, no, no," said Brenda earnestly. "Get the lawyers to show you the will. That was how Uncle Jerry tied it up so there couldn't be a divorce or separation. I mean, it would be no good if we married one week, got the money, and divorced the next week. The fifty thousand is capital. It's invested at between six and eight per cent interest, and brings in close on four thousand a year. Frank was to have the interest on it so long as we didn't divorce or separate. Of course, it was theoretically a joint inheritance, because I was to have an adequate allowance. But it wasn't really; Frank was full of a scheme for putting it all into managing night-clubs; and neither of us could touch the capital unless the other——"

She stopped.

"I see," observed Hadley, examining the point of the pencil. "Unless the other died. So now you've got it all without strings attached. Is that correct?"

You had to admire Brenda's composure, or apparent composure. Her chin was up, and she shook back her hair with a mechanical gesture. She had crossed her kneees, and the toe of one shoe moved sharply, quickly, nervously; that was all.

Hugh was conscious of all things with vividness: the bench on which they sat, like a couple of school children; Frank's tennis racket lying almost at their feet; the tawdry pavilion with the lantern burning inside; even the edge of the picnic-hamper which he could see beyond the open door. He had to make an effort to keep his eyes off that picnic-hamper. *Where had he lost that bit of fingernail?*

"I didn't mean that," said Brenda. "Please, what's the good of suggesting it?"

"I wasn't suggesting anything, Miss White. I was only repeating what you said. Did you know of this proviso, Mr. Rowland?"

"Yes."

"You knew of it. I see." The point of the pencil was at last to Hadley's satisfaction. "Let's leave that for the time being, and go on to the time when all of you came down here to play tennis. I believe, Mr. Rowland, you were overheard to say, 'If we're not careful, there'll be murder done before the day's over.' And Miss White agreed with you."

"Yes."

"What did you mean by that?"

Hugh laughed. "Nothing at all, Superintendent. If your informant heard the rest of it, you'll know we agreed it was only nerves due to the heat before the storm broke." He paused. "Can't you understand that? Didn't you feel the heat yourself? Mightn't it have tempted you into saying or doing something you shouldn't have?"

Hadley swung around.

"Meaning exactly what, Mr. Rowland?"

(Lord knows. Only the arrow whacked the centre of the target again.)

"Nothing at all, Superintendent. Honestly."

"You began to play tennis," pursued Hadley. "I want to be quite clear about this part. You and Mrs. Bancroft were playing Miss White and Mr. Dorrance?"

"Yes."

"Miss White and Mr. Dorrance had the south side of the court. You and Mrs. Bancroft had the north side—that is, the side of the net where Mr. Dorrance's body was later found? Is that right?"

Hugh followed his glance towards the court. "Yes, that's right."

"You played until—when?"

"Until the storm broke, at about a quarter past six."

"And during this time, I'm told, you threatened Mr. Dorrance again?"

"Not exactly. I threatened to hit him."

"But you also used the words, 'I would like to murder you'?"

"Maybe. I don't remember."

"I see," said Hadley, whose eyes never wavered. "Did anything else happen during that game?"

Hugh, coming to a decision, rode straight into the hurricane. "Nothing that I remember. Nothing important, anyhow." He paused. "Except that during the last game, when Brenda was serving, she broke the top of the nail off her middle finger. That was another reason why she wasn't keen on continuing the game."

Silence.

It was a silence so absolute, in fact, that he could hear moths fluttering round the lantern in the pavilion. Every person in that enclosure was looking at him. Again he had to drag his eyes away from the picnic-hamper.

"You don't seem to believe me, for some reason," Hugh said. "I didn't know it was important. But it happens to be true. Isn't it, Brenda?"

"Of course, it's true," answered Brenda, with something like a laugh. "Look!" She held out her hand. "If you've ever played tennis, Mr. Hadley, you'll know it's the middle finger that takes the jar when the racket is held loosely. It pained like fury when I first did it, but I'd forgotten all about it. Why do you ask?"

Another silence.

Hadley walked round in the grass to the other side of the porch, behind them. He picked up what they both recognized as Frank Dorrance's scarf. He returned to face them, drawing the scarf through his fingers.

"Is that so, now?" Hadley said with great satisfaction. "You broke off that fingernail while you were playing?"

"Yes, of course."

"*On* the court?"

"Yes."

"As a matter of fact, I was going to ask you about that. I think we've found the missing bit. Sergeant!"

"Sir?"

"Let me have that envelope, will you? Yes, I think this will fit. If you don't mind, Miss White? Thank you . . . Miss White, you and Mr. Dorrance were playing on the south side of the net. How do you explain the fact that we found this piece of fingernail on the north side, not very many feet from Mr. Dorrance's body?"

"Because," said Hugh instantly, "she was playing on the north side of the net during the last game."

"She was——?"

Hugh contrived to stare at him.

"Yes, of course. We changed sides of the net at the end of the fourth game. Ask Kitty Bancroft, if you don't believe me."

Again Hugh paused.

"Look here, work out the position. The score was five to two in favour of Brenda and Frank. They were on this side of the net; Brenda was serving, and one point had been played in the eighth game. In the last point we played, Brenda served to Kitty. That means she was serving from the service-court on the east side—towards the pavilion—towards us now. So you probably found that bit of fingernail somewhere near all those lines of footprints, maybe ten or a dozen feet from the wire door."

At the end of another silence he added:

"I suppose that's where you did find it, and you're reading some sinister meaning into the whole? Hang it, Superintendent, no! I could have told you about that long ago."

He sat back.

Casually and half-smilingly, he put his hand over Brenda's. Brenda's hand was ice-cold, though she laughed with him. In the background Dr. Gideon Fell, vast and sleepy and also half-smiling, glanced at Hadley and made a gesture as though he were pushing a chess-piece into place.

"Check," said Dr. Fell.

Hadley put the cellophane envelope into his pocket. He was very pleasant.

"Come, now, Mr. Rowland! Do you honestly expect me to believe that?"

"Naturally. It's true."

"I hope it is," said Hadley, looking very hard at him. "We must see whether Mrs. Bancroft knows anything about it. Sergeant! Just step over to Mrs. Bancroft's and ask her to join us. You might get Dr. Young as well." Again he grew very brisk. "When the storm broke, I'm told, all four of you took shelter in this shed——"

Hugh nodded. "Yes. And found a newspaper headlining the attempted suicide of Madge Sturgess. Some outsider had left it there very recently. It had Frank Dorrance badly rattled, though he tried not to admit it."

(It was interesting, he thought, what a strong effect could be produced by mentioning the name of Madge Sturgess. What it meant he had no idea. But it was a suggestion he meant to use, and use, and use again.)

Hadley opened his notebook.

"So you got the impression Mr. Dorrance was rattled?"

"Yes. But it wasn't my impression alone. Kitty Bancroft commented on it, and asked him what was wrong."

"Did he tell you?"

"No. I'm afraid not."

"Then what gave you the idea he was rattled?"

"I can answer that," interposed Brenda. She turned her head round slightly, so that the light from the doorway shone on her eyes, on her half-parted lips, and on the hard hectic flush that had risen in her face as though from a violent reaction. "It was Frank's manner. You couldn't have mistaken it if you'd known him. And then it was from what we'd been talking about. You might as well know this, Mr. Hadley. We started talking about ways of committing murder."

Though he tried not to show it, this clearly was news to Hadley. He jerked up his head.

"Ways of—? Hold on! Mrs. Bancroft didn't say anything about that."

"Probably not," said Brenda, with her eye on a corner of the porch-roof. "Kitty began it by saying she'd been accused of murdering her husband in Winnipeg; and that when she heard you were here this afternoon she was horribly frightened for fear the police had discovered new evidence."

Sensation. Hadley glanced across at Dr. Fell.

"Miss White, is this a joke?"

"Oh, I don't know," Brenda answered fretfully. "Later she said it was, but I've been wondering." Brenda then proceeded to give a detailed account of everything that had been said in the pavilion.

"You see, I had been thinking about strangulation as a method of murder," she explained, her wide blue eyes compelling belief. "That's why I didn't run out on the court as soon as I saw Frank lying there. Do you think, if I had only seen him lying there and nothing else, I shouldn't have run out there in a hurry? I'm not quite such a calculating beast as all that. It was because he had been *strangled*. It was like a nightmare come true. I simply couldn't move."

"So—that's—it," muttered Hadley.

Again he glanced across at Dr. Fell, who grunted. Almost imperceptibly the scale-pans were beginning to dip in their favor. Hadley's expression betrayed little; but it betrayed enough to Hugh.

"I knew perfectly well there was something wrong," said Brenda. "Anybody would have. If you first make a lot of broad hints about garrotting somebody with a silk scarf, and on top of that somebody is garrotted with a silk scarf . . . oh, it's ridiculous and horrible at the same time!"

Hadley was soothing.

"I can quite understand that, Miss White. But how did you come to recognize a footprint made by your own shoe?"

"That's just it. I didn't, at first. Then I thought, 'What's he doing out there?' And I saw the tracks. My mind was on tennis, tennis, tennis, tennis; it was a flat footprint, like a tennis shoe, and I'm the only one hereabouts who wears as small a size as that."

"And you, realized it was a frame-up?"

"Good heavens, no! I never thought of a frame-up. At least,

I didn't then." Brenda opened her eyes. "All I thought of was somebody in my shoes; and that I literally, physically couldn't go near him. You—you saw his poor old face."

"As a matter of fact, that was one of the things I wanted to ask you about," he went on, in tones of such suavity that again an alarm bell buzzed in Hugh's mind. "We'd better get it in order. In the statement you gave me a while ago, there are a few things I still haven't got quite clear."

"Yes?"

"Now, you say here"—he frowned—"that at seven o'clock, after the end of the storm, Mr. Dorrance went home with Mrs. Bancroft and you walked up the drive with Mr. Rowland. You said he was 'going home.'"

"Yes?"

"Well, it's plain Mr. Rowland didn't go home. Where did he go?"

"I don't know," replied Brenda, after a quick look at Hugh. "He got into his car and drove away."

"'Got into his car,'" repeated Hadley, with meticulous concentration, as his pencil moved, "'and drove away.' I see. You went straight into the house, I understand, and back to the kitchen. Now we come to the point that wasn't quite clear. It's about why you came down here to the tennis court afterwards."

Hugh's unspoken voice said to her: Brenda White, if ever in your life you watched your step, watch it now! His scalp tingled with the effort to send her a kind of telepathic warning. The tension in the group was apparent; he could hear the asthmatic wheezing of Dr. Fell's breath.

"You say that the maid, Maria, asked you to come down here and get a—a picnic-basket. Is that correct?"

"No, no. Not a picnic-basket. A picnic-hamper."

"A picnic-hamper?"

"Yes."

"But what's the difference?" inquired Hadley. He was almost jovial. "It's the same thing, isn't it? It always is when my wife drags me off to the country."

"No, no. This was different," said Brenda; and stopped.

"But what is it, Miss White? Where is it?"

It was very obvious. It might have burnt their fingers, inside the pavilion and under the shaky flame of the lantern.

"It's in there," said Brenda, after a brief glance over her shoulder. "In the corner. You can see it."

"That? That suitcase? That thing you've been looking at so often in the past fifteen minutes?" She seemed about to retort, but Hadley forestalled her. He took one step up on the low porch, and peered through the door. "It doesn't look as though it would be much good to anybody. Why did she want it? What's in it?"

Brenda did not move.

"Just one or two bits of china; and—and a thermos flask."

"China," muttered Hadley. Still clinging to the lintel of the door, he craned his neck round and peered out towards the tennis court. He studied the wavering line of footprints there. Then he turned back again.

"You see," Brenda went on, as though by the effort of quick talking she could force his attention away from it, "Maria wanted it. And then I particularly promised Kitty, I gave her my solemn promise, that I would take it up to the house today. I swore I would. Kitty said it was good leather, and it was rotting to pieces."

Hadley was alert.

"You promised Mrs. Bancroft you would take this to the house today?"

"Yes, I did. Didn't I, Hugh?"

"Very much so."

"But you didn't actually *get* it?"

"No. She said it was good leather, and it was absolutely rotting all to pieces down here——"

"I see. Heavy, is it, Miss White?"

"Not particularly."

With a murmured apology, Hadley ducked his head under the door and squeezed himself into the pavilion. They saw his back bend over the hamper. He straightened up. "You're quite right," he added, his voice coming back hollowly. He turned round, bumping into the lantern; and when he edged out again Hugh saw, with a kind of maniacal abstraction, that he was carrying the hamper by two fingers.

Holding it like a box, Hadley undid the clasps. There were no tennis shoes inside, nor was there much of anything else. With the exception of two cups and a cracked plate, the hamper was empty.

XII.

MALICE

At Kitty Bancroft's trim little house round the corner, both Kitty and Nick were in the front garden when the sergeant came to summon them.

Round the little garden ran a whitewashed wall, eight feet high, pierced by a gate in whose arch hung a tiny box lamp. Inside there were rose-trees, bedraggled at the end of the summer, on either side of a lawn with a crazy-paved path. The front of the house was gay with awnings over French windows. Light came from the windows, as dim as the light in the box lamp flickering over the gate.

Nick was in his wheel chair. He had opened his claspknife with his teeth, and was engaged in the delicate task of trying to peel an apple with one hand and in semi-darkness. Kitty sat on the front step; her hands were clasped round her knees, and her head was lowered to them. Nick's quiet, vicious cursing had grown monotonous.

Kitty raised her head.

"You're tired, poor old boy," she said. "I've given you something to eat. Why don't you go home and lie down?"

"Lie down!" said Nick. "That's all anybody ever seems to think of—lie down! How old d'ye think I am, anyhow? If I had my legs, I'd run a mile against anybody in North London. Yes, and fence seven touches with him too."

Kitty cast up her eyes, shivered, and retired to the seclusion of her arms again.

"I won't have it," said Nick. "It's my house. It's my tennis court. They're not going to order me about like that; not while I have any influence left." He was silent for a time. Then she was surprised to hear him chuckling. "Still, you know, maybe it's best. The slow approach—the subtle approach—the dramatic approach——"

Again Kitty raised her head.

"Nick."

"Eh?"

"Who do you think really killed Frank?"

"Mr. Jackanapes Rowland."

Kitty was impatient. "Oh, yes, I know we say he did. But who do you think did really?"

"Mr. Jackanapes Rowland," said Nick. The apple crunched under his teeth.

For perhaps the sixth time that day, Kitty had again changed her clothes. Her late husband used to say that she could get from one outfit into another quicker than any woman he had ever known; and, though his experience had been limited, this may have been true. She had replaced her evening gown with black, unrelieved black, against which the whites of her eyes stood out more clearly than the swarthy skin.

"I don't know what you think," Kitty told him through stiff jaws. "But there's one thing we've got to do. We've got to stop Brenda from telling that lie again."

"You think Brenda's lying?"

"Of *course* she's lying. I'm not clever like some people. I rather distrust these clever people. (And don't you sneer at me, either.) But to me——"

"H'h?"

"It seems so plain. When poor old Frank was killed, don't you see, there were no footprints in the court? Brenda found him after he was dead, and made the tracks herself. Since then she's been afraid to 'fess up, for fear the police would think she did it."

"Won't do," said Nick, with his mouth full of apple.

"Why not? Why not?"

"Tracks too deep. Besides, somebody had to kill Frank. How'd the murderer cross the court and back without leaving footprints himself? Eh?"

"You're so stupid," said Kitty. "I don't mean that really, but you are. How on earth do you suppose poor Frank was persuaded to go out on that court at all? You know how neat he was. You know how he hated getting his shoes mucked up." She spoke with fierce intensity. "It was a bet, that's what it was. Don't you remember that terrible argument Frank had with Hugh Rowland not very long ago, over the gymnastics business? Frank bet him that——"

Nick stopped her.

"I do remember it," he interrupted in a very soft voice. "I remembered it an hour ago. I have been wondering if Rowland does. I particularly want you to remember it."

"That's what I mean. Something like that, only different. Frank was such a *child*. Some ghastly person said, 'I can do so-and-so.' Frank said, 'You can't.' So they tried it. It might just as well have been something that left no marks in the court: like a long jump, for instance. Then again it could have been a pole-jump—or do I mean pole-vault? They always called it pole-vault in Canada."

Again Nick stopped her.

"The world's record for the long jump," he said, "is twenty-five feet eleven and one-eighth inches. Or at least it was ten years ago, which is good enough. You're suggesting the murderer jumped twenty-four feet. No, my one-and-only. No. An Olympic champion in good form, if he first had a long run to give him impetus, MIGHT have made a distance like that. But, to jump inside that tennis court, you would have to stand with your back to the wire and take off standing, without any run. No. That's n.d.g., my one-and-only. It's impossible."

Nick was speaking more rapidly, and in a conspiratorial way. He crunched the apple again.

"As for your pole-vault—good. Very good! But not quite good enough. I suppose you thought of that when you heard about Rowland with the rake in his hands?"

"I never thought any such thing," cried Kitty. "It never occurred to me."

"Ah, but I did," Nick assured her, lowering his voice. "As I say, good. With a rake (or better still, a clothes-prop) you might make a little distance. But not very much distance, and the same objection applies: you've got to have room to run. No, Kitty. No murderer can float through the air with the greatest of ease."

There was a silence.

What might have struck Kitty, almost with a shiver, was that Nick had recovered his old-time geniality. After a brief, bad bout in the sheer ravings of grief, an hour ago, he seemed a different man. Only Kitty had witnessed that brief breakdown; Kitty had

THE PROBLEM OF THE WIRE CAGE · 137

stood by, a rock of strength, holding his head as though he were physically ill, and saying nothing.

Nobody had seen Nick at his best that day. He was again the affable, always-half-joking companion; the host who loved to overwhelm people with hospitality; the good storyteller and the founder of the feast. He had recovered his old-time charm. He added:

"No. Brenda's telling the truth. She wouldn't lie to me."

"But why are you so sure?"

"Because she never has," answered Nick, with obvious sincerity. "Brenda says she didn't make those footprints, and that's all there is to it. Somebody else made the footprints in her shoes— that's simple enough, isn't it? I don't see why you're so opposed to it."

Kitty spoke sharply.

"I'll tell you why. The next thing you know, they may be saying *I* made the tracks."

Nick hooted with derision.

"Yes, of course it's absurd," Kitty flung back at him. "But, in case you don't know it, I can get into a number four shoe. And I made a stupid joke today that's been worrying me ever since. There."

"Who," muttered Nick, "who was it that invented that old *cliché* about conscience making cowards of us all? Bible or Shakespeare, I daresay. That's your trouble Kitty. You! Kill Frank? Not likely! D'ye see, my dear, I know how matters stood between you and Frank."

Kitty spoke even more sharply.

"What do you mean by that?"

Nick chuckled. Settling into the chair, which creaked, he put his head back in comfort; she could see dimly that he was look-ing up at the stars, immeasurable in a lighter sky over the dark well of the garden.

"I wonder where he is now," Nick said. "Gad, he had spirit, that boy! I like to see a lad with spirit! Lord, Kitty, I didn't mind. I knew there were nights when he didn't leave your house until four or five o'clock in the morning. I knew it'd be good for him. Learn things from an older woman. You know?"

He raised his head and blinked at her.

"Good experience," said Nick. "Good for the boy, so long as— mind you—it didn't interfere with his marriage. And I know it wasn't likely to do that. After all, Kitty: eh? You and I are grown up. A little light affair is one thing, if it's not too serious; and, af-ter all, you were much too old for him."

Kitty's eyes were enormous. Her arms were still clasped round her knees, her head down on them; and she looked at him across them as though over a parapet.

"If it comes to that," she said, "you are much older than Bren-da; very many years more than I was older than Frank."

The wheel chair creaked.

"As you say," pursued Kitty, with a raw, harsh edge to her voice which rang in the quiet garden, "you and I are grown up. We're probably the only people hereabouts who are grown up. So we can be frank with each other, can't we?"

"My dear——"

"I've seen you look at her, Nick. They say you had the mother once. Do you want the daughter too?"

Nick looked at her in the gloom.

"Crude wench, aren't you?" he said.

"If necessary," said Kitty, nodding, "I can be. I don't want to be. I like nice things round me: clothes, and flowers, and seeing people happy. But this thing has happened to us somehow. It's got to be faced out. And I've had enough experience in my life to be cruder than anybody you're ever likely to meet. I want to know. Did you want Frank out of the way so that you could get Brenda into a corner?"

"Are you trying to say *I* killed Frank?"

"I don't know," replied Kitty abruptly, and shivered and stared up at the sky.

Nick did not take offence. With his left hand he flung away the apple-core, clumsily, so that it struck a window of the house, spattered there, and whirled off into a rose-tree. Then he spoke to her with such gentleness that she turned to look at him.

"That's the second time today somebody's said that," observed Nick. "Listen to me. What do you think I am? Do you think I've worked and schemed, and worked and schemed (and, by God! how I have!) to get Brenda and Frank married, just so that I could kill Frank a month before the wedding? I'm not likely to have any children. Do you think I don't want any children? Do you think I would kill Frank, of all people?"

Kitty jerked her shoulder. "No, I don't suppose I do, really. Only it seems awfully queer that—that———"

She did not seem to know what she meant herself. She made a gesture towards his bandages.

"I know," said Nick. "Go to fiction, thou sluggard. Always suspect the cripple in the wheel chair. If this were a detective story, I'd have suspected myself long ago. But do you think I went skylarking round a tennis court in my present condition, when I can't even stand upright without using my one good hand to support me? I smacking well *am* a cripple. These fractures are real. They hurt like hell."

He drew a deep breath.

"You can't believe that, Kitty. It's not true. As for Brenda: allow me, in my off moments, to be a sentimental ass. That's all."

There was another silence. Nick was so moved that he got out his handkerchief and blew his nose.

"Well . . ." said Kitty.

"I know. I trod on your toes about Frank."

"But, Nick, the fact remains that somebody killed Frank. Who did?"

"Mr. Jackanapes Rowland," said Nick. "I know how he did it. S-ss-t!"

Both of them, perhaps, were more worked up than either would have guessed. They started guiltily when they heard someone fumbling with the latch of the front gate, and a police sergeant ducked his head under the arch. This was greeted by a din of barking which drowned out even thought. Wriggling frantically, a white wire-haired terrier wormed out through the half-open door, and shot across the lawn. It was followed by another wire-haired terrier, which cannoned into the first so that they sprayed apart, overshot their objective, and had to turn round on it. The dogs, with bright eager eyes and little goatees like statesmen, panted with pleasure. They whirled into the air, making friends with happy maniacal barks, wriggling their hind quarters like Eastern dancers, and making Sergeant MacDougall seem to be surrounded by a dozen dogs. He spoke out of the din.

"Mrs. Bancroft? If you don't mind, Superteintendent Hadley would like to see you at the tennis court. And you too, sir, if it's convenient."

"Ah!" breathed a voice.

Sergeant MacDougall was a conscientious man. He had timed himself, and estimated that to walk from the tennis court to Mrs. Bancroft's took just two minutes. But he was also an interested man; he wanted to see what happened at the tennis court; and his efforts to get the witnesses back in a hurry, particularly since the dogs had taken a fancy to him, were not so successful. When he got the witnesses back, it was with a conviction that he had missed something.

Superintendent Hadley was standing on the porch of the shed. Hadley was shaking open the large leather suitcase. Sergeant MacDougall was too far away to see what was inside the suitcase, but there could evidently be little in it. Hadley's voice rose from a distance away under the bluish lights.

"You're quite right, Miss White," he said. "This is just about as empty as it could be."

Brenda White's voice rose faintly.

"Naturally. What about it?"

"Nothing, nothing! I was getting"—they heard a savage bump as Hadley shoved the picnic-hamper back into the pavilion—"ideas. Very well: I was wrong."

He dusted his hands. Brenda's voice persisted.

"What ideas? What you mean?"

"You can't guess, Miss White?"

"No."

"If that hamper had been full of china," said Hadley, "it would have been very heavy. Twenty, thirty pounds or more. I haven't been altogether satisfied about the appearance of those footprints, though for the life of me I couldn't think what was wrong with them. It occurred to me that if you'd been carrying a hamper loaded with china, and wabbling a little, you would have made prints just as deep as those. Now you know."

Hugh Rowland's voice struck in.

"But, Superintendent——"

"Yes, I know all that," Hadley interrupted curtly. "And the answer is: No, I don't think it's likely that anybody would go out on that court loaded down with a ton of china. It was an idea that had to be investigated, that's all."

"*Nick!*" whispered Kitty Bancroft.

They were waiting by the southern end of the court, looking through walls of wire towards the pavilion. The people on the porch were mere blurs beyond the floodlights. Sergeant Mac-Dougall strode on ahead to announce them, and Kitty seized Nick's arm.

"So that's how it happened," she breathed. "Nick, what on earth is going on? That hamper *was* full of china."

"Was it?"

"Of course it was. Don't you remember? You brought——" She stopped. "Nick, my angel, what precisely are you getting at?"

"You're not going to tell them it was full of china," said Nick.

Kitty backed away from him until she bumped into the wire, which startled her and made her stand upright. She felt along the wire behind her, while she kept her eyes on Nick. She was almost a stately figure. She spoke in a lofty tone but a high, unnatural voice.

"I don't think you can be in your right mind. Of course I'm going to tell them."

Nick sat in the wheel chair and continued to shake his head.

"Do you want to see the real murderer caught?" he asked.

"Of course I do!"

"Do you want to see the real murderer caught now? Within the next few minutes?"

"Naturally."

"Are you sure you want to see the real murderer caught?" inquired Nick, in such a suggestive tone that Kitty's grip tightened on the wire.

"Then pay attention to me," he advised. "Brenda's story is true. Brenda's . . . story . . . is . . . true. There's no hanky-panky about that. She said she never went out on that court at any time, and she didn't. I don't know what all this means about a load of china. *I* didn't steal any china out of there, if that's what you're thinking. When in Satan's name could I have done it? I've been either with you or with Superintendent Hadley every second of the time since Frank's body was discovered. Haven't I?"

"Yes, that's true."

"This business of the china has nothing to do with it. But— Brenda's out of it now. Out of it, d'ye hear? And you're not going to bring her back into it by saying anything about what was in the hamper. Got that?"

He was shivering.

"Nick, I'm trying to do the decent thing! I want to help Brenda. But if you think I'll help her with a flat lie——"

"So? So? A lie, is it? How do you know there was any china in that hamper?"

"Don't talk such silly talk. Of course I know it."

"Well, how do you know it? Come, my handsome Amazon! Come, my pearl of the South Seas! How do you know it? When did you last actually see any china in that hamper?"

"About a year ago."

"A year ago!"

"You needn't try to get round me like that, Doctor Young. I know what I know. At least, I——"

"I shouldn't advise it, Kitty. It's very dangerous to tell the police things you're not certain of. And, as a reward, I'll do as I promised: I'll have the real murderer off these premises in handcuffs within the next fifteen minutes. What do you say?"

"I won't do it," said Kitty.

She turned her head round and looked towards the pavilion. Hadley's voice, urbane but rather impatient, was calling to them to go over there.

XIII.

IRONY

"And now we'll. Hear what you've got to say, Mr. Rowland," invited Hadley.

There are moods when too many surprises have produced complete calmness, even disinterest. Hugh was in one of them. He did not know what traps were being set for him. He did not know where the traps were being set for him. But, now that Brenda had been cleared of all suspicion, he did not much care.

How Brenda had been cleared of suspicion he did not know. His head still sang with the same problem: the disappearance of thirty-odd pounds of china, together with two thermos flasks and a pair of tennis shoes, out of a picnic-hamper which had been full less than two hours before. The glances he and Brenda had given each other had asked the same question and received the same answer. "Did you do it?" "No." "Did *you* do it?" "No." And the same helpless shrug was conveyed by the same helpless glance.

But this was not enough. Kitty Bancroft, he knew, would soon sweep away this piece of luck by telling them the real weight of the hamper. It was therefore with a sort of fascination that he saw Kitty come striding round the corner of the tennis court; that he saw Kitty's smouldering eye, and heard Kitty—under questioning by Hadley—swear that it had been six months since the hamper had contained any china at all.

The world was mad, no less.

Or was it? Wasn't Kitty merely being a good scout? The rush of gratitude he felt towards Kitty transfigured her in his eyes. He tried to convey this to her, but she studiously looked at the ground, or looked at the court, while she flung the words at Hadley. Hugh had got up to give her his seat on the bench beside Brenda; she took it with reluctance, seeming to dislike the centre of the arena. Then, glancing over his shoulder, he saw Old Nick in his wheel chair. And Hugh thought he saw the explanation in one flash.

Old Nick had managed the disappearance of the china, then? Of course. Not a doubt of it! Nick had seen, understood, and acted. Good! Thundering good! Hugh had no illusions regarding how Dr. Nicholas Young felt towards him. But, if Nick had done that, it had been a decent thing to do; and he began to have almost a friendly feeling for Nick.

As for Brenda, she had recovered. In that one moment, when the picnic-hamper had fallen open in front of her, he knew that her nerve had cracked and that she was on the edge of crumpling up in a dead faint. He had seen the sag of her shoulders, the turn of her eyes; and his grip on her arm must have left bruises there. Now she seemed calm enough, except for the rapid rise and fall of her breast.

Hadley was brisk.

"Thank you, Mrs. Bancroft," he said. "That seems all in order. But there are a few points in your earlier statement I want to clear up, so you might stay here with us. And now we'll hear what you've got to say, Mr. Rowland."

"Right, Superintendent."

In other words, Hugh thought, the worst was over. He was never more wrong in his life. Hadley's grim look should have warned him.

"I suppose you know you could get into a lot of trouble for what you've been doing here today?"

The words jerked Hugh upright.

"No; I don't follow that. How?"

"We'll see if we can make you follow it," said Hadley amiably. "Miss White tells us that at shortly past seven o'clock you left her and drove away in your car. Where did you go?"

"Only twenty or thirty yards on, to the other end of the street. I stopped the car there."

"Why?"

"My offside front tire was flat. I hadn't noticed it before. So I got out and changed the wheel."

"You mean you drove clear to the other end of the street without noticing you had a flat tire?"

"Well, I don't know when the puncture occurred. That was when I noticed it. So, as I say, I got out and changed the wheel."

"What time was this? How long did it take you?"

"About twenty minutes. Just as I was finishing, I noticed by the dashboard clock that it was close on twenty-five minutes past seven. If you want to know why I came back here, I came back to get a pump. I discovered there was no pump in my toolkit. And I remembered having seen one in the garage here, so I came back to get it."

"Extraordinary," murmured Old Nick.

Hugh was conscious of a faint chill up his back, a faint shock like that of putting his foot down on a non-existent step. No more; but an omen. If Nick had sneered the word, he would not have minded. It would have helped him to fight off the guilty feeling he was beginning to have in Nick's very presence: the feeling that he had deprived Nick of both Brenda and Frank, the feeling that he was responsible for everything.

But Nick did not sneer. He merely sat and murmured in his wheel chair, patient as a spider.

Hadley wheeled round.

"What's extraordinary about it, sir?"

"Pump," said Nick. "There's a pump in the garage, yes. It's a stationary compressed-air gauge like the ones in public garages. Mr. Rowland would have had some difficulty in using it on a car at the other end of the street."

Hadley's eyes narrowed.

"The last time I was at this house," Hugh told him in a level voice, "I remember seeing a hand-pump in that garage."

Brenda spoke from the porch. "Hugh's quite right, Superintendent. I remember seeing the pump myself."

Nick did not say anything: he merely continued to shake his head.

"Go on," said Hadley stolidly, "with this story about the convenient puncture. You came down to the garage to get a pump. Well, did you get it?"

"No. I didn't get as far as the garage. When I was passing this enclosure, I noticed that the gate in the hedge was open. So I came in."

"Why?"

There was a silence.

"To tell the truth, I don't know."

"But you must have had a reason for coming in here, surely? You were looking for a pump to mend that tire, according to what you tell us. Why should you stop off and come in here?"

Hugh reflected. "The gate was open. I remembered it had been closed when we left. Maybe I wondered who was in there; maybe I half hoped to meet Frank. I can't explain it any clearer than that." He braced himself, for now would come the lies.

"Go on," requested Hadley.

"I walked through. It was darkish, but clear enough to see outlines distinctly. I saw Miss White. She was standing about where I am now: near the door of the court, looking in from outside. She seemed to be in some distress. I ran round here to her. She told me what you've heard: that she had seen Frank's body; but had not gone out on the court, and that the tracks belonged to someone else."

"What time was this?"

"At close on seven-thirty. I can't say exactly."

"Go on. What happened then?"

Crude truth would serve him best here.

"We talked it over. Miss White was, naturally, upset. Truth isn't always believed. I was afraid of the construction the police might put on those footprints, even though Miss White hadn't made them. So I decided to get a rake from behind the pavilion and mess up the tracks beyond recognition."

He was in for a blast of trouble, but he saw that he had said exactly the right thing. He saw Hadley give a significant glance and nod towards the shadow where Dr. Fell waited, a huge shadow. He saw the grim triumph in Hadley's face.

"So you admit that, Mr. Rowland?"

"Yes."

"You—who are supposed to be a reputable member of a reputable firm of solicitors—admit that you intended to commit a serious offence against the law? And were only kept from it because Maria interrupted you. Is that correct?"

"No."

"It isn't correct?"

"No. It was a foolish idea and a dangerous idea; I do admit that, and I apologize. But there were two reasons why I decided not to do it. The first reason was that Miss White herself refused to have anything to do with it; she said she was going to tell the truth. The second reason was that, up to the time I'd actually got the rake in my hands, I hadn't had a close look at the footprints. We both noticed then what Miss White had been too upset to notice before: that the footprints were much to deep for her to have made. I saw that her story proved itself, so there was no need to do anything else, and I sent Miss White on up to the house."

If that wasn't convincing, he thought grimly, nothing would be. It had just the right blend of confession and denial: it expressed a state of mind. Hadley nodded with evil satisfaction.

"You're very wise to be frank, Mr. Rowland. Now let's have the truth about another of your antics." He nodded towards the tennis court. "I suppose it was you who made that third line of tracks out there?"

"Yes."

"When did you make them?"

"After I had sent Miss White up to the house. It may have been anywhere between ten minutes to eight and eight o'clock."

"What made you want to go out there at all?"

Hugh spread out his hands.

"I had to see how matters stood. You can understand that, Superintendent. Here was a devil of a mess for no apparent reason. I wanted to see if there were any clues. I wondered what Frank had been doing on the court at all. I wondered what had happened to his tennis racket and the tennis-balls. I wondered how . . ."

"Hold on!" Hadley said sharply, and pulled back his head. "You mean that tennis racket there on the porch? Do you mean to say you had a good look round this court and still didn't see the tennis racket?"

"No, I certainly didn't see it."

"Or the tennis-balls? Or that book he borrowed from Mrs. Bancroft?"

"No."

Hugh was genuinely puzzled. They were now tripping over a snag not created either by himself or Brenda. All the articles in question were conspicuous. Frank's racket had a frame of polished white wood, the strings dark green; the balls were comparatively new, still whitish in a green net; the book was red-jacketed, with sprawling white letters. Seen under that dazzle of light, they acquired a malignant kind of obviousness. They would stand out for yards. But Hugh, searching his memory, could not remember having noticed them at any time after Frank's death.

"And neither can I," agreed Brenda, meeting his glance. "I was here for quite some time myself, and *I* never saw them." She laughed nervously. "I'm fairly sure I should have remembered a book with a title like. *One Hundred Ways of Being a Perfect Husband,* too. Where were they?"

Hadley hesitated.

"Sergeant!"

"Sir?"

"Step over and show them the place. We found that stuff inside the court. The things were in a heap on that footwide strip of grass, pushed down partly under the wire by a support on the east side. Where the sergeant is standing now: not quite midway along this side, counting from the direction of the wire door. And you say they weren't there when you were here last?"

"I'm positive they weren't," returned Brenda firmly.

"Are you suggesting that somebody put them there later?"

"I don't know."

"What about you, Mr. Rowland?"

"Without swearing to it, Superintendent, I can tell you that I didn't see them."

"Extraordinary," murmured Old Nick.

Hadley surveyed the group with a hard, suspicious eye. "Never mind. We can dig into that later. Now, Mr. Rowland, you went out on the tennis court to look for 'clues.' Did you touch the body?"

"No. Yes," said Hugh.

He slipped, stumbled, and recovered himself so quickly that the two syllables were superimposed on each other, a rapid blur. In the flash of uttering them he remembered that Brenda *had* touched the body: she had further loosened the loose ends of the scarf round Frank's neck, to see whether there was any life in him. And the police would have seen that. Quick as his recovery had been, Hadley was after it.

"What do you mean by 'nyes'? Did you, or didn't you, touch the body?"

"Sorry; I had forgotten. Yes, I did. As a matter of fact, I loosened the scarf round his neck."

"Why did you do that?"

"To see whether there was any life in him."

Hadley's eyebrows went up.

"Is that so? You knew there was no life in him at half-past

seven. Did you think there would be any life in him at eight o'clock?"

This was a bad one.

The awake, alive part of Hugh's brain said to him: Now, you ass, when will you learn to think before you speak, and not rap out with whatever happens to be in your mind? The other part of his brain groped wildly for an answer. But he heard himself replying with great smoothness:

"I expressed myself badly. I knew he was dead, of course. But when there's a violent death, people send for a doctor even though they know the person is dead. That was how I felt. The knot of the scarf was loose; it was only folded over once. I knew he was dead, but I had to make sure."

"Extraordinary," murmured Old Nick.

The wheel chair had crept a few feet closer. It was beginning to have a hypnotic effect.

"Superintendent," said Nick in a gentle, harassed, almost tragic voice, "I don't want to butt in. I'm afraid I've already talked a lot of nonsense today, for which I'm beginning to be ashamed of myself. But may I say something now?"

Hadley eyed him suspiciously. "Depends on whether it happens to be important, sir? Is it?"

"I'm afraid," the other went on, with an attempt at his old bluff manner, "that Old Nick isn't much good to anybody nowadays. Frank's death was a shock to me, naturally. But at the same time I don't want you to think I hold any animus against young Rowland there. I don't. I may have said fool things today, when I wasn't myself, but I don't hold any animus. And the reason is not that I'm forgiving—which I'm not—but just that I want to do the proper thing to make Brenda happy."

"Yes, yes; well?"

"Jerry Noakes and I," pursued Nick, getting out his handkerchief and blowing his nose, "always tried to do our best for Brenda. Yes, so help me, we have, little as it was. If Brenda had come to me frankly and said, 'Nick, I don't want to marry Frank; I want to marry this Rowland fellow,' I'd have said, 'Well, my dear, if that's what you really want, you go ahead and do it. You don't think Old Nick will stand in your way, do you?'"

"Nick, please!" cried Brenda.

She jumped down from the porch and went across to him.

"Now, my dear," said Nick, patting her hand, "I don't want you to think I'm asking for any sympathy. You just understand that! Some of us may not be as young as we'd like to be; and things may not always be as easy as we'd like; but that's not why I'm telling the Superintendent this. No; I'm telling him because . . . There's some matches and a packet of cigarettes in my pocket, my dear. Will you light one for me?"

Brenda complied. Her hands were unsteady in striking the match. Hugh saw her face over the match-flame: flushed, sympathetic, guilty and rather ashamed; and in that look he saw sharp danger to everything he and Brenda had between them.

Nick would win her over yet.

"No!" emphasized Nick, taking the light and settling back so that blue smoke curled up under the flood lamps. "Now, Superintendent, I'm what you could call a theorist. I don't know anything about crime, except in books. But I've always taught Frank, and Brenda too, how to think quickly, and think in the right way, in an emergency. I've been a kind of tutor to them."

"You have, darling," said Brenda in a curious voice.

"Yes, yes?"

"You want to know how a man weighing ten or eleven stone,

with sizable feet, could have walked in number four shoes. I can tell you," said Nick, with a snappish intensity of distress. "But that's the trouble. I *don't* have any animus against young Rowland. I don't want you to think it reflects on him, because it doesn't. It——"

"Just a moment, Dr. Young," interrupted Hadley. "If you have anything to tell us, tell it."

"That's what I was doing. I don't know whether I thought of it myself, or read it in a story. But I was thinking of an acrobatic feat, a kind of bet Rowland had with Frank that he could do it: that's what started me thinking of it. It was a bet they had a fortnight ago." Nick passed the hand that held his cigarette across his forehead. "Superintendent, you're not satisfied with the queer look about those footprints. And (Lord help me!) neither am I. You see how it looks as though the tracks wabble. You said so yourself, didn't you?"

Hadley had nearly lost control of his temper.

"Whether I said so or not, sir, what are you getting at? What was this bet Rowland had with Mr. Dorrance?"

"He bet Frank," muttered Nick, "that he could walk the length of our garden *on his hands.*"

As though a window had opened in Hugh's mind, he saw where this was leading. He remembered that evening in the garden. He remembered how the wager had been interrupted before the test was made. And he saw, in a literal sense, things turned upside down to crush him.

"It's a rotten thing to have to say," complained Nick fretfully. "But any decent gymnast could do it. A man of ten or eleven stone couldn't get his feet into number four shoes. But he could get his hands into them.

"I've been afraid all along that's how poor Frank was killed. The chap who killed Frank said to him, 'Do you want to bet I can't go out on that court in shoes four sizes too small for me?' Frank said, 'You can't.' So the murderer took a pair of small shoes, and put them on his hands, and balanced himself, and walked out there on his hands. That's why the tracks wobble. That's why the murderer had to churn up the ground and make it a mess round Frank's body: because the murderer had to stand upright when he got there. Standing upright, he grabbed poor Frank and choked the life out of him———"

"Nick!" screamed Kitty Bancroft.

"—and then walked back on his hands. I said afraid, and I mean afraid. And why? Because, whatever happens, I want to see Brenda happy. And happy she shall be, whatever it costs me."

The various persons beside the tennis court received that explanation in various ways. Kitty stared as though aware of a dawning conviction. Brenda seemed about to break out into hysterical laughter. But on nobobdy did it have a more curious effect than on Superintendent Hadley. After a long silence Hadley whistled, and then spoke thoughtfully.

"Dr. Young," he said, "I'm much obliged to you."

"You think that's right?"

"Yes," agreed Hadley with the utmost seriousness. "I think that very probably you've hit it. Yes, by George, I do! We already had motive, opportunity, and temperament. Now that we've got method———"

"It's all right, Brenda," Nick assured the girl. "God knows I wouldn't do this to you if I didn't have to! And anyway, Superintendent, I don't see why he should have done it in Brenda's shoes; unless, of course, he first wanted to throw suspicion on her and then be very noble about pulling her out of it. That's quite probable. Psychologically, I know the type. But, after all, Rowland must at least have some affection for her——"

Superintendent Hadley woke up out of a dream.

"Rowland?" he repeated. His voice was incredulous. "Who said anything about Rowland? You didn't, did you?"

Nick, who had tried to stand up, flapped back again. "No. No, Superintendent, of course not. But—I mean—that is——"

Hadley was curt.

"If you can't guess who I mean, sir, it's not my business to tell you. But I thought you did know. I can't think of anything more unlikely than that Mr. Rowland would commit a crime in such a way as to incriminate Miss White. Also, no mere amateur gymnast would ever dare try a trick like that. It would be foreign to him; it would be clumsy for him; and it would be far too risky.

"No. The person I'm thinking of is a professional acrobat. A man I've seen do just that same walk on his hands. A man who does it twenty times a day. A man who is as much at home on his hands as on his feet. A man who was in that shed today. A man who would think of just such a stunt in that way, to incriminate Miss White and get a bit of his own back for Madge Sturgess. A man who said he would kill Dorrance; who was capable of killing Dorrance; and who, to my mind, has done it. Thank you very much. Those footprints, together with the testimony of Miss White and Mr. Rowland, will convict him or I'm a Dutchman."

Brenda and Hugh protested together.

"But——"

"Look here, Superintendent, you can't do that! You don't understand. You've got it all wr——"

"I don't think I need trouble any of you any longer tonight," said Hadley, closing his notebook with satisfaction. "Fell! May I have a word with you in private?"

Twenty-four hours later it happened. Arthur Chandler, who knew no more about the footprints than the Man in the Moon, was arrested and charged with the murder of Frank Dorrance.

XIV.
EXPERIMENT

A warm, dark, wet Sunday, with a laziness which did not extend to Hugh Rowland or Brenda White. For, though Hugh would have doubted that he could get into more difficulties than already existed, fresh troubles piled on him almost as soon as he finished his breakfast. He had had the opportunity for only a brief conference with Brenda before he left Nick's house the night before.

"The trouble is," he stormed, "that none of us had ever heard of this fellow—what's his name, by the way?"

"Chandler, the Superintendent says."

"Chandler. Stop! Come to think of it, I believe I did overhear Hadley mention his name to Nick in the driveway. But I completely forgot about him in our own troubles, and in any case I never knew who he was. An acrobat! An acrobat, of all people! Of course, they may not arrest him. He may be able to prove an alibi. But we can't let a completely innocent man get himself hanged on our own perjured testimony."

"I know we can't," Brenda almost wailed. "What are we going to do?"

"There's only one thing to do. I've got to see my father. Both he and Mr. Gardesleeve are wily old birds, and they may be able to see a way out. Good night, my dear. I'll ring you in the morning."

"I'm in for a night of it myself," said Brenda, shivering. "With Nick, I mean. Don't be too late about ringing me tomorrow."

He kissed her violently enough to express their feelings in every direction. Being in no state of mind to bother with his now-useless car, he went home in a taxi, dreamed all night with unpleasant vividness, and was ready to face Rowland Senior after a late breakfast.

The Rowlands, father, mother, and son, lived in Eton Avenue, near Swiss Cottage: a street of tall, fantastic Victorian houses of which that of Rowland Senior was one of the tallest and most fantastic. It was the habit of Rowland Senior to spend Sunday mornings in his "den," reading the *Observer* and *Sunday Times,* and you must not disturb him during that time. Hugh disturbed him.

Rowland Senior was a little man with large spectacles, and a habit of loading his conversation with old saws and proverbs of the dreariest kind. This habit drove some people to drink, if they needed any encouragement. But it made them under-estimate him, which was what he wanted. Besides being kindly, he was a shrewd and able man. He heard Hugh out without as much consternation as Hugh had expected, though he several times got up to go to the window and make sure that Mrs. Rowland was safely in the garden.

Then he commented. Hugh saw it coming.

"'Oh, what a tangled web we weave, When first we practice to deceive,'" intoned Rowland Senior, shaking his head.

"As a matter of fact, sir," said Hugh, "it's not quite the first time, is it? After all, we faked that defence for Mrs. Jewell——"

Rowland Senior looked pained, and silenced him. His theory was that you could do these things, but you must never refer to them afterwards. Then he reflected.

"We will send your mother to the north of Scotland. That is the farthest we can send her without a passport," he explained. "And there is no time to get one. There will be ructions, Hugh. Yes, I foresee ructions."

"Well, sir?"

"Well, Hugh, I do not know whether to congratulate you or condole with you. You appear to have taken a serious step in several directions. I take it that you are still determined to marry this young lady?"

"If she'll still have me. That's what I'm afraid of."

"I see no objection to that," said Rowland Senior, after more reflection. "The girl has been here to tea, has she not? Yes, yes, I remember. Tall and dark, with a fine graciousness of manner."

"She's small and fair. I don't know about the graciousness of manner."

"It is of no consequence," said Rowland Senior, unruffled. "I remember that I was very favourably impressed, Hugh. *Very* favourably. She struck me as a girl who had character. Yes. As I have so often told you, character is what counts in this world. Fine, sterling character, to face and endure the mountainous vicissitudes of life. Er—I believe you also said that the young lady comes into a considerable sum of money?"

"We're not touching any of that," said Hugh grimly. "That's

Frank Dorrance's. He can take it with him. I've already got enough to support us, thank you."

His father coughed.

"No doubt, no doubt," he agreed. "A worthy sentiment, which does you credit. At the same time——" He took off his spectacles and made a gesture with them.

"But see here, sir! That's not the point. That's not what I wanted to talk to you about. Don't you see, we're in a mess? I want to know what in hell——"

"No swearing, Hugh, if you please. 'He knew not what to say, so he swore.' Byron, I think."

Hugh's estimate of Byron, never very enthusiastic, now dropped still more.

"All right. But about this mess. Admitting that the whole thing is my fault, what do you advise? What do you think I ought to do about it?"

"What do *you* propose to do about it, my boy?"

"Well, sir, I've been thinking about it all night. And, in ordinary common decency, there's only one thing to do. If Chandler is arrested, Brenda and I have got to go to Hadley and tell him the truth."

Rowland Senior cleared his throat. He leaned back in his chair, swinging his spectacles back and forth.

"Are you sure you would be believed if you did tell the truth?" he asked calmly.

Hugh stared at him.

"But the man's innocent!"

"Are you so sure he is innocent, my boy?"

"But——"

"The older I grow, my boy, the more I am impressed by the tragic ironies of life," said Rowland Senior, with a degree of banality which, even in him, was phenomenal. "At the moment I advise nothing. You are apt to be hasty, Hugh. Ve-ry hasty. We must do nothing hastily, lest we repent at leisure. But it has always been my experience that the police know their business. With regard to this man—er——?"

"Chandler. Arthur Chandler."

"Ah, yes. Chandler. Well, there would appear to be a very strong case against him. It is true," he waved aside the detail, "that the police have become convinced of his guilt on the wrong evidence. But is he necessarily innocent? I am inclined to doubt it. Let us suppose that Chandler has committed this murder— murder most foul, as in the best it is; but this most foul, strange, and unnatural—well, Chandler has committed this murder by some means we don't understand. He is safe. There is no evidence against him. But along comes mistaken evidence and convicts the guilty man after all. That is what I mean by tragic irony; or perhaps I should say avenging Providence. Justice would be done, would it not? And we must serve justice, Hugh."

Hugh stared at him, assimilating this.

Then Hugh drew out a chair and sat down opposite him.

"I do not make the suggestion," added Rowland Senior. He glanced across. "But it has occurred to you—ah—that, if the true story appears, it may mean professional ruin for you?"

There was a silence.

"I don't care anything about that."

"You must allow me, however, to care something about it. My boy, you are hasty. Ve-ry hasty."

"But, look here, sir: you don't seriously suggest that I should stick to my story, perjure myself in the witness-box, and let them hang Chandler if they can?"

"Not at all."

"What is it, then?"

"I merely suggest, my boy, that we do nothing in haste. The more haste, the less speed. If Chandler is guilty, as seems probable," continued the other blandly, "we must examine all alternatives. We must see how he really committed this diabolical crime, so that, if necessary, we may be prepared with the proof of it and support our just claims. Now, what is the situation?"

Hugh flapped his arms.

"That's just the trouble. It's a perfectly simple situation. Here's a man dead in the middle of a tennis court, with *no* footprints going out to him: that's all. Brenda walks out to him and makes some footprints. But on top of that we've told one flaming lie on top of another flaming lie, until the infernal thing is now so complicated that nobody knows what's happening. Holy cats, I can't even get it straight myself. Besides, if Chandler did the murder, how did he do it?"

"He is—er—an acrobat, you tell me. Yes?"

"Yes; but even an acrobat isn't gifted with powers of levitation. He can't walk on air."

Rowland Senior swung the spectacles back and forth. "No," he agreed quite seriously, "we shall have to disregard that as a line of approach. At the same time, I was much struck by a suggestion which seems to have occurred to you when you were examining the court." The sharp little eyes, in a wrinkled little face like an apple, swung on Hugh. "You thought that the murderer might have walked out on top of the tennis-net, as on a tightrope."

Hugh felt a violent, uneasy kind of hope.

"Yes, I know."

"Under ordinary circumstances, I agree, such a possibility would be absurd. But, granted a trained acrobat as the murderer, is it so very absurd? Is it even absurd at all? Is it not," said Rowland Senior, warming to his subject, "extremely probable?"

"Well——"

"Also granted, of course, that there is sufficient strength in the net. That is what we must test. I have always told you, my boy (and it is a lesson I wish you to take through life) that to be prepared in these matters is half the battle. This must be tested. Very well, we will test it. Sheppey is here. Send for Sheppey."

Sheppey had been confidential chief clerk to the firm of Rowland & Gardesleeve for eighteen years. He had a standing invitation to midday dinner, on alternate Sundays, at the home of Mr. Rowland and at the home of Mr. Gardesleeve. He always arrived punctually at eleven o'clock, and read the *Observer* and the *Sunday Times* in the library while his employer was reading other copies of them in the den. During eighteen years he had become a little more withered up, a little more in speech like his employers; no more. Rowland Senior greeted him with a frowning brow.

"Good morning, Sheppey," he said. "Sheppey: we are interested in discovering whether it is feasible to walk across a tennis court on top of the net."

"Very good, sir," said Sheppey, who was not to be fazed by a little request like this.

"Are you familiar with the England's Lane Lawn-Tennis Club?"

"I have observed the premises, sir."

"Good. I should like you to go over there, taking . . ." He looked at Hugh. "Have we any information as to Chandler's weight?"

"No. But from the way they spoke of him I should think he was a reasonably hefty sort of bloke."

"Ah; in that case, Sheppey, you had better take Angus MacWhirter." Angus MacWhirter was the odd-jobs man. "Take a step-ladder as well. I want Angus to climb the step-ladder, step off on the net, and attempt to walk it. He need not attempt any difficult feats of balancing. All we are concerned with is the re-action of the net. It is a wet day and I do not think there will be anyone on the courts."

"Very good, sir," said Sheppey. "Are we to conduct experiments with only one court, or with several? I had observed that there are half a dozen courts on the premises."

"I want all available statistics," said Rowland Senior, "as to the strength and resilience of tennis-nets. You are to begin with the first court, and keep on until they catch you. That is all."

When Sheppey had gone, he turned again to Hugh.

"I must ask you to leave me alone for a while. I need time to think. Thought that knits up the ravell'd sleeve of—no, that's something else." (It was the first sign that the old man was worried.) "Do not be unduly alarmed. Your story to the police, as I see it, is fairly safe. Both Mrs. Bancroft and Dr. Young have backed up the story of the empty picnic-hamper; they would not dare retract, and Dr. Young is anxious to protect the girl. No. What troubles me is that Chandler himself may have been near the tennis court at the wrong time; he was certainly there at some time, if he is the murderer: and that he may have seen something he should not have seen."

This was an aspect of the matter which had not occurred to Hugh. New difficulties and pitfalls began to open.

"But most of all," said Rowland Senior, "I anticipate ructions from your mother."

"But why? Why? What's mother got to do with this?"

"Much. I have a feeling that before this is finished the whole thing will be my fault. If it were possible to hold me responsible for the defeat of King James at the Battle of Boyne, I fear your mother would do it. This girl. An admirable lady, as I remember her; admirable; and she will make you, I am sure, a splendid wife. Her . . . er . . . social connexions are satisfactory, of course?"

"Her father shot himself and her mother died of drink."

Rowland Senior rubbed his jaw.

"Well, it might be worse," he said. "She has no relatives doing time in Wormwood Scrubs at the moment, I trust?"

"No."

"That is a relief. At the same time, I am not sure that the north of Scotland is quite remote enough for your mother's holiday. After reflection, I should suggest some place such as Tanganyika or the Arctic Circle. But we must see what we can do. What do you mean to do now?"

"I was going to ring Brenda this morning."

His father considered. "Then you had better ring her immediately. We must keep in touch with what is going on. But——"

Rowland Senior's voice sharpened, and he stood up.

"Whatever happens, Hugh, you are *not* going to be involved in any public scandal or notoriety. Is that clear?"

"Look here, sir. I'll never be grateful enough for the way you've taken this. But I'll tell you just one thing. If things get too hot for Chandler, Hadley hears the truth."

They looked at each other.

"You mean that?"

"I mean it."

"Even," said Rowland Senior calmly, "if it means seeing Miss White in the dock in Chandler's place?"

There was a silence.

"However," he continued with more cheerfulness, "we will

look on the bright side. This sudden passion for telling the truth, which I had not hitherto noticed in you to an embarrassing extent, may be gratified. You persist in missing the point. It is not fatal to tell lies to the police. You are not under oath; you can always retract—*provided* you have reasonable proof of someone else's guilt to put in its place. If we can show (as I am sure we can) that Chandler really did kill young Dorrance by walking out on the net, you and Miss White can cleanse your souls with confession and no damage is done. Otherwise, I warn you frankly, you will have that girl up for murder; and you know it as well as I do. No. Go and make your phone-call, and let us hope that Sheppey returns with good news about the net."

Hugh went out storming. He stormed still more because he knew that what his father said was true. He would, of course, see ten Chandlers hanged in a row at dawn before danger of any sort should come to Brenda. But something awoke and raged inside him at the way things were going. It was again the feeling that the real murderer was having all the luck; that they all had to dodge and duck and lie and trim their courses in terror, while the real murderer laughed.

The real murderer? Chandler? Why not? What his father said there was true too. It would make him still more furious if he had been allowing his conscience to go all over him, and Chandler was the guilty person all the time. The more he thought of it, the more he believed that the trick of walking on the net must be true. It was the only way out. They must prove it somehow.

But this new line of thought brought a worse danger. Again it was as his father had said. If Chandler had been at the tennis court, he might have seen something he should not have seen: Brenda carrying the picnic-hamper, for instance. After all, that tabloid newspaper had disappeared out of the pavilion; which meant that it must have been taken away at some time between seven o'clock and seven-twenty. In other words, the time of the murder. Wow! Chandler's image, like that of a jack-in-the-box, shot up in Hugh's face. From his position as wronged victim, Chandler was assuming more sinister colours. They must find Chandler; they must speak to Chandler; they must find out what Chandler knew.

Sitting down at the telephone in the hall, Hugh dialled Mountview 0440. He remembered that the other phone was in Dr. Young's study, and wondered if he would have to exchange another blast of spite with Old Nick. But it was answered by Brenda—so instantly that Brenda must have been sitting beside it.

"Hello," said Hugh, and felt his throat tighten and his heart begin to thump heavily. The events of yesterday appeared in front of him.

"Hello," said the other voice.

There was a pause, a kind of confusion.

"Brenda: is there anybody in the room with you?"

"No."

"Do you still feel the same as you did yesterday? About us, that is?"

The voice reassured him, with such intensity that the events of yesterday grew scrambled with the present; and Hugh plunged on to other matters before he should say too much.

"Listen: I want you to take the rest of the day off with me. It's very important."

"Hugh, I can't! Poor Nick——"

"Yes, I was afraid of that. But we've got to find Arthur Chandler. I can't explain over the phone, but it's very important. Will you come?"

The voice hesitated. "All right. When?"

"I've got to come up there to get my car. I'll meet you in about an hour, and we'll have lunch in town while I tell you: Right? Good! Has anything been happening?"

"Has anything been happening?" repeated the small voice, dimming and returning as though Brenda had looked away from the phone and back again. "I should say it has! You remember that man Dr. Fell, the one who looked so big and jovial and didn't say one single word the whole night? Hugh— I'm afraid he's on to us."

"What makes you think that?"

"I can't tell you over the phone either," said Brenda hurriedly. "Nick's likely to pop in here at any minute, and all the servants are back and keeping their ears to every door. But Dr. Fell and the Superintendent have been here since nine o'clock this morning, and—well, I think they're on to us. I'll tell you later."

There was another uneasy interval, after which she asked whether he was still there.

"Yes. It's all right, Brenda. Keep your chin up and don't worry. I'll see you in an hour."

He hung up the receiver. For a long time he sat in the telephone corner under the stairs, amid the familiar smell of old coats and umbrellas, considering. Now he did not know whether discovery of his and Brenda's lie would be the best possible thing or the worst possible thing. Again he realized what a persuasive way Rowland Senior had with him. Rowland Senior could charm the legal cobras out of their baskets and make them sway as he pleased. He could convince nearly anyone of nearly any proposition. Rowland Senior, of course, cared nothing for justice; but then neither did anybody else in this case. Each person was trying, for his own separate reasons, to quash truth. Rowland Senior merely wished to see that his own son was kept out of it.

Nevertheless, Hugh was beginning to believe him in earnest. Chandler was the murderer, and the murder had been done by a tight-rope-walking trick on the net. No other explanation was possible. Every fact fitted in—if they could only prove it. If, if, if! Afire with this certainty, Hugh hurried back to his father's den, and arrived there at the same time as Sheppey.

It would not be true to say that Sheppey was flurried or out of breath. He never was. But he looked like a man who had been through much. Rowland Senior rose at him in a fever of dry impatience.

"You are back," he said, "in a remarkably short space of time. Well? Did you find out about the nets?"

"Yes, sir," said Sheppey.

"Well, well?"

Sheppey was not to be hurried.

"At first glance, sir, the proposition would appear to be quite feasible. I may explain that the top of the cloth net is supported either on a length of heavy wire, or a flexible cord composed of plaited steel, strung between the posts and terminating at one of these posts in a very small drum or windlass with a handle, which can be turned to raise or lower the net."

"Yes, yes, I know that. Well?"

"Pursuant to your instructions," continued Sheppey, giving him an injured look, "Angus MacWhirter and I proceeded to the courts, which were at this time deserted. Angus MacWhirter (who, I may say, had shown no great enthusiasm for the project) was persuaded to mount the stepladder and plant himself firmly on the net, holding with one finger to the top of the step-ladder as balance."

"Yes?"

"Unfortunately, sir, the subject of our first experiment was a grass court. I must conclude that the posts supporting the net cannot have been firmly entrenched in the earth. Due to the weight placed on the net, one of these posts came up bodily. As a result of this sudden jerk, Angus MacWhirter—ah—"

"Took a toss?" suggested Hugh.

"That inadequately describes it, Mr. Hugh. I feared for a moment that he had dislocated the base of his spine, and Angus MacWhirter himself expressed no doubts on the subject. He was, however, persuaded to go on to the next court. Here there was no mishap. But the steel cord played out after the fashion of a tape-measure; so that Angus MacWhirter, clinging shakily but valiantly, was lowered bodily until he was standing on the court with the flattened net under him. I attempted to arrest the unwinding of the cord by wedging stones, sticks, and so on, into the windlass; but this would not work."

"Yes?"

"On the third court, sir, the results were not so happy. The cord supporting the net was made of wire, and (I regret to say) broke. Angus MacWhirter was again precipitated into the air, with the additional misfortunte that the court was made of concrete and that this time the base of his spine landed on the overturned step-ladder. The Scotch, however, are a hardy race. We had proceeded to the fourth court— I trust, Mr. Hush, you find nothing to amuse you in this?"

Hugh was whooping. He could not help himself. He leaned back in his chair and roared.

"Hugh," said Rowland Senior, giving him a cold and significant glance. "Go on, Sheppey."

"We had proceeded to the fourth court—leaving, I fear, some-

thing of a trail of ruin behind us—when we suffered an interruption. I observed a figure running towards us from a northerly
direction. This was a man who wore overalls, and appeared to be
the ground-keeper. He was purple in the face, waving his arms
in the air and uttering strange gibbering noises almost unrelated
to human speech. This man stared at us for a moment and then
darted off in a southerly direction. When it became evident that
he had gone to fetch a policeman, we were obliged to curtail our
experiments and depart in a hurry."

"*Hugh!*"

"Sorry," said Hugh. "But I can't help it. Let me laugh. This is
the first pleasant gleam in the whole rotten business. I hope Angus is not permanently damaged?"

Sheppey inclined his head.

"Thank you, sir: I do not apprehend any serious consequences."

"But you did prove," insisted Rowland Senior, "you did prove
that the wire could be walked on? Say by a professional tight-
rope walker?"

Sheppey considered.

"A tight-rope walker, sir? Ah, that is different. Yes. Always provided that the cord could be so tightened or fastened that it did
not unwind at the windlass, I should say it was quite possible."

Rowland Senior and Junior looked at each other; Hugh was
stricken sober.

"Got him!" he said.

"Hardly, my boy. There remains the question of proof. At the
same time, it seems to establish . . . Will you be good enough to
answer that telephone? It seems a pity that even on Sundays we
cannot be free from its ringing. No, not you, Sheppey: Hugh?"

There was a terrible kind of pre-vision in Hugh's mind when
he heard the telephone ring. It was as though by a sort of telep-

athy he saw a new blow coming. It became certainty when he heard Brenda's voice again over the wire.

"Hugh, I'm sorry to bother you"—it was excited and a little incoherent—"but I *know* they're on to us now."

"How?"

"They've just had a man down there at the tennis court trying to walk on the net. He's a professional tight-rope walker."

"A professional tight-rope walker?" yelled Hugh, with such power that he heard the door of his father's den open.

"Yes. I sneaked in to get a good look, but they caught me and tossed me out."

"And could he walk on the net?"

"No! They got hold of old Matty Parsons—you don't know him; he built the court for Nick—and they've established that it can't be done. It seems that the court's made of a composition of sand and gravel built up on a concrete basis, and that the posts holding the net ought to be sunk in concrete. But they're not. They're just stuck in like stakes, and if anybody weighing more than a few stone gets up on the wire, both posts come out and the whole thing collapses. And that's not all. If you're thinking of Arthur Chandler: Chandler can't walk a tight-rope. It's not his line. They've found out——"

"But it's got to be, Brenda! It's got to be."

"Darling, I only know that it's absolutely and definitely impossible." Her voice sharpened. "I've got to ring off, Hugh. That Dr. Fell's coming up the stairs now."

Back went the receiver; the connection was severed, and Hugh stood amid the ruin of another plan. He went back to the den, where Rowland Senior was now swinging his spectacles with sharp jerks. Rowland Senior shut the door carefully, suspecting the imminent presence of Rowland *mère*. Though his expression did not change when Hugh told him the news, a certain grimness was apparent.

"There is gammon in this," he declared, after reflection. "As the elder Weller would put it, my boy, we are the victims o' gammon. Someone is trying to outmanoeuvre us: this cannot be allowed. Chandler *must* have walked on that net."

Hugh shrugged his shoulders.

"I don't know. I only know what Brenda just told me; that it's absolutely and definitely impossible."

"H'm. H'm. I must see Gardesleeve," muttered Rowland Senior, sitting down by his desk and beginning to tap his knuckles on it. "It would also cheer me if I could decide what was going on in the heads of Messrs. Hadley and Fell. I fear that last-named gentleman, Hugh. Old King Cole or Father Christmas present a terrifying aspect when they appear in the guise of a detective. His penchant for investigating miracles should be satisfied over this affair. And you must keep out of his way while I have time to think. Hugh, are you convinced that Chandler is the murderer?"

"I am. But——"

"Yes. Precisely. No doubt now exists in my own mind that this nimble gentleman in some fashion killed young Dorrance. But how did he do it? As you say yourself, he cannot be gifted with powers of levitation. He did not jump. He did not, according to you, walk on the net. This is a problem which will drive Gardesleeve mad. By the great and vanished snakes of Ireland, Chandler is guilty! But how?" Rowland Senior smote the desk a blow with his fist. "How?" He smote the desk again. "How?" He smote it a final, shattering whack. *"How?"*

XV.

HUMOUR

IN THE orchestra-pit at the Orpheum Theatre, Charing Cross Road, the leader lifted his baton. Though the vast auditorium was empty on Sunday afternoon, and a stage pared of backdrops showed a dreary brick wall behind, there were twenty glowing cores of light in the orchestra-pit. It lay yellow-gleaming, flat as a plate, while a dozen black fiddle-bows rose over it in unison, like spiders' legs. Cymbals clashed hard on the opening bar. Swinging with pendulum-movement, faintly derisive, the full music smote out against vacancy:

> *O-oooooh!* (the cymbals struck again)
> *He floats through the air with the greatest of ease,*
> *The daring young man on the flying trapeze;*
> *His actions were graceful, all girls he could please ——*

At the back of the dim auditorium, Hugh Rowland automatically began to whistle it, until he realized what it meant, and broke off to swear. Brenda swore in sympathy.

From the first they had never thought of the theatre itself as a possible place of finding Chandler on Sunday. Lunch, at a restaurant in Soho, has been a meal at which Hugh sat beside her and tried to keep his mind on business.

Brenda looked tired, as though she had been up most of the night; as, in fact, she had. She wore white, with a white hat, and her white, small-fingered hands were restless.

"Drink that," said Hugh, indicating the cocktail before her. "And then tell me what's up."

Brenda complied, draining the cocktail almost at a gulp. Then she spoke surprisingly.

"Hugh, do you think this Dr. Fell is insane?"

"Did he strike you as being insane?"

"Yes, he did, a bit."

"I don't know what it means," said Hugh, "but I don't like the sound of it."

"That's what I thought. As I said, they got to the house at nine o'clock this morning. I saw them go down the drive and turn in at the tennis court. They were having the most terrible argument, swearing at each other and waving their arms. Dr. Fell seemed to be trying to persuade the Superintendent of something, and the Superintendent wouldn't have any of it. Every so often the Superintendent would stop dead and glare at him, and Dr. Fell would wave his stick in the air again."

"Yes?"

Brenda waited until the soup was in front of her. "Well, I followed them," she admitted, with a half-guilty smile. "After all, with all those trees and hedges and things, it's fairly easy to hide inside the enclosure— What did you say?"

"Chandler!" groaned Hugh, striking the table as his father had done. "Brenda, we were a pair of feather-witted goops not to realize something was up when we left that tabloid newspaper in the pavilion at seven o'clock, and it wasn't there when you came back at twenty minutes past! Never mind! I'll tell you in a minute. Go on."

She hesitated.

"I don't know what they were doing," she explained. "They seemed to have been searching the pavilion when I got there. Of course they'd searched it the night before, but they were having another go. Dr. Fell was too big round to go through the door of the pavilion, and that annoyed him. They didn't find anything except an old sweater of mine, and a pair of ice-skates that belonged to Frank, and the basket of clothes-pegs. Dr. Fell chucked the ice-skates at the wire net, and began throwing the clothes-pegs all over the place like a lunatic. Then the Superintendent got mad and picked all the stuff up. Dr. Fell kept saying, 'A whacking great object like that? Gone? Where is it, then? Where is it?'"

"What were they talking about?"

"I don't know. But wait! It was the next thing he said that made me nervous. He said, with a kind of gesture like an orator"—Brenda illustrated— "'Now we have here a huge stretch of unmarked sand.' You see? *Unmarked* sand."

"H'm, yes. What did Hadley say?"

"He said, 'It's not sand exactly. We've been calling it sand because that's more convenient than saying a-composition-of-sand-and-gravel-built-up-on-a-concrete-basis.' And at that Dr. Fell practically reared up on his hind legs and trumpeted. He said, 'Precisely. That's what I have been attempting to drive into your head. It's not like sand at the seaside. You could draw your finger across it without leaving a mark; but apparently you couldn't walk on it without leaving footprints.'"

Hugh had lost his appetite for soup.

"Accent on the 'apparently'?" he inquired.

"No, not that I noticed. But immediately after that he picked up the ice-skates and started looking at them with an expression like a pirate ordering somebody to walk the plank."

"The ice-skates?"

"As heaven is my witness," declared Brenda, lifting her hand with some fervour, "the ice-skates. Next he asked the Superintendent whether they could get a tub of water. Poor old Hadley was madder still by this time, but there's a water-tap in the garage and Dr. Fell insisted. They filled a tub and carried it back. Dr. Fell lugged it out on the court and tipped it up in one spot, mostly on his own shoes and the Superintendent's. Then he took one of the skates and tried to run it very lightly over the wet spot."

Hugh was finding even less appetite for the lobster-mayonnaise.

"I'm only glad," he said, staring, "they didn't try that game at the England's Lane Lawn-Tennis Club. I shouldn't like to answer for the groundkeeper's sanity if a second pair of maniacs got loose on his courts in the same day." He felt his own reason swimming. "But look here: are we all off our respective chumps? Is it being suggested—now—that the murderer went out there on a pair of ice-skates?"

"I don't know."

"But how could it be? The thing's not reasonable!"

"I don't know. All I know is what I saw. After that they went away in the Superintendent's car, and were gone a couple of hours. They said something about finding Chandler. When they came back they seemed terribly excited again, and had a man to try to walk the tennis-net. Hadley left again almost immediately; but Dr. Fell (in fact, while I was still talking to you on the phone the last time) came up to see me."

"So?"

Brenda looked uncertain.

"Yes, but he didn't say one word about the murder. Mostly he talked about himself. When he starts a chuckle, and looks at you as though you were a kind of refreshing phenomenon he'd never seen before, and gradually gets to such a guffaw that there are tears in his eyes, you find yourself laughing in spite of yourself. I thought he was an ordinary medical doctor like Nick, but it seems he's a doctor of philosophy. He's been a schoolmaster and a journalist and heaven knows what. He kept asking me all sorts of questions about what we all did, and how we employed our time, and so on. I couldn't see any harm in any of them. All through the questions he kept telling me a series of the funniest (and most incredible) stories I'd ever heard. In the middle of it Nick came in with a face like death, and asked us what was so funny in Frank's murder. Ugh!"

Hugh brooded.

"There is dirty work here," he decided, and told her about Chandler. The recital lasted until the coffee, at which time Brenda was not laughing.

"I'm afraid you're right," she murmured. "You think we ought to——?"

"Find Chandler! We've got to!" He lowered his voice. "My old man doesn't know anything about this move, and he'd probably try to stop it. Unfortunately, all sources of inquiry about Chandler are stopped up today. We could try to trace him through Madge Sturgess, by getting on to the hospital where she was taken; but that may take too long. The first possibility is the phone. There are three columns of Chandlers in the directory, including twenty-one 'A's' and five Arthurs. Also, we've got no reason to suppose he's on the phone; a theatrical boarding-house is more likely. But it's the first faint hope."

Chandler was not, in fact, on the phone; but his parents were. Crammed together in the telephone-box at the restaurant, the investigators wasted pennies and heard negatives until at the fourth try—this unlikely Chandler being a photographer in Fulham—a woman's voice spoke so sharply that the carbon cracked against Hugh's ear.

"He's not in," said the voice. "Who is that speaking, please?"

Hugh looked triumph at a white-faced and gesticulating Brenda.

"My name is Sturgess. I'm speaking for my sister Madge. Can you tell me where he is?"

The telephone was silent for so long that Hugh thought he had made a bad howler.

"If you're Madge's brother, how is it you don't know where he is?"

"I don't Mrs. Chandler. You're his mother, aren't you?"

For some reason this not-very-complicated deduction appeared to reassure her. "I'm sorry if it's all right, I'm sure. But that's the third time somebody's been after him today. First it was the p-police, and then some woman. What is it? Is he in more trouble?"

"We hope not, Mrs. Chandler; but——"

The telephone grew frenzied, cracking and rattling the carbon. "Oh, God, nothing but trouble, trouble, trouble; and him going to that grand school his father was so set on, and even Cambridge if you please; and now *look* at him! Can't even keep a job among a lot of loose-living painted-faced *music-hall* people; sacked because he wasn't there yesterday and only got his job back because he went down on his bended knee and said he was with Madge, which he wasn't; I can't put up with this; I *won't;* you tell him for me——"

"I know, Mrs. Chandler. Where is he?"

"He's at that place. The Orpheum. Rehearsing a new turn. You tell him from *me,* not as if his father had any spunk——"

"Thanks, Mrs. Chandler. I'll tell him," said Hugh, and hung up. "Which means," he continued, as they plunged up Shaftesbury Avenue at a pace that made Brenda protest, "which means, a hundred to one, Chandler was at the tennis court all right."

"Yes; but are you sure what we're doing is right?"

Hugh stopped short.

"Right? How?"

"If Chandler's at the music-hall," said Brenda, "that means the police won't be far off. Didn't your father tell you to keep away from them? Suppose we run into Chandler and Hadley together; what are we going to tell them?"

"I don't know," growled an exasperated Hugh. "It doesn't seem to matter a curse what we tell them. All I know now is that I want to talk to Chandler more than anybody else in the world. And if I find him——"

They did find him.

The Orpheum, in Charing Cross Road just north of Cambridge Circus, is a relic of more spacious Edwardian days. It is very large, very grimy, and amazingly hideous outside. Bills on the glass doors to the foyer announced that it would open Monday, August 12th, with a new programme, including the Flying Mephistos, Schlosser & Weazle, Tex Lannigan and his whip, Gertie Folleston, and other names which meant nothing to Hugh. He had a vague idea that they ought to go to the stage-entrance. But the glass doors to the foyer were wide open, so they simply walked in.

Inside was a spectral darkness, stuffy with heavy theatre-smell overladen by damp, and silent except for a vague rumbling somewhere ahead. Nobody stopped them; there was nobody about. But, when they pushed open padded doors ahead, a dozen sharp brittle little noises struck out at them, hollowly.

"*Hup!*" said a voice.

There were perhaps twenty people moving or lolling in the first few rows of orchestra-stalls. Rows of seats, shrouded in white dust-covers, stretched from darkness at the back down a long opera-glass mile to the lighted naked stage. Somebody struck three notes on a xylophone. There was the faint patter of a tap-dance. Faces would appear from the wings, and draw back again. The heavy gilt Cupids and nymphs on the proscenium-arch, the heavy gilt light-brackets by the boxes, seemed to tremble to this pattern of sounds as a glass trembles to a note in music.

"*Hup!*"

On the stage, looking pallid and unreal despite their scarlet tights, the acrobats had tumbled into a pyramid, and tumbled apart like falling cards. Creaking, four trapezes in the form of a square were lowered from the flies. Four of the Flying Mephistos, two men and two women, darted up silvery ladders held by the other two. They slid nimbly over the trapeze-bars, seeming to land and swing for impetus in the same moment. The orchestra played one verse before the chorus; and then, with the cymbal-clang as a signal, one of them launched himself into the air.

O-ooooh! (the symbals banged)

He floats through the air with the greatest of ease——

In the darkness behind curtains at the back, Brenda whispered.

"Which is Chandler? Do you know?"

"I think he's the rather lanky one with reddish hair, the one on the trapeze nearest us. He's thinner and a little bit taller; most of 'em look like Italians."

"Do you think they would toss us out if we just sat down? Oh!"

She shied a little. A tall, lean figure, shadowy in the dimness, was coming up the red-carpeted aisle. This resolved itself into an even taller man in a white ten-gallon hat. To the waist his costume was an ordinary lounge-suit, except that he wore two cross-belts supporting holsters and pearl-handled .45 revolvers. Under this he wore leather chaps over high-heeled, spurred boots, and he was carrying in his right hand a long, heavy black-snake whip. He would have been a startling figure, his face rather like a horse's, and seeming of the colour and consistency of the leather chaps, if it had not been for two exceedingly mild eyes peering down at them.

"Howdy," said the apparition. "Y'all in thishyer show?"

Brenda gave him a smile that raised his hair.

"I'm afraid not. But do you think they'd mind terribly if we sat down for a minute?"

Hugh knew the effect of that smile. The new comer swept off his ten-gallon hat. He was almost shivering with gallantry. His lanky arms and legs seemed to have come all apart.

"Sho'!" he crowed. "Sho'!" He was not attempting to use the word, 'sure'; he was merely uttering an exclamation of astonishment.

"Lady," he added with fervour, "as far as Ah'm concerned, y'all can have enathing you like. You want to sit down?"

"Please."

"Sho'!" said the new comer. His arm jerked back; the long whip uncoiled blindingly, with a crack so exactly like a light rifle-shot that everyone who heard it jumped. The music jarred and went sour. The end of the whip appeared, with magic suddenness, coiled round one of the white dust-covers on the stalls. He whisked off the dust-cover and pulled it towards him.

"That's for you," he explained. "Thishyer"—*crack*—"thishyer's for the gent. Thishyer"—CRACK—"thishyer's for me. Sho'!"

"Thanks so much," said Brenda. "I expect," she smiled at him, "you're from the West?"

The other's huge mirth changed.

"Texas ain't the West," he said, with passion. "Lady, Ah shonuf have had a time tellin' people that since I been in thishyer town. Texas is the South. Ah'm a Southerner m'self. Sho'!"

None of them, least of all Tex Lannigan, had noticed the dead, hollow silence that had fallen on the theatre. The orchestra had stopped. The trapezes ceased to swing.

"Shut that scarlet row!" a voice bawled at them, blasting through a microphone. "Who's the adjectival so-and-so that's making that adjectival row?"

Tex Lannigan looked mildly astonished.

"That," he yelled back, "ain't language to use in front of a lady."

"I'll cram it down your adjectival throat," said the other, a short, squat acrobat with a blue chin. "Want 'em to break their necks, do you? All right, Professor. All right, boys. Same again."

"Ah'm right sorry," said Tex mildly. "But Ah still say: that ain't——"

"Please!" urged Brenda, in a furious whisper. "Please! Sit down. Here!"

"All right, ma'am. Enathing you say."

One night to his tent he invited her in,
Filled her with confidence, kisses, and gin,
And started her out on the road to ru-in;
She made——

"Ah was forgettin'," said Tex, leaning across to whisper. "Did you want to see enabody, lady?"

Brenda was incautious. "Shh! Yes. One of the acrobats. I don't know which one. His name's Chandler."

Tex uncoiled himself and got to his feet; and, for attention, he made the whip crack with the noise of a service-rifle. Somebody dropped a cymbal in the orchestra pit. A fat man in shirt-sleeves, wild-eyed, popped up from the first row of stalls.

"Any of you fellows," shouted Tex, in what he imagined to be the tongue of Dante, "allee samee catchee name Chandler? Lady want him."

"Kviet!" howled the fat man in shirt-sleeves. "Oi, oi, oi, oi, oi! Iss it to de bughouse you are sending me gradually, no? You vant my hacrobats should lose de tempo hoff de music and fall hoff de bar, yes? I vill not haff it. Oi, dese foreigners!" He hurled a sheaf of papers into the air. "Alessandro, it iss no good ve go on. Take a fief minute break, yah? Phooey!"

"Nice quiet little place," said Hugh.

"Sho'!" scoffed Tex. "Look. Y'all like to see me take that cigar outen his kissen with thishyer whip?"

"For heaven's sake, no!" cried Brenda, clutching at his arm. "Please! Sit down. Everybody's looking at us."

"Recokn *so*," said Tex, unimpressed.

"I say, though, Hugh. The red-headed one is Chandler all right. Look at him. And look down there!—six rows ahead of us, on the aisle."

It was a girl, sitting alone. She had turned round to glance at them with such a look of cold malevolence that Hugh started. Even though it was too dim to se much else, you could see or at least feel the malevolence. Hugh had a vague feeling of having seen her before, when the association of ideas gave him the face at once. Though he had seen it only in a newspaper photograph, the face was Madge Sturgess's.

The acrobats had dropped with soft thuds to the stage. Their looks were professional masks; but the leader seemed to be addressing some blistering remarks to Chandler, who only nodded.

"He's going off stage!" muttered Brenda. "Dou you think he's——?"

But he was not. In a few moments Chandler reappeared from the iron door leading backstage out of the pit. He wore a long scarlet cloak which made a vivid moving spot in that gloom, and he was carrying something under his arm and under the cloak.

"Reckon Ah'll be pullin' m' freight," said Tex, getting up. His formal courtesy was overpowering. "If Ah can be of any further service to you, ma'am, or to you, sir, just you signal like thishyer." He let out a reverberating whistle which caused two Negro tap-dancers, who had taken the stage, to glare at him. Then he thrust out his hand. "Lannigan's mah name. Clarence Lannigan," he added defiantly, "of Houston, Texas. And don't nobody go callin' it Howston, neither. Now just you watch me go and git old Margetson's goat."

He shambled away as Arthur Chandler briskly threaded through the rows of stalls.

Only stopping to whisper a brief word to Madge Sturgess, Chandler came straight up to them. He was smiling. He had a bony, shrewd, apparently good-natured face which suggested the phrase "too clever by half"—but only half. He seemed on a wire of uncertainty, though he tried to conceal this. His eyes, long and light-blue in the high, shiny frame-work of the face, looked reddish and sanded at the lids; they roved into corners of the auditorium. On closer inspection, his scarlet cloak appeared a trifle soiled and shabby like himself. But Hugh rather liked the look of him.

The orchestra was playing again, for the tap-dancers, so that his words were inaudible a few feet away. He leaned over and spoke in a pleasant voice.

"Good afternoon," he said. "Come to have a word with the murderer?"

Brenda half got to her feet, and sat down again when Hugh put a hand on her arm.

"That's direct enough, anyhow," Hugh admitted.

Chandler threw back his head and laughed. Then he leaned forward still more confidentially.

"It's all right," he assured them. "I've already confessed to the murder, you know."

XVI.

PRIDE

"Would you mind," said Hugh, leaning forward himself with great attention, "repeating that again?"

"I've confessed to it," said Chandler, "or practically so. I'm under arrest, or practically so. They'll be taking me to the Bridewell this evening."

On the stage the Negro tap-dancers were bending to curious positions: their shoes, like polished black mirrors, seemed to flicker with a diabolical life of their own. *Ticka-tack, ticka-tack, ticka-tack* ran the noise under the swing of the orchestra. Across it, now, cut a whip-crack so loud and venomous that Brenda, Chandler, and Hugh all jumped.

Tex Lannigan had declared war. Whether he was merely trying to get Mr. Margetson's goat, or whether (like all Southerners) he had decided views on the color-question, was not clear. But he was standing across the auditorium and making the whip talk. Unperturbed, the dancers flickered across the stage, and flickered back.

Arthur Chandler slipped into a seat in the row in front of Brenda and Hugh. He twisted round and grinned at them.

"Under arrest," muttered Hugh. "Doesn't that bother you at all?"

"No, not much."

"You see," said Brenda, "we'd better explain who we are. We——"

Again Chandler threw back his head and laughed.

"Oh, I know who you are. In fact, I was wondering whether you would be honouring me with a visit today. I hoped you would." The heavy box or parcel, which he had been carrying under his red cloak, he now lowered to the floor beside him. "I've been wanting to return this infernal china. I mean the load of china I removed from the tennis pavilion last night."

His grin grew ever broader.

"I'm a friend of yours, don't you think? But it's only a nuisance to me, and won't be any good at all when I'm in gaol."

Crack! went Tex Lannigan's whip.

Hugh turned to meet Brenda's wide eyes under the brim of the tilted white hat.

"It is possible to argue," Hugh said, "that this is the biggest miracle of all. So it was you who stole that stuff?"

"Obviously. Here are the dibs." Chandler kicked at the parcel and made it rattle.

"But why?"

Chandler ignored this.

"I also thought," he went on, "that there was something you both ought to see. Look here."

Reaching under his cloak, and under the neckband of the red tights, he drew out a piece of glazed paper only a few inches square. He passed this across the back of the seat to Hugh. Hugh peered at it in the gloom; he snapped on the flame of his lighter to peer more closely; and, holding the photograph down under cover of the line of seats, he felt a slightly queasy feeling in his stomach.

"My father is a photographer, as you may know," Chandler explained easily. "I developed that late last night. Only a snapshot, of course, and a rotten bad light; but I was using the new K Panchromatic, which is fast enough to take a fairly good snap in anything less than total darknes."

It was.

The photograph, taken from the west side of the tennis court outside the wire wall, was a view pointing obliquely across the court. It showed, in the foreground, Frank Dorrance's body lying in a sickly greyish expanse smeared with rain-water puddles. But most clearly it showed Brenda White.

Brenda was facing the camera, though not looking at it. She was looking at Frank's body. One wave of hair had fallen across her face; her eyes were open and dilated even in that mimic greyness; her mouth was pulled down as though in a grotesque parody of herself. She seemed to crouch. She was holding, with both arms in front of her as though the arms were dislocated, a picnic-hamper which seemed to bang against a blur of legs. The camera had caught her running—running towards Frank's body, and a dozen feet away from it—violent action and emotion frozen and blurred in cold print, as the camera will catch sea-spray rising against rocks.

Crack! went Tex Lannigan's whip, cutting through the music and the *ticka-tack, ticka-tack* of the dancers.

"Good, don't you think?" grinned Chandler.

"Very good," whispered Brenda. She put her hand across Hugh, and pressed down the top of the petrol lighter so that the flame went out. He could feel her breath against his cheek.

Chandler's voice changed.

"Steady, my lad. Don't get the wrong idea. This isn't blackmail, you know."

"Then what is it?"

"Well, *I* should call it an uncommonly friendly gesture," grinned the other. He was now kneeling on the seat like a lean red goblin. They saw faint light along his sardonic jaw. "Though you evidently don't regard it as such. The role of guardian angel is new and queer to me, I admit, but it's notorious that those who can't take care of themselves can always take care of other people. Whisk! I wave my wand. Whisk! Suspicion is removed from you. Damme if I don't think that rates at least a word of thanks, at least!"

"Thanks?" repeated Brenda. "How?"

"See here," said Chandler. "Just now I've got no time for anybody's troubles but my own. And among ourselves I'll admit that nothing I've done was done out of altruism. But, instead of holding that thing as though it would bite you, why aren't you cheering? Don't you see it proves that Miss Brenda White had nothing to do with this business?"

"Does it?" said Brenda.

"Don't take my word for it. Just look at it. If there's one thing it does show, it shows Dorrance dead—and no tracks coming near him except his own. Now look at yourself. You're quite a long distance back from him. You haven't even reached him yet. There are his tracks, and nobody else's. Aside from an alibi witnessed and testified to by the Lord Chief Justice and the Archbishop of Canterbury, what better proof do you want?"

The theatre was intensely hot.

"Is he right, Hugh?"

"He is."

"Then——"

"There's no question of a fake about this," said Hugh, who wondered why his collar was so warm and why a subconscious fear had been erased at last. "It can be enlarged and compared with the official photographs. Look here, Chandler; many thanks, and several apologies. But would it seem like biting a friendly hand if I asked what in blazes you were doing there with a camera? Or even what you were doing there anyhow?"

Chandler grinned again. They could sense his vitality, a wiry and half-savage kind of vitality.

He waved his hand.

"Ah, that would be telling."

"Is there any objection to telling?"

"Don't splutter, my boy. Bad for you. As for the photograph," said Chandler magnanimously, "keep it. It's yours. Superintendent Hadley already has a copy of it."

(*Crack!*)

They had to lower their voices to a mutter. The music of the orchestra had died away, leaving a vast hollow under the roof, as the tap-dancers flickered off-stage. Tex Lannigan was now using his whip to pull off, at long range, the pink shades of the wall-bracket lamps beside the boxes. Mr. Margetson the manager, after carefully placing his spectacles on the floor and jumping on them, had run over to threaten or expostulate. A pair of cross-talk comedians, composed of a little man with a red nose, and a fat, gouty Colonel Blimp on crutches, had begun to speak thinly. And Tex, who had evidently no animus against Schlosser & Weazle, for the moment left off his whip-practice.

"So Superintendent Hadley has a copy of it," muttered Hugh in a hollow voice. "Just like that! Since when?"

"Since noon today. He and an obese old blighter named

Fell ran me to earth in my favourite pub. I was expecting them. I'd printed off several copies of that little snapshot, you see. I thought they might come in useful."

"Hadley knows?" cried Brenda, instinctively looking over her shoulder. "But he never said anything about it to me."

Chandler was sardonically grim. "He will. Madam, he will. I can assure you of that."

"Wait," said Hugh. "What did you tell him?"

"I told him," answered Chandler coolly, "that I was the public-spirited citizen who killed Mr. Francis Ruddy Dorrance."

"Well? And did you kill him?"

"Ah, that's the question again. Speaking strictly among ourselves: perhaps I did, and perhaps I didn't. In any case they'll have to prove how I did it, and that will take some doing." He seemed to grow serious. "Now see here. This will be the only chance I have to talk to you before I am haled off to clink. It should happen at any minute now, which will further infuriate my boss and further please me——"

"But, hang it all, you seem to WANT to be arrested."

"I do. However, let me finish what I was going to say. I just want to warn both of you; for your own good, don't stick to that old wheeze about Miss White not having made the tracks at all, and recall the beautiful fancy that I might have worn the shoes by walking on my hands. It would be an act of ingratitude to your guardian angel, and a source of severe discomfort to you. I have evidence to blow it sky-high. In fact, I have blown it sky-high."

"Admitted. Well?"

Chandler grinned like a wolf.

"Now that story could have been bad for me. I *could* have walked on my hands. I had to dispose of it, and I did. Once that's gone, however, the sky's the limit and I don't care what you say. All I ask is that you don't harass your guardian angel with too many questions. Never mind why I was there with a camera, or why I pinched the china, or how long I was there, or how much I know . . ."

Hugh interrupted him.

"Those are rather important questions, though."

Chandler hesitated.

"I'll tell you what I'll do," he decided. "I'll tell you just what I told Hadley, no more and no less. But, since I regard you as allies of mine—" He stopped. His red-rimmed eyes narrowed. "By the way, I understand it wasn't you who concocted that story about me walking on my hands?"

"No. That was a gentleman named Dr. Young."

Again Chandler's eyes narrowed. "Young? Young? That's the old geezer, isn't it? Owns the house? Sort of guardian to Dorrance? Yes, I've heard of him. So it was his brilliant idea, was it?"

"It was; but he wasn't trying to put a rope around *your* neck. He had other game at the time."

Chandler seemed convulsed with inner amusement. "Sort of internal politics, I take it? Bless you, my children. Well, since I regard you as allies of mine, I will do a little better than that. I will tell you——"

"Not the truth, by any chance?" suggested Brenda, with ineffabale sweetness. "I don't think we could stand it by this time."

"Why not? I will quote you the statements I gave Hadley. And after each one, in the fashion of the newspaper questionnaires which list Gorgonzola as a Spanish composer, a cheese, or a mountain in Greece, I will add the word, 'true' or 'false.' Listen carefully.

"I said I had heard at Dorrance's flat on Saturday afternoon that he had gone on to the old geezer's house in Highgate to play tennis. (True.) I said I had followed, and inquired my way of a policeman who looked at me very rummily when I asked for details of Dr. Young's place. (True.) I said I arrived in the grounds at about twenty minutes to six. (True.) I said I had found the tennis court, and left the newspaper conspicuously in the pavilion to give Dorrance something to think about. (True.) I said I intended to kill Dorrance. (False, oddly enough.)

"I said I had heard people coming to the court, so I withdrew behind a tree and watched. (True.) I watched a game of tennis until the storm broke. (True.) Then, not being a duck, I took shelter in the garage until the rain stopped. (Very true.) I heard the mixed doubles separate, and heard Dorrance's intention to go to Mrs. Bancroft's and cut back in a hurry by the same path. (True.) I then waited patiently in the garage until a few minutes later I heard Dorrance coming back—alone. (True.)

"He was whistling, the little swine," added Chandler. "He didn't whistle much longer. Oh, I forgot: true."

Chandler stopped.

The pure venom in his voice startled his hearers. He had a trick of making things vivid by the pitch of his voice or the slight turn of a wrist. They were not in the theatre any longer. They were back by the garage, and they heard Frank whistling.

"I said I saw him, through the window in the garage, stop outside. (True.) I said I saw him go into the enclosure. (True.) I said I saw him go in there alone. (False.)"

The scene had become diabolically vivid. Brenda was brought up sharp on it.

"But if you saw him go in there," she said, "you must have seen who killed him."

"You're forgetting. *I* killed him."

"'The murderer is Arthur Chandler'—True or false?"

"Ah, that's another of the things you mustn't ask yet. But, you see, it's what worries the police. It's what keeps me safe. I admitted all this to Hadley. I said I must have killed the fellow; on careful thought, I rather supposed I had. The big snag in their way was that they couldn't tell how I had done it."

There was play-acting in this. Hugh felt convinced of it. Its core was shoddy; it smelt of the scarlet cloak. What he could not decide was whether it was the play-acting of guilt or the play-acting of innocence.

"But what happened then?" he prompted. "After Dorrance went in to the court—not alone?"

"Sorry. The story stops there."

"To us, or to the police?"

"To everybody."

Hugh's wits were working furiously; or, at least, he was trying to make them work. "There are," he said, "several dozen puzzles. But the biggest of them is why you are so infernally keen about getting yourself arrested."

"Can't you guess?"

"No. Unless——"

"Unless?"

"Unless, of course, you're not guilty and you've got evidence up your sleeve which will absolutely clear you at the trial." He paused. "You may think the notoriety of being tried for murder, especially a 'miracle' murder, will help you up to the place in the world you want: whatever that is." He paused again. "You may be right, though it's a devil of a risk, I warn you."

Somebody's breath whistled. If he had pressed hard on a broken nose, he thought he could not have got a more violent reaction; yet Chandler did not move.

"The man's barmy," grinned Chandler. "It's more probable, isn't it, that I'm guilty and have got a foolproof method of
murder that they can't prove on me? When better murders are
built——"

"Chandler will photograph them," said Hugh. "That's what
I meant by evidence. If you got a snapshot of Brenda after the
murder, there's no reason why you shouldn't have got a picture
of the murder itself. And the murderer. And the method. That
would be the *real* goods."

As he said this, he was not looking at Chandler. He was looking past Chandler, down a few rows of seats to where the lights
from the stage shone on the edges of Madge Sturgess's hair. It
was brown hair, somewhat fluffy. All he could see of Madge
Sturgess was that she was a thin girl in a print dress; but again
she turned round to look at them. Her look did not now seem to
be of anger or malevolence, but astonishment.

Now it would be impossible for her to have overheard a word
at that distance. The turn, the look, must have been caused by
something else, though it fitted in with uncanny precision to
Hugh's words. In any case he forgot it. For, Chandler spoke in a
voice so normal, so human, and so charged with violence that it
was difficult to realize he whispered.

He said:

"Good God, is it as obvious as all that?"—and, not acting now,
he wrenched at the top of the seat as though he tried to wrench
it up from the floor.

Hugh reached out and seized his arm.

"So you have got a photograph of it?"

Chandler shook it off.

"No!"

"Sure?"

"I've told you. What's the fatality about it?" said Chandler. "Why is everything always so difficult for me, and why was it always so easy for that little swine?"

"Yes, but——"

"Ever since I was so high," said Chandler, putting his hand near the floor, "I've been dreaming about what I would do. All sawdust. None of it ever worked. I've told Madge I would fill a top-hat with five-pound notes one day and toss it in her lap. Have I? No. Give me a chance to shine in the dock, at least."

Practical certainty smote Hugh.

But he did not argue too much.

"It's your own affair," he said. "And the same thing has been done before, of course. I remember the case of a man who deliberately confessed to a murder (which he didn't commit), and then went into court and produced evidence to show conclusively he wasn't guilty. He explained that a whispering-campaign had accused him of the murder for so long that he was going both mad and broke; and the only way to clear himself was to clear himself before the eyes of the world in open court."

Hugh paused.

"If you're confessing to this because you want the notoriety of a trial," he went on, "maybe that's all right. They can't do anything to you for lying, unless you lie in court. But you've got to be certain you can prove your innocence. I want to warn you, as a lawyer, that it's full of deadly risks. The judge won't like a stunt of that sort. The jury won't like it. Be sure of your bluff before you start, or they'll think it's the other kind of bluff; and they'll hang you."

"I don't know what you're talking about!"

Brenda had caught the cue. He could see the line of her eyelash, the soft line of the jaw, the tense line of the shoulders.

"Hugh's right, Mr. Chandler," she said. "With all due respect to our guardian angel, you're not a very good liar."

"Ho!"

"You're not, though," Brenda insisted, shaking her head mesmerically. All the pleading of her voice went into it. "You're too honest; or, maybe, too afraid of being caught. I know one whacking liar"—the disgust she felt with herself was suddenly so apparent that Hugh wondered how long she had been feeling it— "I know one whacking liar who couldn't get away with it. And you can't either."

Chandler looked at the floor. After a while he spoke abruptly.

"Maybe you're right. I wish I knew. It's been worrying me silly all day."

"Believe me, we're right," said Hugh. "Don't you think there will be enough notoriety, and safe notoriety, if you just tell the truth? That is, if you yourself show the proof? You'll be the hero of the day."

"You think so?" demanded Chandler, jerking up his head with a ghoulish kind of hope.

"I know it."

Chandler seemed to come to a decision. After glancing quickly round the auditorium, and seeming to make sure that Madge Sturgess was out of earshot, he bent over them impressively.

"Listen!" he said . . .

"*Flying Mephistos!*" bawled a voice from the stage. "*Places! Number four there! Hoy! You!*"

Chandler, while Hugh and Brenda sat with their hearts in their throats, stopped speaking, moistened his lips, and turned round.

"Half a tick!" he yelled. "I only——"

"Wow!" said the voice from the stage. The squat acrobat, who seemed to be the leader of the turn, was not content with ordinary speech. His face looked pale. He ran to a microphone at the side of the stage; and the amplified voice blattered and tore at them.

"I've stood enough," the voice said. "Nobody can stand any more. If you're not in place in three seconds, while I count, out you go. You hear me?"

"But——"

"You'd better go," advised Hugh. "If you're not going through with that scheme, you'd better keep your job."

"One. Two. And you can tell that Texas so-and-so"—hollow, calm and evil the microphone-voice rose—"that he can crack his adjectival whip till Doomsday, for all these ladies and gentlemen care. It wouldn't bother a flea. We've heard peanut-eating in Manchester that was louder. One. Two——"

With the whirl of a scarlet cloak, Chandler's boneless figure swept over the seat in a one-handed vault, landed lightly in the aisle, and ran down towards the stage.

A plunk of tuning fiddles issued from the orchestra pit.

"Hugh, he knows," muttered Brenda. "There's no doubt at all about that. He knows who the murderer is, and how it was done. We shouldn't have let him go. If he has time to think about it, he may change his mind again."

"Yes. And if we don't let him go, that bloke 'Alessandro' will sack him and he'll be desperate enough to stick to his old story. Let it be. He won't have time for much personal thinking while he's doing his act."

"That," said Brenda, turning round so that her narrowed eyes met his, "is what worries me too. Hugh—that work is dangerous.

He's in no state of mind to do it. I say: it would be rather horrible if his hand slipped, or something, wouldn't it? They're fifty feet over the auditorim, and no net."

They stared at each other.

It was a new danger, a new greased board for uncertain walking. But they had no time to think about it. Someone walked quietly down the red-carpeted aisle and touched Hugh's shoulder from behind. Contemplating them, with a very curious expression, was Superintendent Hadley.

XVII.
PITY

"Er—sit down, Superintendent," invited Hugh, moving over.

Events had moved so fast that he had not had time to readjust himself to a new, and very much more ominous, aspect of Hadley. But if he had expected a blast of anger, or even a look, he did not get it. There was only a thick, constrained pause. Hadley glanced at Hugh. He glanced at Brenda, who was hastily stuffing the photograph into her handbag.

"Ah?" murmured Hadley.

He struck a match to see his way in the gloom. It showed the aisle seat turned up, with a white metal plate inscribed in black letters, 'This seat is fitted with Tonophone apparatus for the convenience of the deaf.' He blew out the match and sat down. The thick, constrained pause went on.

"The fact is, Superintendent," said Hugh, "the fact is——"

"Yes?"

"Well, damn it, the fact is we didn't tell you the whole truth."

"So I've heard, young man," observed Hadley, as though a little surprised. "So I've heard."

He continued to look at the stage, where the Flying Mephistos were assembling.

"I only wanted," insisted Hugh, "to explain——"

"No explanation is necessary," said Hadley. He added: "Thank you very much."

"Yes, I know I deserve a kick in the pants. All right; you can kick me from here to the Marble Arch and welcome. But you don't understand. I'm telling you this because now—at long last—we can help you. We've found out something. We're on to the real truth."

"Is that so, now?"

"Yes. We've found—" Belatedly, the whisper of Hadley's tone meant something to Hugh. Hugh stopped short. "You don't seem exactly receptive, Superintendent."

"Well, well, well!" said Hadley. "So I'm not receptive, eh? I'm not bloody well receptive. Is that it?"

"You still don't understand. This isn't a trick. It's the truth."

"As I hope to live and breathe," urged Brenda. "If you'll only listen to us, Mr. Hadley, you'll have the real murderer under lock and key before the day's over. Chandler knows. Chandler's got a photograph of the real murderer."

"You've made a slight mistake, haven't you?" asked Hadley, turning round to look at her for the first time. "He's got a photograph of *you.*"

"No, no, this is another photograph. Chandler was there and saw the whole thing. He practically told us so himself."

"I'll bet he did."

"But won't you listen to——"

"Just one moment," said Hadley. Drawing a deep breath, he seemed to loom over them; but he spoke in the same quiet, curt voice. "We'll forget what's past. It was my own fault. I always prided myself on being a judge of liars. But my wife is quite right. I'm not. At least, as far as women are concerned. After thirty years in the police force, I'm still a blundering, blistering babe in arms."

He paused impressively, looking so hard at Brenda that she drew back.

"So it's too bad I'm not receptive. If I were, I could sit here and let you tell me another little pack of ghost stories to pass the time. But it's a pity I'm not. Young lady, I wouldn't believe you if you told me I had egg on my tie or that the sun would rise tomorrow morning. If you two have concocted another song-and-dance to distract attention from yourselves, forget it. I don't want to hear it. It's not necessary."

(*Crack!*)

Even Hadley stirred at the vicious whip-noise across the theatre. Tex Lannigan's white hat was in evidence again. The Flying Mephistos, going through their ground routine, moved in a quick, scarlet Catherine-wheel which rolled and dived to a series of soft slaps and thuds. They paid no attention.

(*Crack!*)

"Hugh, that's got to be stopped," said Brenda, getting to her feet. "Stop what's-his-name: Clarence. Whistle for him! Don't you see? Chandler! That poor man's as nervous as a cat. If the whip keeps going while he's on the trapeze, heaven only knows what will happen. This is rather awful."

"Is it?" said Hadley, settling comfortably. "You kept saying a lot of things were that last night. What is 'awful' now?"

"Chandler! He'll fall."

"I hope not," said the Superintendent comfortably. "I want

him to be in good shape when he goes along with me. But since he's only been doing this routine six or seven years, I think he can last out now."

Hugh interposed.

"Hold on! You're not going to put Chandler under arrest?"

"He *is* under arrest, even if he doesn't know it." Hadley contemplated the stage. "Have a good time, my bucko," he added with satisfaction. "You had a good deal of fun taking Fell and me over the jumps this morning. We'll see how you like a bit of your own treatment tonight."

(*Crack!*)

"But you can't do that, Superintendent! He isn't guilty, and he knows who is. He's got a photograph of the murderer. Besides, it'll be no good arresting him anyway if you can't show how he did the murder."

"Oh, I think we know that," said Hadley.

To ancient storm-music from the William Tell Overture, pitched in a louder key than was necessary, two of the Flying Mephistos were doing a series of back-flaps across the stage.

"Then how did he do it?"

Hadley spoke almost absently, his eyes on the acrobats. "He walked on the net. That's rather a good turn. I almost hate to break it up."

"He couldn't have walked on top of the net," insisted Hugh. "That's impossible. The net was too weak to support anybody; and, in any case, Chandler doesn't do wire-walking. Brenda saw your experiments. She also overheard you say——"

This time, as Hadley gave them his attention, his expression was genuinely sinister.

"So you saw and heard that too, Miss White? Well, well, well! There isn't much you miss, is there?"

"That's true, though," Brenda pointed out.

"Once and for all," said Hadley. "I am going to warn you to keep out of this. I have at least a hundred questions I want to ask you, and a hundred things *you* are going to make clear to *me*. That can wait. But, at risk of having two people who have no more moral sense than a trapeze interfering still more in this case, I'll make you a proposition before I stick you both in gaol on the first charge I can think of. If I tell you how he did it, will you stop getting in the way of people who are trying to get at the truth?"

(*Crack!*)

"Yes."

"He walked on the net," repeated Hadley. "Not in the way you mean. As a matter of fact, you'll have to hear about this, because we shall want your evidence against him."

"Our evidence? But I'm damned if I know anything, and neither does Brenda!"

"I think you do." The Superintendent spoke grimly. "But I won't lead your minds. You're going to tell me. Now, when you began to play tennis yesterday afternoon, what was the height of the net?"

"The usual height. The top was one racket-length plus one racket-width above the ground."

"Yes. But what happened after the rain had been hammering on it for three quarters of an hour? It sagged, didn't it?"

Hugh remembered only too well that crumpled arc hanging down. "It sagged a good deal, yes; but———"

"You also tell me there was a lot of wind blowing, both before the storm and during it? Yes." Hadley nodded. "Well, there's your answer if you just stop to think about it. Given both those two circumstances, what would happen?"

It was Brenda who spoke out clearly here. "They're going up to those trapezes. Look at Arthur Chandler! He's as white as a ghost and he nearly missed his grip on that silver ladder when he started. If you're not going to stop our friend Clarence, I am. Let me pass."

(*Crack!*)

The orchestra, as before, would play one verse before the chorus, to give the performers time to mount and get the trapezes in motion. The full music swept through the theatre as Brenda started to push her way past Hugh's knees.

"Look here, Brenda: no! Sit down. Those people are old hands. They know their business; they were only grousing at Lannigan. But if *we* start raising a rumpus now, there may really be trouble. Superintendent, I still don't see what you're getting at."

> Oh, once I was happy but now I'm forlorn,
> Like an old coat that is tattered and torn;
> Bereft in this wide world to fret and to mourn,
> Betrayed by a maid——

As Brenda pushed past into the aisle, Madge Sturgess also got to her feet. Lightly, with something of the walk of a mannequin, she moved up the aisle towards the dark rear of the auditorium. She and Brenda passed each other. And they gave each other a quick, comprehensive look.

"Brenda! Here!"

"Sit down, Mr. Rowland!" said Hadley impatiently. "If she thinks she can stop that fool with the whip, let her go. So you still don't see what I'm getting at?"

"Yes. No," babbled Hugh, struggling with indecision.

"A tennis-net," said Hadley, "is heavy, isn't it? Yes. And, if it sagged as much as all that, about three or four inches of it would be lying on the ground, wouldn't it? Yes. Including the weighted cloth border of the underside, the border being over an inch wide? Yes. You agree?"

"All right. Brenda!"

> Now this girl that I loved she was handsome,
> And I tried all I knew how to please——

"But what else happens?" inquired Hadley. "What else happens if the weather is blowing? The net does more than drag on the ground. It flaps back and forth on the ground. Consequently, if the sand surface of the court is soft enough during a thunderstorm, the flattened net leaves marks. It leaves a trail of its own clear across the court. You look at that trail; and you never think twice about it because it looks so natural. You don't count it as a mark at all.

"But a man could walk along the underside of that net, couldn't he? He could walk on the border that lay flat on the court, and leave no footprints of his own? More than that—he could jump or spring on it. Starting with a long spring from the side of the court (such as Chandler could manage easily), he would land on the nearest edge of the net. Two more springs, and he's at the middle. He makes no marks, because the trail has already been made for him. That's how our acrobatic friend did his acrobatics; and it's going to hang him."

> But I never could please her one quarter as well
> As the man on the flying trapeze . . .
> OO-HHH!——

Shatteringly, the cymbals banged as the music soared to a break; and the first acrobat hurled himself into the air.

It had begun.

Hugh, standing up, searched the blur of the auditorium with his eyes. He could see neither Brenda's white dress, nor Tex Lannigan's white hat.

"And that," concluded the Superintendent, "if you could give me any of your attention, is what we have to establish."

"Superintendent," said Hugh, "I don't believe it."

"No? Why not?"

"What about Chandler's weight? Admitting"—he still stared out over the auditorium—"admitting Chandler could have done that without leaving marks, still at the few places where he did land there would be deep marks in the trail left by the tennis-net. Did you find 'em?"

Hadley was unmoved.

"There needn't be anything of the sort, necessarily. He was walking on a soft, spongy sort of bundle (meaning the net itself), with the area that took the pressure distributed. It wouldn't be like the sharp edges of marks left by shoes, which allow the weight to sink. I'm afraid you'll have to accept it, young man. There's no other explanation."

(*Crack!*)

Hugh, though he had no technical knowledge of what he saw, yet realized that he was watching an aerial display of the first order. He did not wonder that the Flying Mephistos had been touchy. The novelty of the turn lay in the four trapezes set like a square, with two teams working at once. One person of each of the teams was always in the air, flickering past each other with such shuttle-effect that it seemed they would collide at any moment. If so much as a shoulder had brushed a shoulder in that weaving, darting play, it would have meant disaster. Timed to a hair-line, heels always flashed past as hands and head dived.

(*Crack!*)

Despite himself, Hugh felt a jerk at his nerves at each twist in the air. Brenda was right. Lannigan ought to be stopped. Lannigan was a fool. Lannigan was a danger. Lannigan was——

(*Crack!*)

"Sit down," snapped Hadley. "You don't do this usually, do you, when you see a turn in a music-hall? Anyhow, that's the position. Chandler is the murderer, and that's all there is to it."

"Does Dr. Fell agree with you?"

"That's of no consequence. Fell never agrees with anybody but himself. If he wants to play the bear with the sore head, he can. Chandler is the murderer because he had motive, opportunity, temperament, and method; and because he's the only person who could be guilty."

(*Crack!*)

Hugh heard that final, vicious lash dimly, because the orchestra was banging with exaggerated loudness to drown out the whip. But he heard it just as he looked behind him—and saw Brenda standing in the middle aisle, staring, with Tex Lannigan's coiled whip in her hands.

Since his eyes were away from the stage, Hugh did not see it begin to happen. But he saw the rest of it.

Chandler had returned his partner to the trapeze-bar, where she caught and, magnificently, held his weight while he gained impetus to swing back. They were on the trapezes facing the audience, and Chandler's was nearest. He swung and spun, his hands out, towards his own trapeze-bar and towards the auditorium. They saw his face, pale and glistening, with a stupid look under the overhead lamps.

Then it seemed to happen in slow motion. The arch of his body had a slow, easy curve. The extended tips of his fingers passed several inches beneath the trapeze-bar; they sagged at the elbows, but did not fall until he began to fall himself. It was as though, a red attacker, he were leaping out at the audience. He missed the orchestra pit, struck head down across the aisle-seat of the first row of stalls with a rattling thud, crumpled up across it like a piece of burnt paper, and rolled over on his back in the aisle.

He was dead, of course, when they picked him up. Since he was wearing red tights and had red hair, it was a minute or two before anyone noticed the three bullet-holes in his corpse: two through the body, and one through the crown of the head.

XVIII.
INSPIRATION

AT TEN o'clock that night, Dr. Gideon Fell was sitting at the desk in the study of his new home at Hampstead, patiently trying to build a cardhouse.

The old flat at Number 1, Adelphi Terrace, was no more. What is humorously known as Progress has destroyed that noble street, to make room for new blocks of offices whose polished pegs were not the place to support Dr. Fell's shabby shovel-hat. He did not in the least mind the change; it is not even certain that he noticed it. The house at Hampstead was comfortable and quiet, as he liked such things. There was room for all his books, which is saying a great deal.

There was a garden with an iron bench strong enough to support him, and room enough to play croquet in case any sane person should feel an inclination for that extraordinary pastime. But the old flat had been full of memories: of pipes smoked, or beer drunk, of good work written and bad work torn up, of conversations held far into the night, even of criminal cases coming to their curious ends.

And then, too, there was the business of moving. Dr. and Mrs.

Fell had been in the new premises for a month, but the Doctor's study—at least—was still in a state of chaos.

Just when some of the books were being transferred nicely from packing cases to shelves, he would come across an old and (for the moment) extremely curious book which he had not seen for a year or two. He would have to sit down while he glanced through it, puffing with surprised interest. So it had taken him three weeks to unpack the books; and, since he always put the book down just where he happened to be sitting or standing at the time, stacks had accumulated. They hid his tobacco-jar, covered the grand piano, and stood up in shaky piles by all the chairs; so that one wall of the room was still full of vacant shelves. But Dr. Fell wandered among the lumber, peering at things, and was content.

So at ten o'clock on Sunday night he sat at his desk, under the powerful drop-lamp, with a cigar in his mouth and a pint of beer at his elbow, trying to build a cardhouse. Every time it fell to pieces he would swear in an absentminded way. Then he would make a note with a pencil, on the pad beside him, as though it were a building-specification. Once he left off building for some minutes to scowl at these notes. He did not seem satisfied.

And to him at shortly past ten o'clock, angry and dispirited and even less satisfied, came Superintendent Hadley.

Hadley studied the room while Dr. Fell rang for sandwiches and more beer. "I see," remarked Hadley, after a careful inspection, "that your settling-in tasks for today are done. You've hung the Colombian devilmask over the mantelpiece, and put that shield between the windows. If my eyes don't deceive me, there are also at least a dozen more books on the shelf since last week. Congratulations."

Dr. Fell grunted. "We are not amused," he said, without looking up. He frowned, puffing out his cheeks over the work, until cigar-smoke got into his eye and he had to leave off. "Well, Hadley?"

"You mean Chandler?" asked the Superintendent.

"I do."

"It would be a nasty whack," said Hadley, throwing his briefcase on the piano, "if I had to admit you were right without even knowing what it is you say. I don't know what your blasted case is. I haven't got the ghost of a guess. All you could do today was rave on about a missing——"

"Chandler?" interrupted the doctor, with patient insistence.

"Regarding Chandler, I can tell you in a word what we've got. We've got another miracle murder."

Dr. Fell raised his head. His big face hung under the lamp, incredulous. "Miracle? Nonsense! Impossible."

"Yes," said Hadley bitterly. " 'It is impossible for a miracle to be impossible.' Work that one out. All right: look at the facts. I gave you the gist of them over the telephone. Again they're simple enough, if it comes to that. Chandler was shot three times with a very small calibre weapon, probably a .22 revolver. These shots were fired from the rear of the auditorium, where it was very dark.

"If the murderer was an outsider, access would have been very easy. All the murderer had to do was walk in from the street. Every door was open. The foyer was dark. The gangway at the back of the orchestra stalls has a curtained rail eight or nine feet high. The murderer could have blazed away through those curtains, at Chandler on a lighted stage, and walked out again. He could have done this unheard because some maniac of a Wild West performer kept on cracking a whip through the show.

"Now, here's the point. The murder was definitely *not* committed by anybody inside the theatre, unless it was committed either by Madge Sturgess or by Brenda White. The reason is that everybody else was gathered in a kind of group close to the stage. They have a corporate alibi. They're all in a position to swear that none of them could have drawn a revolver and fired three times at Chandler, with intervals of a few seconds between the shots, without being seen. You can wash out any idea like that.

"But Madge Sturgess and Brenda White are in nearly as good a position, as far as being cleared of suspicion goes. No weapon has been found either on them or in the auditorium; and there's no place to hide one. Though both women were towards the back of the theatre, they weren't very far back; and it's in the highest degree unlikely that either could have fired three shots without being seen by anyone in the group at the wings of the stage, facing out towards the audience. Take the Sturgess girl first. Just before the Flying Mephistos began their aerial turn, she got up from her seat towards the front and moved much further back; because (she says) she was still feeling ill and the light on the stage hurt her eyes. But she was the first to reach Chandler's body when he fell, and she hadn't time or place to hide any weapon. Besides, she, of all people, had no motive in the world to kill Chandler."

Hadley pondered. "As for Miss Brenda White——"

"Stop a bit," rumbled Dr. Fell, taking the cigar out of his mouth and holding it up. "You're not still chasing *that* particular hare, are you?"

Hadley eyed the floor. He seemed to meditate landing a swift kick on a rather rare copy of *Hocus Pocus Junior, or The Anatomy of Legerdemain* (4th edition, 1654), which was lying invitingly at his feet, and sending it across the room as though to begin a football match.

He shook his head. "I can't tell you," he admitted. "When I think of the baby-faced act she put on for my benefit yesterday, I could believe she was capable of anything.

"But again, look at the evidence! When the Flying Mephistos got steam up, Brenda White was afraid Chandler would fall and break his neck. She says she wanted to get the whip away from this crazy Westerner. She got up and went to him. He was then at the back of the house on the other side. She asked him in her most winning way for the whip. He handed it over without a murmur, and walked forward to join the corporate alibi by the stage. She went between the stalls to the centre aisle, passing behind Madge Sturgess, whom she says she didn't notice. The shots must have begun about then. But, when the final shot was fired, she had come forward and was standing in the aisle a few feet behind Rowland and me. She couldn't have done it. It's out of the question. And there you are."

"Well?" prompted Dr. Fell.

Hadley was exasperated. "I've just told you."

"Perhaps I do not make myself clear," said Dr. Fell. "To put the matter in more elegant language: so what? You establish that nobody in the theatre killed Arthur Chandler. So it was an out-side job. Where's the miracle?"

"It's this. We've proved that no outsider could have commit-ted the murder either."

Dr. Fell sat for a time wheezing gently, his mouth open, his face growing even more pink and polished under the drop-lamp, and his eyes slowly widening. The he said, in a thunderous whis-per like wind along an Underground tunnel: "Hadley, this won't do. What's your evidence?"

"The only way an outside murderer could have come in," said Hadley, "was through the front entrance of the theatre. That's the only entrance or exit which wasn't guarded. Without going into details that would take half the night, you can accept that from me as a fact. So the murderer must have come in by the front entrance. Only—he didn't."

"Why are you sure of that?"

"Witnesses. The Orpheum is in Charing Cross Road just above Cambridge Circus. At three o'clock on a Sunday afternoon, that neighbourhood is deserted. Across the street, on the corner of Cambridge Circus, there's a Sunday-newspaper-seller who has a pitch there. Directly across the street there's a tobacconist. Both these fellows took great interest in the Orpheum, especially on a dull day.

"Now the theatre has been closed for a month or two. But the new turns have been rehearsing for a little while for the opening tomorrow. Most of the people employed about the theatre, and even the performers who are old hands, are known by sight. They'll come out for a breath of air, or pop round to the pub for a minute, or come across to buy cigarettes from the tobacconist. In any event, both the newspaper-seller and the tobacconist are prepared to swear that *nobody*—no stranger of any sort—either entered or left the theatre after two o'clock in the afternoon, with the exception of Rowland, the White girl, and myself.

"You can't shake them, Fell. I've tried. So have Sergeant Betts and Morris. But it's no go. And the murder was committed at a quarter to three."

"Which," muttered Dr. Fell, staring in a singularly crosseyed fashion at the card-house, "is impossible."

"Of course it's impossible. But that's what happened. Nobody inside killed Chandler; but nobody outside did either."

"There's a flaw in it, Hadley."

"You," asked the Superintendent, "are telling me? Naturally

there's a flaw in it. What I want to know is, where the hell is the flaw?"

The sandwiches and beer had arrived. Vida, the maid, put the tray on a table, clearing off the table a pile of hunting-prints, and a (loaded) revolver which she carried out of the room holding it far in front of her by the trigger-guard, as though it were a dead mouse.

Still Dr. Fell did not speak.

"All right," growled Hadley, attacking the sandwiches. "Say it!"

"Eh? Say what?"

"That I've got to climb down about this. I was sure Chandler was guilty. Who wouldn't have been, when you heard the fellow practically admit it to us? But——"

"You don't think so now?"

"No. It's possible, I admit, that Chandler may have killed Frank Dorrance and that somebody else killed Chandler. But I don't believe it. It would be stretching coincidence to the bursting-point. No: these two murders are the work of one and the same person."

"Agreed without a struggle," said Dr. Fell.

"And again," blazed Hadley, a difficulty feat with his mouth full, "who would have been mug enough to believe Rowland and the White girl when they jumped at me with that cock-and-bull yarn about Chandler knowing who the murderer was, and maybe having a photograph of him. That's what makes me maddest of all."

"They said what?" demanded Dr. Fell, galvanized.

Hadley explained. "I thought I wasn't mug enough to believe it," he added. "All women are liars. It's just a question of degree: part-time lying or whole-time lying. But, probably for the first time in her life, that girl must have been telling the truth. Chandler knew too much. So the murderer polished him off with a little gun, and had to plug him three times to make him fall off the trapeze."

"But what about these photographs? Did he get a picture of the murderer? Is that possible?"

Hadley hesitated. "I don't know. I'm afraid to hope. Betts and Morris and I went round to his home afterwards. We had a bad time with the parents, and we'd already had a bad enough time with Madge Sturgess. His father is a photographer, keeping a photographic supply-shop . . ."

"Yes?" prompted Dr. Fell murderously, as again Hadley hesitated.

"It's like this. Chandler was at the tennis court yesterday. All right: what was he *doing* there? What was he doing there, carrying a camera and also a large piece of white canvas like a sack? Yes, it's quite true. His father says that he left home early yesterday afternoon, taking with him a new Arundell camera, two rolls of the new K Panchromatic film, and that shapeless piece of canvas. The canvas solves the mystery of how he carted away a load of china. But he didn't go there to cart away china, surely? He didn't go there to take photographs of a murder, certainly? It's the same point that bothered us this morning, you remember. Chandler had a peculiar sense of humour; but I can't believe anybody's sense of humour is as peculiar as that. Anyhow—hold your horses, and stop puffing and blowing!—we found a few things among his effects. We found several more prints of photographs off the same roll he showed me this morning. All the pictures were of Brenda White or Rowland, or both. *But we also found a finished, sealed roll of K Panchromatic which hasn't yet been developed.*"

"Wow!" said Dr. Fell. "Where is it?"

Hadley pointed. "In my brief-case. I'm taking it along to the Yard to get it developed."

"I don't suppose," said Dr. Fell, puffing fiercely at his cigar, "it would have occurred to you to mention this in the first place. Will you also tell me why you are pulling such a long face over it? Archons of Athens! There's your evidence. Why do you want to weep into it?"

Hadley did not seem to know himself. "Because I don't believe it," he admitted, with pessimism. "I'm half afraid to have the film developed; and that's a fact. It can't be. It's too good to be true. After being hoaxed and flum-diddled by White, Rowland, Chandler, and everybody else——"

Dr. Fell grunted. "Well, it is easily settled. We can develop it here. And, by thunder, we're going to develop it now! What in the name of Bacchus are we waiting for?"

"No, you don't," said Hadley sharply.

"Hey?"

"Sit down," the other ordered, with a measured grimness. "You don't touch that film for just a minute yet. There are a couple of questions I want answered, and answered straight. First: do you think you know how Frank Dorrance was murdered?"

"I think so," said Dr. Fell, muttering. "Mind, I say I think so. If only we could find——"

"Yes. I suspected that was coming. Now I'll tell you why I ask. You remember the 'missing article' you were kicking up so much fuss about this morning, the thing that disappeared out of the pavilion?"

"I do."

"Sergeant Betts found it in the drawer of the dressing-table in Arthur Chandler's bedroom," Hadley told him grimly. "And on the knob at one end of it there is a fine set of fingerprints."

There was a pause.

Dr. Fell sat back in the vast leather chair, breathing slowly and noisily. A twitch went over his face, and agitated his small nose. He puffed out his cheeks. He stared back at Hadley through the eyeglasses. Then, with the same slowness of movement, he picked up his crutch-handled stick and waved it mesmerically over his head. "That's torn it," he said. "My answer to your earlier question is now, with my hand on my heart, yes: an unqualified yes."

"Good!" said Hadley. "Before you go any further, you are now going to tell me how, why, and who." He raised his hand. "I won't say for my own part, mind you, that I haven't got a dim idea of the line you're working on. I have, particularly after that incident . . . but you tell it. Or, so help me, that blasted film goes out of this house and stays out."

Dr. Fell indicated a chair.

"Sit down," he said seriously. "Light a cigarette. And, if you like, I will tell you how, why, and who."

A dim-voiced clock struck the half-hour. It was very quiet in the big, high room whose windows looked out on a balustrade and a hill of twinkling lights. Dr. Fell, settling his shoulders, let a puff of cigar-smoke drift up into the lamp and watched it curl there. There was a vacant expression on his face. When he began to speak, it was not with his usual fiery argumentativeness, but with an air of rapid apology.

"The trouble with this case," he said, "is that the truth has been too obvious to be seen. It obtruded itself too much; and therefore nobody noticed it. It has been a hundred years since the Chevalier Auguste Dupin pointed out this primary habit of people failing to notice something that was too big to be seen, but we persist in doing it all the same. And when a thing is not only very large, but very familiar as well, it becomes completely invisible."

Hadley groaned. "Just a minute," he interrupted. "I don't want any lecture, and I don't want any paradoxes. Stick to the facts. Is there anything in this affair that has been both too large and too familiar to be seen?"

"Yes. The tennis court," answered Dr. Fell.

He let another puff of smoke drift up towards the light, watching it. And he looked doubtful.

"I daresay," he went on, "I can claim to have solved this problem. But I may add that this is the only case I have ever tackled in which I solved the problem before I knew what the problem was. As I told you, I looked at that court last night, and I let my imagination soar. I envisioned (fine thought) an expanse of sand in which there were no footprints except those of the dead man."

"But why?" demanded Hadley.

"Why, because it would make such a thundering good problem, that's all!" retorted Dr. Fell, sitting up. "That's the only reason. There was no logic in it. But, curiously enough, the closer I looked at it the more I saw that all the logical evidence supported my flight of pure fancy.

"I tried to point this out to you this morning, before we saw Chandler. You would have none of it. You could quite reasonably say: 'What in blazes is the good of supposing a court without footprints when we can see for ourselves there *are* footprints?' After which we saw Chandler. And Chandler at one sweep disposed of your hard facts by showing, with the aid of a photograph and a sackful of china, that there had been no tracks in the court until Brenda White made 'em after the murder.

"At which I suddenly realized, in a dazed kind of way, that my imagination had shot the bottle clean off the fence. I had imagined a situation; and it was right. I had conceived of a method of murder to fit that situation; and that looked right too. I had hunted the snark and got the tiger instead. I had solved the problem before I knew what the problem was.

"Now, Hadley, you shall guess the answer for yourself. It's not hard, and you are an intelligent man. You will guess it easily when I mention a few small points you have seen for yourself; and you will see it with unco' clearness when I give you one other point which you don't know but which everybody else in the case does. Here are the hints."

Again Dr. Fell contemplated cigar-smoke.

He spoke vacantly.

"*One.* How was Frank Dorrance persuaded to go out on the tennis court? Hold on! I know it has been suggested, over and over, that it was a wager. But don't you see that this still does not answer the question? Suppose the murderer had said to him, 'I can walk on the net; I can dance a jig on my nose'; any fantastic wager you like. Dorrance would have accepted the wager. But would he have gone out on the court?

"Why should he? Dorrance, we know, was an immaculate and rather dandified young man who hated getting his shoes mucked up. Why should he have gone on the court? Couldn't he have got just as good a view by standing on clean grass and watching from there? The voice of common sense whispers that he could. What, therefore, enticed him out as far as that?"

Dr. Fell paused, looking at his companion with a hard, suggesting eye.

"Go on," said Hadley.

"*Two,*" pursued Dr. Fell. "The article stolen from the pavilion, later found by you in the drawer of Chandler's dressing-table. Think about it.

"*Three.* I call your attention to the way in which a common or garden variety of tennis court is built.

"*Four.* This point is a repetition of something we debated to-day. The surface of the court is made of a composition of sand and gravel built up on a concrete basis. It is not, as you said your-self, proper sand such as we find at the seaside. In this connexion I most earnestly direct your attention to my experiments with a pair of ice-skates.

"*Five.* H'mf! Haah! Here's a very important one. I mean the exact position in which three articles—Frank Dorrance's tennis racket, a bag of tennis-balls, and a book—were found just after the murder. They were found on the narrow strip of grass inside the wire, not quite half way along the east side, at a very interest-ing point indeed."

Superintendent Hadley stopped him.

"You know," Hadley grunted, frowning at a fresh page of his notebook on which he had not made any notes, "I've got a feel-ing—" He stopped. Then he roared out at the doctor. "I've got a feeling that I ALMOST see what you're talking about. That's the maddening part. I'm just on the edge of it; just groping; just got it; and then it goes."

"Steady."

"All right. Have you got any more of these points?"

"Just one," said Dr. Fell. "The last."

"Well?"

Hadley's mind, if he told the truth about it, was less a whirl of facts than a whirl of images. He seemed to see someone and something, against the background of the tennis court. Then he saw fog.

Again he prepared to make notes.

"*Six,*" said Dr. Fell. "Who loosened the front of the scarf round Dorrance's neck after he was dead? Hugh Rowland told us that *he* did, to see whether there was any life in the man. But he slipped up there; and, in the light of our present knowledge, I think we can safely say it was Brenda White. She did this, clearly enough, when she ran out on the court at about twenty-five minutes past seven. Rowland was merely repeating her story, and telling us what she had told him: the first thing that came into his head.

"But what I find significant in that," urged Dr. Fell, beginning to fire up in spite of himself, "is the choice of words, whoever was telling the truth. And, by thunder, I say it is significant! If you will ponder on the matter, I think you will agree. There are six points to determine the method of the murder. I trust you now appreciate what I mean?"

There was a long silence, while. Hadley leafed back through his notebook. He studied first one page, then another page.

Abruptly his voice cracked.

"By—the living——"

"Come on, Steve," chortled Dr. Fell, with the gesture of one urging the reins of an imaginary horse. But his expression was less than of a jockey than of a brigand, ghoulishly set as he leaned forward. "'As chief who hears his warders call, To arms! the foemen storm the wall, The antlered monarch of the waste——'"

"Be quiet," said Hadley curtly. He looked Dr. Fell in the eye. "Stop that bilge and tell me one more thing. What is the piece of information you mentioned a while ago: the thing that everybody else knows but I don't?"

Dr. Fell told him.

"Got it?" inquired the doctor.

"Got it," said Hadley, and flung his notebook with a flap on the table. His head was full of a kind of incredulous horror, as he might have felt if a toy pistol had exploded and fired a real bullet into a child's brain.

Dr. Fell spoke with sombre emphasis.

"You observe, my lad, that we have been making a mistake. What we have been regarding as a kind of slap-dash, crash-bang, spur-of-the-moment crime is (in actuality) as cold-blooded and carefully planned a piece of deviltry as we have yet encountered. Not one detail was neglected, as you can see for yourself if you care to look under the ferns at the entrance to the tennis enclosure. At the first shallow glance, you would not even think the person in question capable of such a thing. Which is interesting."

Hadley glanced across the table.

"Then the method of the murder was—" He made an illustrative gesture with his hands.

"Yes."

"And the murderer is———?"

"Yes," said Dr. Fell.

XIX.

DISCLOSURE

MISS MADGE Sturgess walked by the tennis court.

It may be remembered that in the late afternoon of Monday, August 12th, the heat was again intense. The burning day had reached that slope of afternoon when wits are thickest and the sun is most level.

Looking into the enclosure, you would have needed a close inspection to see the humps of tracks in the baked, yellow-brown court. The net had bloomed out in drying and assumed a more normal appearance. Otherwise, except for a near-absence of white lines, it looked the same as it had looked when the mixed doubles composed of Frank Dorrance and Brenda White v. Hugh Rowland and Kitty Bancroft began their game. Heat stifled the poplars, brilliant in the middle of the court and thick even in shadowy corners where midges stung. And Madge Sturgess, alone, Walked up and down by the pavilion, her feet swishing in the crisp grass.

It might have been difficult to tell what Madge was thinking. She was clearly nervous. But there were other elements too. She wore a decorous dark frock and her hair had been waved that day. She had a faintly modish, pouting, spoiled manner; good-natured and easy-going, you would have diagnosed, perhaps somewhat weak. Full of life if she had not been ill, with a sparkle in her brown eyes, and a tireless talker. You might have thought that the death of Arthur Chandler would lie lightly on her. But several times she looked at the tennis court, and looked away again, and pressed her hands together as though her eyes would fill with tears. The silence of the enclosure, disturbed only by the ugly noise of a wasp, was getting on her nerves.

"Hullo!" she called aloud suddenly, as though to experiment and see if there were anybody about. There was no reply. It seemed to disturb her nerves still more. She walked to the opening in the wall of poplars, and out to the gate in the hedge, which was swinging open. There she stood for a time, hesitantly, and scuffed at the edge of the gate with her shoe. That was how she happened to kick a clump of ferns by the hedge, and disclosed something else. It was a padlock, open, with a short chain and the key still in the lock. Though it had been rained on heavily, and was beginning to turn rusty at the clasp, it was still new.

Madge looked at it for some little time, as though for want of something to do. Then, without haste, she kicked the ferns back again to hide it.

"Hullo!" interrupted a new voice—a voice of such briskness, clarity, and robustness that it might have been a late answer to Madge's hail. There was friendliness in the voice. Kitty Bancroft, her hands on her hips, came swinging round the path beside the garage and strode over to the gate. Madge started, kicked at the ferns again, and assumed a manner of freezing aloofness. She had, or had cultivated, one of those ultra-refined voices in which 'I' becomes 'Ay' and 'me' becomes 'muh.' "Oh!" she said. "I'm sorry! You startled me," and tilted up her head.

Kitty regarded her with open curiosity. Though certain harsh ravages had not worn off Kitty's face, though her skin had a leathery look, she had recovered something of her usual manner. She was full of friendliness. She smiled.

"I do barge about," she admitted, though her eyes did not leave Madge. "Phew! It's been another snorter of a day, hasn't it?" She glanced up at the sky. "I say, excuse me: but haven't I seen you somewhere before?"

"Oh?"

"Yes, I'm positive I have! Forgive this staring, but——"

"I've been in the papers," said Madge, regarding the ground but conscious of importance.

"Oh, good Lord!" Kitty cried, and snapped her fingers. Her deep contralto voice was full of contrition. "Of course I know you now! You're Madge Sturgess, aren't you? I'm a dense sort of jackass!" She paused, and floundered. "I mean, it must be pretty beastly for you. That is—Frank. And then this other—I mean——"

"I had no interest in Mr. Dorrance, thank you," said Madge, flaming coldly.

Kitty hesitated. "Well, forgive me anyway," she urged. She took a quick look round, and lowered her voice with sympathy. "And I do think, from what I've heard, that the young imp played a disgraceful trick on you. Tell me. You're all right, aren't you?"

The cold flame increased. Madge straightened up.

"Really!!" she said. "Well, really!"

"Oh, Lord, I've put my foot in it again! No, no; I didn't mean that. I didn't mean what you thought I meant. I mean—money, and all that? Your job?"

Madge seemed appeased. "I have a new position. I applied for the post this morning, and got it. In a beauty-parlour. They gave me a perm for nothing."

She patted the back of her head. Again she hesitated, seeming impressed by Kitty's obvious friendliness.

"But I don't think I—Miss—Mrs.——?"

"Bancroft," said Kitty. "Mrs. Bancroft. Call me Kitty."

"Oh, you're Kitty Bancroft," said Madge. She studied Kitty, and smiled slightly as though with a memory. Her manner thawed. When she spoke again it was in a voice of relief and almost without trace of the elaborate accent. "It's a good job, you know," Madge confided. "A damn good job. Shez Suzy in Oxford Street; you know? Only that's what worries me."

"Why should it worry you?"

"Because I talked too damn much to get it," confided Madge, after a quick look round. "I talked and talked and talked. I told them things I wasn't supposed to know. That is, things I didn't tell the police. About why poor Archie (that was Mr. Chandler) came here on Saturday——"

Kitty's forehead was pitted with wrinkles. "But, I say: speaking of being here, why on earth are you here now? Not that you're not welcome, of course." She laughed. "But what ever possessed you to come here?"

"That's it," wailed Madge. "The police told me to."

"The police?"

The thick, hot air burnt on their faces outside the trees. It was another such day as Saturday, with the same oppressiveness against the brain. Grass-blades, under that sun, were as individual as swords; and Madge Sturgess turned her face away from it.

"Yes! They said, be at the tennis court at seven o'clock. Of course they said, 'If you don't mind,' or, 'Would you mind,' or

232 · JOHN DICKSON CARR

something; but I have a whacker of a good notion what that means, haven't you? I thought of marching straight up to the front door of the house and ringing the bell. But at the last moment, I couldn't muster up the cheek. Why not, though? Why not?" said Madge, tossing her head. "They're not such grand people!—not if they can send you cheques and have 'em returned by the bank! But, 'Be at the tennis court at seven o'clock.' It's hardly a quarter to seven yet, and yet I couldn't stay away. Do you think they've found out? I mean, about what I told my boss? Do you think my boss will tell on me?"

Kitty regarded her in a curious way.

"You're rather a naive young lady," Kitty smiled. "So Mr. Chandler was here at the tennis court on Saturday?"

Made gave a toss of impatience.

"He was here for hours! And they never caught him. Do you know why? Look!" She put out her hand to the hedge that was as tall as a man.

"Archie was an aerial artist. He could go over these hedges as easy as winking. What he called a tail-spin or a barrel-roll or something. But, whup! and hu! and over he went, landing on his feet and not making a sound. If he was inside the hedge, and anybody came near him, all he had to do was flip over to the outside again. He said he enjoyed that. Anyway, he said he had to go over the hedge when he first went in, because there was a padlock on the gate. That's true. I noticed the padlock just now."

Her eyes strayed towards the ferns.

"It sounds tremendously interesting," said Kitty. "What was he doing here, though?"

"He—" Madge stopped. "I *can* trust you, can't I?"

"You can," smiled Kitty. "But what makes you think you can?

A minute ago you said, 'Oh, you're Kitty Bancroft,' as though you'd heard of me. Where did you hear of me?"

Madge was defiant.

"From Mr. . . . ah, why be so stuck-up?" she said bitterly. "From Frank. You don't mind, do you?"

"Mind! Of course not! What did he say about me?"

"He said you were one of the best, only——"

"Only?"

"Nothing!" Madge flushed.

"A bit old, perhaps?" suggested Kitty. "I'm not really, you know; though I dare say I must seem so to your nineteen or twenty."

"He said 'long in the tooth.' Frank," Madge went on in a quiet, cold voice, "was just 'bout the nastiest bit of work that ever lived. I mean that, though I didn't know it until later. Let me tell you what Archie was going to do. When he heard about a certain thing that Frank did, he was wild. He knew about Frank Dorrance already. He said it was no good trying to get him in an argument; because he'd only make you lose your temper and laugh at you. He said it was no good giving Frank an ordinary beating-up; because he'd only have you in law-courts and Archie couldn't afford that again. Archie said the only way to handle him was to make him look royally foolish. You see?"

Kitty smiled, a motionless figure. "No, I'm afraid I don't."

Madge lowered her voice still more. "But that's it! He was going to waylay Frank here. Somewhere, when there was nobody about to inferfere. First, Archie was going to give him an awful hiding; and serve him right! While he was still passed out from the hiding, Archie was going to do the rest of it. Archie had a big canvas thing like a bag with armholes and a headhole cut in it, and on it he'd painted in black letters, 'Big He-Man; All Women Fall For Me.' He was going to stuff Frank into that, and prop him up looking silly, and take a lot of photographs of him. Archie said he would get a lot of them printed as his professional cards, with his name and address on them; and circulate them among the gang. Only—well, you know what happened."

"Yes. I know what happened."

Madge was looking rather white.

"Archie did it for me," she said. "At least I think he did; he talked so foolish, sometimes."

"Did he?"

"Yes. And when he came back, and said he'd seen everything, and that he was going to give me a top-hat full of five-pound notes when he'd confessed to the murder, I fainted. I've always been delicate. Still, I thought it was nice. The top-hat, and all." She nodded her head.

The baked stones of the crazy-paving steps up the terrace; the concrete drive; the corrugated metal roof of the garage; these swarm in a shimmer of heat before the eye, like the individual burning blades of grass. It pressed the back of the brain. It made chill-blooded people gasp for breath.

"Well, Madge," said Kitty, coming to life in her bustling and cheerful way, "what can't be cured must be endured. And we mustn't stand here any longer, or we shall have sunstroke. In you go!—to the tennis court."

"Yes-s. It's still early, though, isn't it?"

"Never mind. The more time to talk."

"But you won't tell, will you? I've said rather a lot."

"Now don't get the wind up!" urged Kitty, as the uneasy face turned towards her. "I believe you're seeing things already. Didn't you tell me you saw a padlock on this gate?"

"No, not on the gate. Under the ferns there."

"How terribly odd! I never knew this gate to be locked. So it is! A new padlock! We'll just rescue it. I dare say Archie told you everything he saw here on Saturday?"

"No," said Madge doubtfully, "except that he saw you."

Kitty stood very still. "Saw me? When?"

"Oh, long after Frank was killed, when Archie was just leaving himself. He said he saw you come in here and speak to Mr. Rowland, and tell Mr. Rowland that that *Miss White,*" her tone was venomous, "had told the police she didn't make any footprints, and somebody walked in her shoes. Archie said he practically whistled out loud when he heard that. He said he supposed she was depending on china being heavy to support her story—whatever that means. He said *Miss White,*" the jealous note flashed again, "had sex appeal; and had had a lot of trouble already, so he thought he'd just pinch the china and give her a hand up. The reason I know is that he tried to give the china to me. I wouldn't have it, though it was lovely china. But he didn't tell me anything else. He said I wasn't discreet."

"You're sure he didn't tell you anything else?"

"Of course I'm sure! Wouldn't I be?"

"Hello there! KITTY!" shouted a voice from the top of the terrace. Brenda White and Hugh Rowland came down the stairs. Hugh, in fact, had been so surprised to see Madge that he yelled louder than was necessary. Even so, he had not expected to see them jump. Madge instantly assumed the air of cold aloofness that puzzled him so much.

"I hope I do not intrude?" inquired Madge, with a crushing manner which again completely floored Hugh. "I am under instructions, you see. I was asked to come."

"By the police?" inquired Hugh sharply, and Madge whirled

on him. "I only mentioned it," he added in some haste, "because I was asked. By Superintendent Hadley. He says they're going to arrest somebody."

"We were all asked," said Brenda. "Hullo, Kitty. What's that you've got there?"

"It's a—a lock," said Kitty. "A padlock," she went on, turning it over in her hand. She pressed it, and the lock closed with a loud snap. "Madge here says it was on the gate when Frank was killed."

"You promised!" screamed Madge.

"Come inside here, all of you," Kitty said abruptly.

No air stirred under the poplars inside. It was quiet except for the buzz of a wasp which hovered over the tennis court. The sun flashed on its striped body. When they reached the pavilion, Kitty turned round with an air of decision.

"Now, Madge, my dear," she said briskly, with colour under her eyes, "I sympathize with you. I do. But we mustn't be stupid about these things. It was very wrong and foolish of you not to tell the pol——"

"Oh, you cat!" cried Madge, backing away. "You prom——"

Kitty seemed to smile and frown at once, like a schoolmistress. "No, my dear, I didn't promise anything. And it can't do any harm to tell what you know, can it? After all, it isn't as though your Archie told you what he saw. It's a question of what's our *duty*, Madge."

Madge stared at her. "Duty be bothered! I won't tell anybody anything." She directed a defiant look at Brenda, who was puzzled. "I won't tell her anything. I don't believe the police asked me to come here at all. I believe it was all a flummox you got up yourself. I won't——"

Five minutes later, sitting on the edge of the pavilion porch, she was again pouring out the story of Arthur Chandler. And Hugh, who had exchanged meaning looks with Brenda, found the pattern taking form with deadly clearness. They were approaching something.

"And we were right!" said Hugh, smacking his fist into the palm of his other hand. He felt hot, excited, and, for some reason, a trifle queasy about the stomach. "Chandler got those photographs after all."

"Of the murderer. Didn't he, Miss Sturgess?"

"He didn't say anything about any photographs," Madge complained. "Why don't you listen? He was going to take pictures of Frank; not of anybody else. He only said, be quiet; that's all."

And they were all quiet, for they heard voices. Bumping, Old Nick's wheel chair emerged through the opening in the poplars; and Nick's expression, which seemed to be heightened by the buzzing of the wasp, was one of deep satisfaction. Behind him lumbered Dr. Gideon Fell.

Dr. Fell had put aside his cloak and his shovel-hat. He wore a loose, shapeless suit of black alpaca, shiny at the seams and with the pockets bulging; and he walked, very slowly as though in doubt, leaning on his ivory-headed stick.

"Did anyone here," murmured Brenda, so low that Hugh hardly heard, "ever have a psychic feeling? Something's going to happen. And happen soon."

But Kitty heard it.

"Nonsense," Kitty said. "It's the heat. Don't you feel that?"

The two doctors, of different professions and perhaps different views, stopped in the grass a little way from the pavilion. "Good evening," said Dr. Fell, inclining his head politely. "We are—harrumph—grateful that you could see your way clear to assisting us today."

"Assisting you," said Hugh sharply, "in what?"

"In showing how Dorrance was killed," answered Dr. Fell. "It is necessary that you all be present to see it. Where is the switch that controls the floodlights?"

Brenda frowned. "Floodlights in the daytime? Why?"

"Because you will then," explained Dr. Fell, "see much more clearly how the thing was managed. We were all looking at it on Saturday night; but unfortunately,"—he massaged his hot forehead with one hand; he seemed disturbed and a little nervous—"unfortunately, like other things here, it was much too big to be seen. Er—we must wait for Hadley. He will be here in a moment."

A little way behind Dr. Fell's elbow, Hugh could see Nick's face. On it, as Nick looked at both him and Brenda, was a sneer of such positive pleasure that apprehension struck again. Were the frame-ups over, after all? Were they? Could they be?

Hugh moistened his lips. "Is it true," he asked, "that someone is going to be arrested? Here? Now?"

"Yes," said Dr. Fell. "The evidence in the case," Dr. Fell went on, clearing his throat with a rumbling noise, "was clear and complete last night. But it has taken today definitely to establish motive. The prosecution is not bound to prove motive in a court of law, but we thought the trial would be tidier if it were produced . . . I think that's Hadley coming now," he added, turning round.

Hugh felt a singing in his ears, a roaring of blood in the head.

"Can you tell us," he said, "what the motive was?"

"Eh? Oh, yes. Financial gain."

"Financial gain?" cried Kitty. "But——"

She stopped. Superintendent Hadley, brisk-stepping and followed by two men who remained at the gate, entered the enclosure. In one hand he carried both a brief-case and a small suit-case. They followed every movement he made until he reached them.

"Good evening," Hadley said. "Miss White. Miss Sturgess. Mrs. Bancroft. Mr. Rowland." He turned to Nick. "Is your name Dr. Nicholas Young?" he asked.

Nick jerked his head round. "You know damned well it is, Su-perintendent. What about it?"

"It is a formality, sir," answered Hadley. His voice was colour-less. "At the end of this interview, I must ask you to accompa-ny me to Dale Road police-station, where you will be formally charged with the murders of Frank Dorrance and Arthur Chan-dler. I must therefore warn you, Dr. Young—"

Hugh Rowland, who had been lighting a cigarette, dropped both cigarette and match. Very slowly, they all turned to stare.

XX.
THE MIRACLE EXPLAINED

THE SNEER on Nick's face did not change, except that it grew mixed with incredulity. He kept himself poised in the chair. The crutch was across his lap, his posture easy. He uttered a hollow, unbelieving snort. Then he threw back his head and laughed at them.

"Rot!" he said. "Stop joking and get on with it."

"Sir," said Dr. Fell, "this is not a joke."

"You keep out of this," snapped Nick, flinging his head round and flinging it back again quickly. "It's no bloody business of yours."

"Sir," said Dr. Fell, with heavy and dangerous quietness, "the business is exactly as you describe it; and it is not of my making. However, since I have had some part in finding out what you did, I now propose (with Hadley's permission) to give myself the pleasure of telling you where you get off."

"And where's that?"

"The gallows," said Dr. Fell. "They are going to hang you." The heavy and paralyzed silence which held the others was not broken. But Nick laughed at him.

"Old Nick!" he scoffed. "Me!" His eyes sought Brenda. "They're having a lot of sport with a poor cripple, aren't they, my dear. Brenda! There's a packet of cigarettes and some matches in the side pocket of my coat. Will you . . ."

"No, sir," said Hadley quietly. "Stay where you are, Miss White."

Dr. Fell turned to the others. "I should now like," said Dr. Fell, "to tell you some home truths about this charming, hospitable, bluff, hail-fellow-well-met gentleman. That is why you are here. You in particular, Miss White, must hear it. It won't be pleasant hearing; but it will release you out of bondage. You must have a look at what is really inside his head. By thunder, but he's a beauty!"

"So I've got to deal with you, have I?" asked Nick coolly.

Dr. Fell did not remove his eyes from Brenda.

"Listen to him, Miss White," he said. "Don't you hear Frank Dorrance in his voice? If it never occurred to you to wonder about Mr. Nicholas's real character, didn't it occur to you when you observed Frank Dorrance? Who moulded Dorrance? And if the pupil was such a cold and fish-blooded product who knew the softest side of the bed to lie on, what do you think of the master?

"He never cared a rap for Frank Dorrance. Dorrance was to him only the subject of a psychological experiment in moulding characters. His exaggerated devotion to Dorrance, his exaggerated devotion to you, his sentimental dream of a rosy union between you and Dorrance, was all a thundering piece of acting (like his snivels) which only began when he saw how it could profit him financially.

"The truth can be told in three words: he is broke. In spite of his house and his cars and his pictures and his plate, his hasn't a farthing left. When he began to go downhill we don't know. But it began long before the late Mr. Gerald Noakes made that freak will.

"Now, Nicholas Young wasn't instrumental in making that will. But he saw afterwards, and probably not long afterwards, how it could profit him—if he didn't mind murder. Well, how could it profit him? It couldn't—if Dorrance lived. Every penny of the money, we know, was settled on Dorrance. Dorrance (as we heard you say, Miss White) was full of a scheme for putting all of it into the opening of night-clubs. The pupil had been taught too well. If there was one thing in the world Dorrance was mean about, it was money. Miss Sturgess can tell us that. Let us suppose that a desperate Nicholas Young had come to Dorrance and said, 'For God's sake, you've got to help me; I'm in debt and I can't get out.' Dorrance's reply would have been, 'Sorry, old boy; but it's your own fault, isn't it? I've got projects of my own to look after, and I really can't help you.' But suppose, on the other hand, that all this money were to be inherited by Brenda White?"

Dr. Fell paused.

Brenda's face was so pale that the eyes seemed to have turned a darker colour. Hugh felt her seize his arm, and hold it hard; after which she became so embarrassed that she could not look at Nick.

Dr. Fell spoke very quietly.

"Can you—any of you—think of any person more likely to be influenced by sentimental appeals than Brenda White? I ask you that now. Our friend Nick already had the hold. Hasn't he been at you persistently, Miss White? Wasn't the real reason why you refused to marry young Rowland when he first asked you, that you were counting on your 'allowance' in the marriage with Dorrance to help out valiant, uncomplaining Nick? Hey? Weren't all these hints he's been pulling you with, 'I've tried to do my best for you,' and, 'Things may not always be as easy as we'd like'—weren't they all hints about money?"

Brenda still could not reply. She opened her lips, and closed them again.

"You understand," pursued Dr. Fell, "he hoped to marry you." (Brenda started, and her face grew scarlet and incredulous.) "Oh, yes. We mustn't underestimate this gentleman's vanity. He is stuffed with vanity. That's why he won't grow old. That's why he smashes racing-cars and challenges people to running-matches. He looked in the mirror and saw no reason why he shouldn't be the husband of a rich and grateful wife: presently, when the fuss had died down. In the meantime, preparing the way by romantically agitating for the marriage of Brenda White to Frank Dorrance, he sat down to consider how he could kill Dorrance."

"Prove it," said Nick, and laughed in their faces. "I don't think you'll get Brenda to believe that. Will they, my dear?"

"We will trace it from the beginning. It was his motorsmash, of course, which gave him the idea. Those fractures are perfectly genuine fractures. He honestly has not got the use of either his right arm or his left leg. But we see, popping into his mind with brilliant inspiration, the sudden realization that he can kill Dorrance in perfect safety. That had been the horrible difficulty: he must not be under *any* serious suspicion.

"He can now kill Dorrance in safety, provided Dorrance is strangled—provided, that is, it is the sort of murder which Nicholas Young himself could not possibly have committeed. 'A cripple like that strangle a full-grown man?' people will say. 'Nonsense; impossible!' But he could and he did. For he thought of a method, which entailed the use of a tennis court and the silk scarf Frank Dorrance wore in dressing for tennis. And for a week he patiently set about preparing for it.

"Now, when should he commit this murder? Obviously, on a Saturday. First, it was one of the days when tennis was usually played. Second and more important, it was the one day when all the servants were out of the house except Maria. And, if anything went wrong and he were seen, Maria was an old flame of his who would protect him.

"And the time to commit it? Just before dinner on Saturday evening, when the tennis would be finished and he could waylay Frank alone. You follow the position? At that time the only two persons in the house would be Brenda White and Maria Marten. Both of them (by an iron-bound household law, as we know) would be preparing dinner in the kitchen. If he let himself out of the house and went down the drive with the use of his crutch, still further protected by that high bank and the trees, it would be impossible for anybody to see him. Nor could anybody detect his absence from the house. By another iron-bound household rule, it was forbidden to disturb him in his study between tea-time and dinner. (And this we know only too well, since Maria refused to disturb him even for a Superintendent of Police, who arrived on urgent mission just before half-past seven.)"

Dr. Fell paused.

The court was darkening, though it remained hot. Nobody moved, except Nick pushed his wheel chair an inch back.

"Let us," Dr. Fell said almost affably, "try to follow him on the Saturday afternoon. It is the perfect day and time for his plan. The time by the clock is a few minutes past six. The dupes are playing tennis. He is sitting in his study, with all the windows open, and Hadley is just telling him that a man named Chandler may try to murder Dorrance."

Dr. Fell's gesture conjured up the picture: the long, low study with the green-painted walls; the low book-shelves with the bronzes on top of them; the clock ticking; the windows open to a noise of tennis rackets in the distance.

"If we can imagine this astute gentleman hugging himself, he must have hugged himself then. This was perfect. He was being provided with a red herring in Chandler. He got rid of Hadley in a good deal of a hurry. All his other preparations were made. The west windows of his study—as we know—command a clear view of the tennis enclosure, the drive, the garage, and the path to Mrs. Bancroft's house. From this look-out tower, he could see the tennis players when they left the court; and he could see where they went.

"Only one thing might wreck his plan. And, for the moment, it did. That was the storm which was threatening to break. That would upset all his calculations; it kept him in agony. Almost as soon as he got rid of Hadley, the storm did break. He sat down, in a fury, to ponder what had best be done. And he concluded, philosophically, to wait till it blew over and see what happened. So (he tells us) he lay down on the couch to read *The Trial of Mrs. Jewell.*"

Dr. Fell made a slight gesture.

Superintendent Hadley moved out and stood in front of Nick, whose wheel chair had creaked back another inch.

"I'll ask you, sir," said Hadley, "to answer me a couple of questions about the time you spent in your study then."

Nick was unruffled.

"Sure, though I've already given you a statement."

"Yes; these are other questions.—When the storm broke, did you close the windows?"

"Naturally."

"I see. When did you open them again, Dr. Young? They were open when I saw you next."

"If it's of any interest to you, I opened them when the storm blew over. At seven o'clock, or thereabouts."

"What did you do then?"

"Superintendent, how many times have I got to repeat this? I went back to my couch; I lay down again; and I read a dull book."

"You did not leave the study at any time between seven o'clock and seven-thirty?"

"No, I did not."

"I see. Then how is it," asked Hadley, "that you failed to hear the telephone ring during that time?"

"Eh?"

Hadley was patient. "The only reason why I paid your house a second visit on Saturday afternoon," he said, "was that I could not get you on the telephone. I tried. I rang for fully three minutes; and nobody answered. That telephone is on the desk in your study. Why didn't you answer it?"

The faint, sceptical, contemptuous smile was still on Nick's mouth. He shook his head in a fishy and derisive way.

"That won't wash, my fine flatfoot. Perhaps I was asleep."

"You slept, in an afternoon nap, through three minutes of a telephone ringing only six feet away from you?"

"Or perhaps," said Nick coolly, "I just didn't choose to answer it. We're under no obligation to, in case you didn't know it, even for high and mighty lords like you. I was comfortable where I was. So I let it ring."

"You did hear it ring, then?"

"I did."

"When did it ring, sir? At what time?"

There was a very slight pause. "Come to think of it, I couldn't be bothered to remember. I took no note of the time. Not wanting to get up and see——"

"That won't do," said Hadley, so sharply that a jump went through the group. "The clock on your desk, I can testify myself, faces straight across towards the couch."

"I still can't be bothered to remember."

"You could give us an estimate, though. Come sir! That's easy, isn't it? Was it—say—nearer to seven, or nearer to seven-thirty? There's a whole half-hour to play in."

The shrillness in Nick's voice was now perceptible. "I didn't regard it as important. So I regret to tell you I took no notes."

"If you won't tell us," said Hadley, still endlessly patient, "we must tell you. Go on, Fell."

"At seven o'clock," pursued Dr. Fell, addressing Brenda as though the whole story were for her, "this Nick of yours got up (as he says) to open the windows in his study after the storm. From his look-out tower, he saw the rest of you leave the tennis court and separate. He saw Dorrance and Mrs. Bancroft go one way, he saw you and Rowland go another way. And his heart was uplifted with mighty gladness, for the victim was delivered to him.

"Dorrance would be coming back soon—alone.

"But I think Our Nick took one precaution first. The house was empty except for Maria in the basement. Still, he must make sure that Rowland left the premises first, and that Miss White was safely in the kitchen with Maria. So he went into a front bedroom and peered out over the street. He saw (as he thought) Rowland get into a car and drive safely off. He saw Miss White run back into the house. But I am wondering if he saw anything else."

Brenda spoke for the first time. She swallowed hard.

"Do you mean," Brenda said, "do you mean—when Hugh kissed me just before he went?"

"Look at the man's face, all of you!" snapped Dr. Fell.

That look was gone in a flash, and Nick presented to them a vast, fishy calm which nothing could shake. But Hugh, imagining that face peering down from behind a lace curtain in a dark window to a darkening street, felt that more than a wish for money had let loose a murderer then.

"So," continued Dr. Fell, "he thought he was safe. He slipped out of the house, moving clumsily but steadily on his crutch. He went down the drive in the gloom of the after-storm. By the garage he met Frank Dorrance coming back from Mrs. Bancroft's. Time, about six minutes past seven. He used a certain pretext—a certain pretext—to get Dorrance into this enclosure. Here he killed Dorrance."

Again Dr. Fell drew a deep breath.

"Last night Superintendent Hadley and I discussed six points which seemed to lead us conclusively to the way in which this 'miracle' murder was done. I should like to discuss them with you now. The first was a query: How was Dorrance persuaded to go out on the tennis court? And we can suggest to you something rather more convincing than a wager. You can help us here, Miss White."

"*I* can?" cried Brenda.

Dr. Fell blinked at her. "In fact, you have. I asked you a number of questions on Sunday as to your habits, though I am not sure whether you remember the answers you gave me. For instance! You play a lot of tennis here, don't you?"

"Well, we try to. But——"

"Exactly! But you find it difficult to get in as many games as you'd like?"

"Yes."

"Now tell me," pursued Dr. Fell quietly. "Did Nicholas Young ever promise to invent you a 'tennis robot'? In your own words, 'a dummy that will return your strokes so that you can play alone'?"

Brenda stared at him. "Yes, he did. I mentioned it to Hugh on Saturday. Nick's been making promises about it all week. He said, if possible, it was going to be life-size and work just like a real player. Frank was wildly enthusiastic about it. Frank nagged him to get on with it, because Frank was a first-rate player and couldn't get in enough practice."

"Did our friend Nick ever tell you how he intended to invent this dummy?"

"No."

"I imagine not," said Dr. Fell grimly. "He couldn't invent any such thing. But then he didn't have to, because he had his reputation for wonderful ingenuity to sustain him. All he had to do was persuade Dorrance that he had invented it.

"He met Dorrance outside the gate. He said to Dorrance, 'Well, I've got the idea for your tennis dummy, and I know how to make it work. But I've got to get the exact measurements. If you want your robot, you've got to help me; and do it now.' Would Dorrance have jumped at that? I think it very probable he would.

"He let Dorrance precede him through the gate. Then, softly and without noise, he made them safe and cozy against interruption. He took a new padlock out of his pocket, and locked it on the gate so that no intruders should be inconvenient witnesses. Next he went to the pavilion here,"—Dr. Fell gestured—"and fetched out of it a certain article which has been missing since Saturday night.

"Searches both on Saturday night, and on Sunday morning, failed to disclose that article. It was not there; and yet in ordinary household management it should have been there. Maria (as we know) uses this tennis court to hang up the washing. The basket of clothes-pegs was there. The tall clothes-prop was there, at the back of the pavilion among the rakes. What had happened to the clothes-*line?*"

He nodded towards Hadley. Hadley opened the suitcase he had brought with him, and took out a coil of clothes-line. It was a large, heavy coil which must have contained fifty feet of line. At one end was a wooden knob, set there for purchase to pull; but the other end was ragged as though it had been cut with a knife.

Dr. Fell did not look at it.

"I now want you to take a careful look at the tennis court. We have seen such courts so often that we tend to forget how they are constructed. How is that wire netting held up? It is held up by tall iron poles, set at intervals of ten feet or so apart, and driven deep into the ground.

"Now did you notice, on Saturday night, the curious effect of shadows produced on the court by floodlighting? If someone will turn on the floodlamps now, we shall get the same effect. Being of a scatter-brain type myself, I was intrigued by it. The court was striped with shadow, like a griddle, all down its narrow side. This was because shadows of the iron poles on either side of the court—east to west—met in the middle. If they met in the middle, it meant that the poles were set exactly opposite each other across the width. And one of those shadows made a streak straight across the feet of Frank Dorrance's dead body."

Somebody in the group let out a kind of strangled gasp.

It was not Nick; but Nick's eyes had begun to turn.

"Look again," said Dr. Fell. "Now (h'mf) observe the surface of the court. This is not proper sand. No. Over and over have I shouted that fact. You could not walk on it, if the court were wet, without leaving footprints. But you could (say) draw your finger across it without marking it. I experimented with this. I soaked a part of the court with water and drew across the wet place the blade of an iceskate—which is, by the way, about the same breadth as a clothes-line. I still say IF a length of clothes-line were to fall on that wet surface, and to be drawn across it like a snake, that clothes-line would leave no mark."

Kitty Bancroft's voice burst out.

"What are you saying?" she almost screamed. "What are you getting at? I've got a horrible, dim kind of idea that I can see what's coming, but——"

Dr. Fell stopped her.

"Next let us note, from the facts, the position in which we found three articles: a tennis racket, a net of tennis-balls, and a book entitled *One Hundred Ways of Being a Perfect Husband*. There was much argument as to whether those articles were, or were not, on the grass inside the wire at the time of the murder. But that's not the point! Miss White and Rowland said they were not there, simply because they did not remember having seen them. But why should they have seen them? At the time their attention was called to the articles later in the evening, floodlights of enormous power were blazing down on them and bringing out the colours of racket, balls, and book. That is very different from seeing them in semi-darkness, poked down half under the wire, where there is a hollow that tennis-balls seek anyway. "No. I tell you, the important thing is their position. Suppose Dorrance is carrying those articles when he enters these grounds. What must he have done? Look! Before walking out on the wet sand at all, he steps on to the foot-wide grass strip just inside the netting. He walks along on that strip, carrying these things. He stops. He puts the articles down—where? As Hadley showed you Saturday, on the grass just beside one of the iron poles, or supports.

"But, after walking along the grass strip, putting his tennis racket and the rest of it down on the grass beside this post, what does he do? Does he walk *straight out* on the court from that position? Not at all. He walks back along the grass strip to the wire door. Only then does he go from the wire door—setting his feet in the wet sand—and walk out in an oblique line across the court.

"To where? To the middle of the court. And to where else? To a point where, when he falls, his head is ten feet from the net. So his feet are fifteen feet from the net . . . along the center line . . . as though he were playing tennis.

"Dr. Nicholas Young, the murderer, had said to him: 'I will show you how my tennis robot will work. But I must have the exact dimensions, so that the dummy will be correct. And, since I am incapacitated, you shall do it for me. Just follow my instructions.'

"Now watch the scene take form! Dr. Nicholas hands Dorrance the coil of clothes-line. At Nick's direction, Dorrance walks along the grass strip to the designated iron support. Here, at a designated height up from the ground—in fact, at about the height of his own neck—Dorrance ties one end of the clothes-line tightly to the pole. He then takes the coil of clothes-line (at Nick's direction), and flings it out into the centre of the court. Not wishing to get his shoes more messy than necessary, Dorrance walks back to the wire door. From here he goes out into the court.

"They are having a lot of fun, these two. It is a great lark, constructing the lines on which the robot is to work. In the centre of the court, Dorrance picks up the coil of clothes-line. He flings it the rest of the way across the court, to the west side, where Nick is waiting outside the wire. Nick fishes up the end of it, by reaching under the wire with his one hand. He raises it to the iron support.

"They have now constructed a sort of tight-rope which stretches straight across the court. It is the trolley (Dorrance thinks) on which a tennis robot will hang and run. It is about the height of his own neck. He has no idea of how it is to work. But he is fascinated, and wild with enthusiasm. This is good. Old Nick will make him a dummy. Old Nick's ingenuity will not fail. For remember: Frank Dorrance was with the one person in the world he really trusted.

"And Old Nick says to him: "The measurements must be right. We must know the size of the dummy's neck.'

"It is still a good joke. Dorrance is holding up the rope in the middle, to keep it from sagging to the ground. He will impersonate the dummy. 'I want,' says Nick, 'to get the rope tight, so that it won't sag. But I don't want you to chafe your neck. You are wearing a thick, soft scarf with a band an inch and a half wide. Pull the scarf as tightly as you can without discomfort, and nestle the rope in against it.' Dorrance complies. With his right hand—as he faces the net—he takes the right side of the rope, lifts it over his head, wraps it round his neck in a loop, pulls the left side of the rope tight, and settles the loop against the scarf...

"*You* could do that, you people. Any of you. You could persuade a wife or a husband or close friend to walk into the same trap, without the ghost of a suspicion ever entering their heads. The essence of successful murder is that the victim sees a smiling face. A domestic scene? A homely tennis court? A little experiment to see whether a 'comeback' can be made? I do not advise you to try it. But I think you would find it would work.

"Nicholas Young has an inordinately powerful hand and arm, as any one will agree who has seen him propel his wheel chair. He has only one hand; but he needs only one. He now has Frank Dorrance's neck caught in a loop between two supports. One end of the rope is tied to an iron pole across the court. The other end is drawn against the opposite pole, like a pulley, and is then wound twice round that powerful left hand. Standing outside the wire mesh, he supports the weight of his body against the pole. Clothes-line is very light, but it is also very strong. A twitch on that rope will cause Dorrance discomfort. A sudden, blinding, powerful pull——" Dr. Fell swept out his arm.

"You'd better stop, sir," said Hugh. He was afraid Brenda was going to be sick. She was shaking all over. He put his arm round her.

"No, wait!" cried Brenda, turning to him with a kind of frenzied remembrance. "The *loose* part of the scarf! The *loose* knot at the front, that was only folded over once! It was loose when I found him."

"Steady."

"Don't you see?" demanded Brenda. "The rope pressed in the scarf all round Frank's neck, just as though some body's hands had pulled the knot tight and strangled him. But the rope couldn't make the folded ends of the scarf any tighter. That's what I thought was so queer when I found him. I told you——"

Dr. Fell nodded massively.

"You did, Miss White. You told Mr. Rowland. And he, in turn, told us in your own words. That's precisely what made us suspect hocus-pocus with the scarf. Once you came to suspect the scarf, the whole secret was out. We were led back inevitably through all the steps I have just outlined.

"Nor does anyone want to dwell on the ugly details of that scene. But some things you must know for the sake of clearness. Frank Dorrance was, to all intents and purposes, hanged. And there is one thing a hanged man always does: he kicks. Unless they are tied, his feet thrash in a wide circle—a circle, you note—and his heels dig the earth. Dorrance was swinging on that hell's line, wider and wider in a circle, as the murderer clung to him. Dorrance's own feet made the blur round his body, later added to and still more messed up by Miss White. And his own fingernails tore at the scarf which the murderer had closed round his neck.

"It was soon over. The whole performance, from entering this enclosure to murder, took less than ten minutes. Our worthy Nick stopped in the twilight, his labours well done. He listened. He dropped his end of the line. He hobbled round to the other side of the court.

"There he cut the knot in the rope which Dorrance had tied round the opposite iron support. He did this with the clasp-knife he always carries; and which, I am told by those who have seen him pare apples with one hand, he can open with his teeth. He then began, swiftly, to snake in the line. You recall that Dorrance had been *rolled*—rolled over several times. When Nick began to pull in the rope from this side of the court, the body was rolled over as Nick jerked at it to free the line from the neck.

"There was no fear, of course, of dislodging the scarf itself from the neck. As usual in cases of strangling, it adhered deep into the neck. But the rope was loose, and came back without trouble. The murderer folded up an innocent-looking coil of clothes-line and replaced it in the pavilion. He gathered up the few inches of cut line. And he made only one real mistake.

"Mind you, our friend never intended to create a 'miracle' murder. All he wanted to do was leave a strangled corpse which could not be the work of Nicholas Young. If he had chosen dry weather, we might never have had cause to suspect the kind of strangling this was. But he couldn't wait; he had to take the moment that blazed. He never for a moment dreamed that serious footprints, identifiable footprints, can be left on a tennis court even when it was wet. And once he had begun the job it was too late.

"He was back up in his study before twenty minutes past seven. He was not only emotionally exhausted, glutted with triumph; he was physically done in as well. He fell on that couch and slept with outward peacefulness; though I should not be surprised to hear that his dreams were horrible, or that, when he was roused up, the strain he had put on his mending bones burnt him with the pain of the damned.

"Maria woke him there, in a state of physical sickness, at twenty minutes to eight. His acting powers were still of the first ability—until he heard from Maria that Brenda White had been caught in the trap. Then it was not acting. The pretense cracks across; and he becomes a madman. He was a madman when he talked to Hadley a little later. He was a madman when he tried, at any cost and even in defiance of common sense, to fasten the murder on Hugh Rowland. But then, you see, he thought he had to. He had seen his whole scheme endngered by witnessing one love-scene outside the gate of his house.

"He was a madman when he tried to support his pose as bluff, sympathetic Old Nick by sending a 'little cheque' to Madge Sturgess. He had got her address from Hadley on Saturday afternoon (you recall?), and promised a cheque. He was fool enough to send this, even though he must have known the bank had clamped down on his overdraft and would not honour it——"

Madge Sturgess spoke, pale with fury.

"You bet they wouldn't. And I told Mrs. Bancroft so. They're not any such grand people! They——"

"And he was a madman at his very worst," concluded Dr. Fell, "when without plan, rhyme, reason, or any protection whatsover, he shot Arthur Chandler at the Orpheum Theatre yesterday."

Even Hugh protested at this. "Sir, he couldn't have! We heard all about that yesterday. No stranger went in or out of that theatre."

It was Hadley who answered him. "Did you ever hear of a pair of comedians called Schlosser & Weazle?"

"Well, *I* have," snapped Madge. "Cor knows they've been doing the same stuff for years. They were on yesterday, for dress-rehearsal. Schlosser is a comic colonel on crutches, with his leg done up in bandages to show it's gout——"

Hugh's memory opened. "Wait! I remember seeing—"

"That's the whole story," said Hadley grimly. "We dug it out today when we weren't so swamped with miracles. Two people across the street on a dark, wet day swore they saw no strangers leaving the theatre. What they thought they saw was Schlosser, an old-timer, coming out of the place and ducking round the corner to the pub for a quick one before closing-time. (The time was a quarter to three.) What they really saw was something else altogether."

He took a step forward.

That, Dr. Young, is the outline of the case you'll be expected to meet. You've heard it all; and we've also"—he glanced at the shorthand reporter, who nodded—"we've also got enough confirmation from these witnesses to justify our calling them. Do you want to make any statement?"

It had grown much darker by the tennis court. The poplars were thin weights of shadow against the sky; the wasp had gone with twilight. But someone threw the switch for the floodlights, and the deathly bluish glare lit up every corner. The bars of shadow sprang out across the court, and two of them met in the middle at the edge of the scuffed circle where Frank's body had lain.

Nick took one look round at it, and jerked his head back. His face was bluish, the colour of skim-milk, and they heard him breathe.

"You're a pack of dirty liars," he said through stiff jaws. "You'd all rat on me. Nobody's got any friendliness for me. *You* don't believe this, do you, Brenda?"

"I'm afraid I do," said Brenda.

"Then you can go to hell," said Nick, "for a dirty crooked little piece of goods who would——"

"Steady!" said Hadley, as Nick finished the sentence, and even Kitty went a little white. The explicit and obscene coldness of it would not be washed out. "We'll have no more of *that*, my friend. We'll hear about evidence from you, if you feel disposed to talk. For instance: how much did you know about what Chandler knew about you?"

"Try to make me tell you."

"You knew," said Hadley, "that he'd been at the pavilion. You guessed it as the rest of us guessed it: by the fact that the newspaper left in the pavilion was there at seven o'clock and gone at seven-twenty. So you decided Chandler knew too much. You got Maria to ring him up on the telephone—that was the woman who inquired over the phone on Sunday—and find out where he was. And you shot him. Is that, or isn't it, correct?"

"Get me out of here, Hugh," said Brenda, and choked.

"By all means," said Nick, "get her out of here. I can't stand the sight of the lying harlot who'd let down her old guardian and believe he did all this muck when I'm innocent and the whole dithering lot of you can't prove any different. You talk very high and mighty, don't you? You're very sure of your ground, aren't you? 'Nick did this, and Nick did that'"—he wagged his head in grotesque parody—"and all the time you're bluffing and making a ruddy rotten bluff of it too. I'd skin the hide of all of you if I had both my hands and legs. How do you know what I did? I suppose you've got a big gold-framed picture of me, all hanging up and ready to display?"

Hadley opened his brief-case.

"It's not exactly gold-framed," he said. "But they're all enlarged. It might interest you to look at the eight photographs of you killing Dorrance. Chandler took them from various angles on the east side of the court, and this one of the expression on your face when you faced the camera——"

He stopped. Nick's eyes seemed to have retreated into his head. Nick surged up out of the chair. The crutch was across his lap, and he flung a blow at Hadley's skull that almost broke Hadley's arm before the crutch was wrenched away. It was the last word he said. He was weeping at his own sad plight when they took him away.

POSTSCRIPT

In the good old-fashioned novels that our fathers read, there was never any doubt at the end of the story as to what happened to all the characters afterwards. The author always conscientiously sketched out the subsequent history of everybody concerned, even to minor characters whom no reader could remember. Nor was there any nonsense about not rewarding good and evil. It was noted that the faithful servant who brought the horses now kept a flourishing public-house. If a minor villain appeared for two pages in chapter six, to take a pot-shot at the hero, that miscreant later fell off Hammersmith Bridge, or something of the sort; but was, in any case, satisfactorily dead.

Nowadays this practice is thought to be inartistic, or perhaps too much trouble. Most stories end in mid-air, with a row of dots: to show, as someone has pointed out, that life is continuous. But sometimes it happens—as, it must be confessed, is the case here—that the author gets rather fond of his people. And if the greatest living dramatist can do so at the end of a play, telling you explicitly how all the characters would act afterwards, and pouring scorn on the cad who says they wouldn't, then the liberty of the practice may surely be extended to this unimportant chronicle.

Well, it was nearly a year after the foregoing events before Brenda White and Hugh Rowland were married. Some of the events in between were not pleasant to remember, notably the dark November morning which saw the end of Nick. Nick had surprised everybody by pleading guilty even though Sir Edward Gordon-Bates had been briefed in his defence; and the trial, therefore, caused little notoriety.

But domestic upsets were frequent. Hugh's mother retired to a nursing home in a fit of the megrims. Rowland Senior went instantly to see that Brenda's financial affairs were in order, spent two hours telling an approving bank-manager that a penny saved was a penny earned, and assured his wife that all was well that ended well.

Indeed, Brenda had no stouter champion than Rowland Senior. At the wedding he was the most popular and outstanding figure. As Brenda and Hugh came down the aisle to well-known strains, his face beamed like a thousand-watt bulb, and no glossier top-hat has ever been seen inside the premises of St. Jude's. He presented the young couple, as wedding gifts, with a handsome silver cigar-humidor, a complete set of the Works of William Shakespeare, and a receipted bill for forty-six pounds eighteen and a tanner from the England's Lane Lawn-Tennis Club. Afterwards there was a party at which even Sheppey got drunk. Rowland Senior made a speech, in which his partner Mr. Gardesleeve estimated that he went on for fifty-two minutes without introducing an original observation of his own. The young couple were packed off to Paris, extremely happy and also slightly tipsy; and even to this day (all this was two years ago) contrive to remain almost indecently happy.

Superintendent Hadley sent his regrets that he could not attend the wedding, since somebody was passing dud banknotes in Putney. But Dr. Fell was there, and talked almost as much as Rowland Senior. The servants were laying bets that no living human being could drink up so much beer; and the caterer who had his money on Dr. Fell cleaned up a packet. Kitty Bancroft wept all through the ceremony, but cheered up afterwards. It is nowadays reported that she has been going about a good deal with a young Australian, and appears quite content with life in general.

To this day Brenda has not touched the fifty thousand pounds, which is the only thing that grieves Rowland Senior. A part of it was used to settle up Nick's debts, and some more to set up Madge Sturgess with a beauty-parlour of her own.

As a final note, it may be mentioned that only a fortnight ago Brenda and Hugh went to the Orpheum Theatre. They were startled to see a familiar name on the bill. Whatever the cause of the extraordinary and magical effect always made on Tex Lannigan by Brenda, it is to be recorded that he saw her in the fourth row of the stalls, recognized her, and went wild. To the uproarious delight of the audience, he danced Chicken in the Breadtray; took the baton out of the orchestra leader's hand with his whip; and punctured the bass-drum with a real bullet. This was so successful that it has all, with the exception of the drum-busting, been included in his regular programme.

The comment of Rowland Senior on the whole affair may be imagined. It began, "It's an ill wind——" But he had just made a *bon mot;* on being informed that his bath was ready, he had been able to reply, in sepulchral tones, "Ay, there's the rub"; and he was so delighted with this that he may, perhaps, be excused for not being up to his usual form.

DISCUSSION QUESTIONS

- Were you able to predict any part of the solution to the case?

- Aside from the solution, did anything about the book surprise you? If so, what?

- Did any aspects of the plot date the story? If so, which ones?

- Would the story be different if it were set in the present day? If so, how?

- What role did the setting play in the narrative?

- What sort of detective is Dr. Gideon Fell? What special skills make him a great investigator?

- Can you think of any contemporary mystery authors who seem to be influenced or inspired by John Dickson Carr's writing?

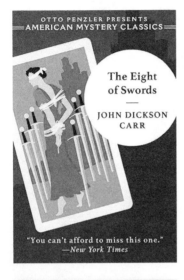

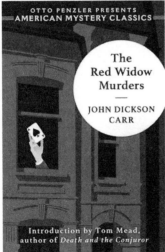

All titles are available in hardcover and in trade paperback.

Order from your favorite bookstore or from
The Mysterious Bookshop, 58 Warren Street, New York, N.Y. 10007
(www.mysteriousbookshop.com).

Charlotte Armstrong, *The Chocolate Cobweb*. When Amanda Garth was born, a mix-up caused the hospital to briefly hand her over to the prestigious Garrison family instead of to her birth parents. The error was quickly fixed, Amanda was never told, and the secret was forgotten for twenty-three years … until her aunt revealed it in casual conversation. But what if the initial switch never actually occurred? **Introduction by A. J. Finn.**

Charlotte Armstrong, *The Unsuspected*. First published in 1946, this suspenseful novel opens with a young woman who has ostensibly hanged herself, leaving a suicide note. Her friend doesn't believe it and begins an investigation that puts her own life in jeopardy. It was filmed in 1947 by Warner Brothers, starring Claude Rains and Joan Caulfield. **Introduction by Otto Penzler.**

Anthony Boucher, *The Case of the Baker Street Irregulars*. When a studio announces a new hard-boiled Sherlock Holmes film, the Baker Street Irregulars begin a campaign to discredit it. Attempting to mollify them, the producers invite members to the set, where threats are received, each referring to one of the original Holmes tales, followed by murder. Fortunately, the amateur sleuths use Holmesian lessons to solve the crime. **Introduction by Otto Penzler.**

Anthony Boucher, *Rocket to the Morgue*. Hilary Foulkes has made so many enemies that it is difficult to speculate who was responsible for stabbing him nearly to death in a room with only one door through which no one was seen entering or leaving. This classic locked room mystery is populated by such thinly disguised science fiction legends as Robert Heinlein, L. Ron Hubbard, and John W. Campbell. **Introduction by F. Paul Wilson.**

Fredric Brown, *The Fabulous Clipjoint*. Brown's outstanding mystery won an Edgar as the best first novel of the year (1947). When Wallace

Hunter is found dead in an alley after a long night of drinking, the police don't really care. But his teenage son Ed and his uncle Am, the carnival worker, are convinced that some things don't add up and the crime isn't what it seems to be. **Introduction by Lawrence Block.**

John Dickson Carr, *The Crooked Hinge*. Selected by a group of mystery experts as one of the 15 best impossible crime novels ever written, this is one of Gideon Fell's greatest challenges. Estranged from his family for 25 years, Sir John Farnleigh returns to England from America to claim his inheritance but another person turns up claiming that he can prove he is the real Sir John. Inevitably, one of them is murdered. **Introduction by Charles Todd.**

John Dickson Carr, *The Eight of Swords*. When Gideon Fell arrives at a crime scene, it appears to be straightforward enough. A man has been shot to death in an unlocked room and the likely perpetrator was a recent visitor. But Fell discovers inconsistencies and his investigations are complicated by an apparent poltergeist, some American gangsters, and two meddling amateur sleuths. **Introduction by Otto Penzler.**

John Dickson Carr, *The Mad Hatter Mystery*. A prankster has been stealing top hats all around London. Gideon Fell suspects that the same person may be responsible for the theft of a manuscript of a long-lost story by Edgar Allan Poe. The hats reappear in unexpected but conspicuous places but, when one is found on the head of a corpse by the Tower of London, it is evident that the thefts are more than pranks. **Introduction by Otto Penzler.**

John Dickson Carr, *The Plague Court Murders*. When murder occurs in a locked hut on Plague Court, an estate haunted by the ghost of a hangman's assistant who died a victim of the black death, Sir Henry Merrivale seeks a logical solution to a ghostly crime. A spiritual medium employed to rid the house of his spirit is found stabbed to death in a locked stone hut on the grounds, surrounded by an untouched circle of mud. **Introduction by Michael Dirda.**

John Dickson Carr, *The Red Widow Murders.* In a "haunted" mansion, the room known as the Red Widow's Chamber proves lethal to all who spend the night. Eight people investigate and the one who draws the ace of spades must sleep in it. The room is locked from the inside and watched all night by the others. When the door is unlocked, the victim has been poisoned. Enter Sir Henry Merrivale to solve the crime. **Introduction by Tom Mead.**

Frances Crane, *The Turquoise Shop.* In an arty little New Mexico town, Mona Brandon has arrived from the East and becomes the subject of gossip about her money, her influence, and the corpse in the nearby desert who may be her husband. Pat Holly, who runs the local gift shop, is as interested as anyone in the goings on—but even more in Pat Abbott, the detective investigating the possible murder. **Introduction by Anne Hillerman.**

Todd Downing, *Vultures in the Sky.* There is no end to the series of terrifying events that befall a luxury train bound for Mexico. First, a man dies when the train passes through a dark tunnel, then it comes to an abrupt stop in the middle of the desert. More deaths occur when night falls and the passengers panic when they realize they are trapped with a murderer on the loose. **Introduction by James Sallis.**

Mignon G. Eberhart, *Murder by an Aristocrat.* Nurse Keate is called to help a man who has been "accidentally" shot in the shoulder. When he is murdered while convalescing, it is clear that there was no accident. Although a killer is loose in the mansion, the family seems more concerned that news of the murder will leave their circle. *The New Yorker* wrote than "Eberhart can weave an almost flawless mystery." **Introduction by Nancy Pickard.**

Erle Stanley Gardner, *The Case of the Baited Hook.* Perry Mason gets a phone call in the middle of the night and his potential client says it's urgent, that he has two one-thousand-dollar bills that he will give him as a retainer, with an additional ten-thousand whenever he is called on to represent him. When

Mason takes the case, it is not for the caller but for a beautiful woman whose identity is hidden behind a mask. **Introduction by Otto Penzler.**

Erle Stanley Gardner, *The Case of the Borrowed Brunette.* A mysterious man named Mr. Hines has advertised a job for a woman who has to fulfill very specific physical requirements. Eva Martell, pretty but struggling in her career as a model, takes the job but her aunt smells a rat and hires Perry Mason to investigate. Her fears are realized when Hines turns up in the apartment with a bullet hole in his head. **Introduction by Otto Penzler.**

Erle Stanley Gardner, *The Case of the Careless Kitten.* Helen Kendal receives a mysterious phone call from her vanished uncle Franklin, long presumed dead, who urges her to contact Perry Mason. Soon, she finds herself the main suspect in the murder of an unfamiliar man. Her kitten has just survived a poisoning attempt—as has her aunt Matilda. What is the connection between Franklin's return and the murder attempts? **Introduction by Otto Penzler.**

Erle Stanley Gardner, *The Case of the Rolling Bones.* One of Gardner's most successful Perry Mason novels opens with a clear case of blackmail, though the person being blackmailed claims he isn't. It is not long before the police are searching for someone wanted for killing the same man in two different states—thirty-three years apart. The confounding puzzle of what happened to the dead man's toes is a challenge. **Introduction by Otto Penzler.**

Erle Stanley Gardner, *The Case of the Shoplifter's Shoe.* Most cases for Perry Mason involve murder but here he is hired because a young woman fears her aunt is a kleptomaniac. Sarah may not have been precisely the best guardian for a collection of valuable diamonds and, sure enough, they go missing. When the jeweler is found shot dead, Sarah is spotted leaving the murder scene with a bundle of gems stuffed in her purse. **Introduction by Otto Penzler.**

Erle Stanley Gardner, *The Bigger They Come.* Gardner's first novel using the pseudonym A.A. Fair starts off a series featuring the large and loud Bertha Cool and her employee, the small and meek Donald Lam. Given the job of delivering divorce papers to an evident crook,

Lam can't find him—but neither can the police. The *Los Angeles Times* called this book: "Breathlessly dramatic … an original." **Introduction by Otto Penzler.**

Frances Noyes Hart, *The Bellamy Trial.* Inspired by the real-life Hall-Mills case, the most sensational trial of its day, this is the story of Stephen Bellamy and Susan Ives, accused of murdering Bellamy's wife Madeleine. Eight days of dynamic testimony, some true, some not, make headlines for an enthralled public. Rex Stout called this historic courtroom thriller one of the ten best mysteries of all time. **Introduction by Hank Phillippi Ryan.**

H.F. Heard, *A Taste for Honey.* The elderly Mr. Mycroft quietly keeps bees in Sussex, where he is approached by the reclusive and somewhat misanthropic Mr. Silchester, whose honey supplier was found dead, stung to death by her bees. Mycroft, who shares many traits with Sherlock Holmes, sets out to find the vicious killer. Rex Stout described it as "sinister … a tale well and truly told." **Introduction by Otto Penzler.**

Dolores Hitchens, *The Alarm of the Black Cat.* Detective fiction aficionado Rachel Murdock has a peculiar meeting with a little girl and a dead toad, sparking her curiosity about a love triangle that has sparked anger. When the girl's great grandmother is found dead, Rachel and her cat Samantha work with a friend in the Los Angeles Police Department to get to the bottom of things. **Introduction by David Handler.**

Dolores Hitchens, *The Cat Saw Murder.* Miss Rachel Murdock, the highly intelligent 70-year-old amateur sleuth, is not entirely heartbroken when her slovenly, unattractive, bridge-cheating niece is murdered. Miss Rachel is happy to help the socially maladroit and somewhat bumbling Detective Lieutenant Stephen Mayhew, retaining her composure when a second brutal murder occurs. **Introduction by Joyce Carol Oates.**

Dorothy B. Hughes, *Dread Journey.* A big-shot Hollywood producer has worked on his magnum opus for years, hiring and firing one beautiful starlet after another. But Kitten Agnew's contract won't allow her to be fired, so she fears she might be terminated more permanently. Together with the producer on a train journey from Hollywood to Chicago, Kitten becomes more terrified with each passing mile. **Introduction by Sarah Weinman.**

Dorothy B. Hughes, *Ride the Pink Horse.* When Sailor met Willis Douglass, he was just a poor kid who Douglass groomed to work as a confidential secretary. As the senator became increasingly corrupt, he knew he could count on Sailor to clean up his messes. No longer a senator, Douglass flees Chicago for Santa Fe, leaving behind a murder rap and Sailor as the prime suspect. Seeking vengeance, Sailor follows. **Introduction by Sara Paretsky.**

Dorothy B. Hughes, *The So Blue Marble.* Set in the glamorous world of New York high society, this novel became a suspense classic as twins from Europe try to steal a rare and beautiful gem owned by an aristocrat whose sister is an even more menacing presence. *The New Yorker* called it "Extraordinary … [Hughes'] brilliant descriptive powers make and unmake reality." **Introduction by Otto Penzler.**

W. Bolingbroke Johnson, *The Widening Stain.* After a cocktail party, the attractive Lucie Coindreau, a "black-eyed, black-haired Frenchwoman" visits the rare books wing of the library and apparently takes a head-first fall from an upper gallery. Dismissed as a horrible accident, it seems dubious when Professor Hyett is strangled while reading a priceless 12th-century manuscript, which has gone missing. **Introduction by Nicholas A. Basbanes**

Baynard Kendrick, *Blind Man's Bluff.* Blinded in World War II, Duncan Maclain forms a successful private detective agency, aided by his two dogs. Here, he is called on to solve the case of a blind man who plummets from the top of an eight-story building, apparently with no one present except his dead-drunk son. **Introduction by Otto Penzler.**

Baynard Kendrick, *The Odor of Violets.* Duncan Maclain, a blind former intelligence officer, is asked to investigate the murder of an actor in his Greenwich Village apartment. This would cause a stir at any time but, when the actor possesses secret government plans that then go missing, it's enough to interest the local police as well as the American government and Maclain, who suspects a German spy plot. **Introduction by Otto Penzler.**

C. Daly King, *Obelists at Sea*. On a cruise ship traveling from New York to Paris, the lights of the smoking room briefly go out, a gunshot crashes through the night, and a man is dead. Two detectives are on board but so are four psychiatrists who believe their professional knowledge can solve the case by understanding the psyche of the killer—each with a different theory. **Introduction by Martin Edwards.**

Jonathan Latimer, *Headed for a Hearse*. Featuring Bill Crane, the booze-soaked Chicago private detective, this humorous hard-boiled novel was filmed as *The Westland Case* in 1937 starring Preston Foster. Robert Westland has been framed for the grisly murder of his wife in a room with doors and windows locked from the inside. As the day of his execution nears, he relies on Crane to find the real murderer. **Introduction by Max Allan Collins**

Lange Lewis, *The Birthday Murder*. Victoria is a successful novelist and screenwriter and her husband is a movie director so their marriage seems almost too good to be true. Then, on her birthday, her happy new life comes crashing down when her husband is murdered using a method of poisoning that was described in one of her books. She quickly becomes the leading suspect. **Introduction by Randal S. Brandt.**

Frances and Richard Lockridge, *Death on the Aisle*. In one of the most beloved books to feature Mr. and Mrs. North, the body of a wealthy backer of a play is found dead in a seat of the 45th Street Theater. Pam is thrilled to engage in her favorite pastime—playing amateur sleuth—much to the annoyance of Jerry, her publisher husband. The Norths inspired a stage play, a film, and long-running radio and TV series. **Introduction by Otto Penzler.**

John P. Marquand, *Your Turn, Mr. Moto*. The first novel about Mr. Moto, originally titled *No Hero*, is the story of a World War I hero pilot who finds himself jobless during the Depression. In Tokyo for a big opportunity that falls apart, he meets a Japanese agent and his Russian colleague and the pilot suddenly finds himself caught in a web of intrigue. Peter Lorre played Mr. Moto in a series of popular films. **Introduction by Lawrence Block.**

Stuart Palmer, *The Penguin Pool Murder*. The

first adventure of schoolteacher and dedicated amateur sleuth Hildegarde Withers occurs at the New York Aquarium when she and her young students notice a corpse in one of the tanks. It was published in 1931 and filmed the next year, starring Edna May Oliver as the American Miss Marple—though much funnier than her English counterpart. **Introduction by Otto Penzler.**

Stuart Palmer, *The Puzzle of the Happy Hooligan*. New York City schoolteacher Hildegarde Withers cannot resist "assisting" homicide detective Oliver Piper. In this novel, she is on vacation in Hollywood and on the set of a movie about Lizzie Borden when the screenwriter is found dead. Six comic films about Withers appeared in the 1930s, most successfully starring Edna May Oliver. **Introduction by Otto Penzler.**

Otto Penzler, ed., *Golden Age Bibliomysteries*. Stories of murder, theft, and suspense occur with alarming regularity in the unlikely world of books and bibliophiles, including bookshops, libraries, and private rare book collections, written by such giants of the mystery genre as Ellery Queen, Cornell Woolrich, Lawrence G. Blochman, Vincent Starrett, and Anthony Boucher. **Introduction by Otto Penzler.**

Otto Penzler, ed., *Golden Age Detective Stories*. The history of American mystery fiction has its pantheon of authors who have influenced and entertained readers for nearly a century, reaching its peak during the Golden Age, and this collection pays homage to the work of the most acclaimed: Cornell Woolrich, Erle Stanley Gardner, Craig Rice, Ellery Queen, Dorothy B. Hughes, Mary Roberts Rinehart, and more. **Introduction by Otto Penzler.**

Otto Penzler, ed., *Golden Age Locked Room Mysteries*. The so-called impossible crime category reached its zenith during the 1920s, 1930s, and 1940s, and this volume includes the greatest of the great authors who mastered the form: John Dickson Carr, Ellery Queen, C. Daly King, Clayton Rawson, and Erle Stanley Gardner. Like great magicians, these literary conjurors will baffle and delight readers. **Introduction by Otto Penzler.**

Ellery Queen, *The Adventures of Ellery Queen*. These stories are the earliest short works to feature Queen as a detective and are among the best of the author's fair-play mysteries. So many of the elements that comprise the gestalt of Queen may be found in these tales: alternate solutions, the dying clue, a bizarre crime, and the author's ability to find fresh variations of works by other authors. **Introduction by Otto Penzler.**

Ellery Queen, *The American Gun Mystery*. A rodeo comes to New York City at the Colosseum. The headliner is Buck Horne, the once popular film cowboy who opens the show leading a charge of forty whooping cowboys until they pull out their guns and fire into the air. Buck falls to the ground, shot dead. The police instantly lock the doors to search everyone but the offending weapon has completely vanished. **Introduction by Otto Penzler.**

Ellery Queen, *The Chinese Orange Mystery*. The offices of publisher Donald Kirk have seen strange events but nothing like this. A strange man is found dead with two long spears alongside his back. And, though no one was seen entering or leaving the room, everything has been turned backwards or upside down: pictures face the wall, the victim's clothes are worn backwards, the rug upside down. Why in the world? **Introduction by Otto Penzler.**

Ellery Queen, *The Dutch Shoe Mystery*. Millionaire philanthropist Abagail Doorn falls into a coma and she is rushed to the hospital she funds for an emergency operation by one of the leading surgeons on the East Coast. When she is wheeled into the operating theater, the sheet covering her body is pulled back to reveal her garroted corpse—the first of a series of murders **Introduction by Otto Penzler.**

Ellery Queen, *The Egyptian Cross Mystery*. A small-town schoolteacher is found dead, headed, and tied to a T-shaped cross on December 25th, inspiring such sensational headlines as "Crucifixion on Christmas Day." Amateur sleuth Ellery Queen is so intrigued he travels to Virginia but fails to solve the crime. Then a similar murder takes place on New York's Long Island—and then another. **Introduction by Otto Penzler.**

Ellery Queen, *The Siamese Twin Mystery*. When Ellery and his father encounter a raging forest fire on a mountain, their only hope is to drive up to an isolated hillside manor owned by a secretive surgeon and his strange guests. While playing solitaire in the middle of the night, the doctor is shot. The only clue is a torn playing card. Suspects include a society beauty, a valet, and conjoined twins. **Introduction by Otto Penzler.**

Ellery Queen, *The Spanish Cape Mystery*. Amateur detective Ellery Queen arrives in the resort town of Spanish Cape soon after a young woman and her uncle are abducted by a gun-toting, one-eyed giant. The next day, the woman's somewhat dicey boyfriend is found murdered—totally naked under a black fedora and opera cloak. **Introduction by Otto Penzler.**

Patrick Quentin, *A Puzzle for Fools*. Broadway producer Peter Duluth takes to the bottle when his wife dies but enters a sanitarium to dry out. Malevolent events plague the hospital, including when Peter hears his own voice intone, "There will be murder." And there is. He investigates, aided by a young woman who is also a patient. This is the first of nine mysteries featuring Peter and Iris Duluth. **Introduction by Otto Penzler.**

Clayton Rawson, *Death from a Top Hat*. When the New York City Police Department is baffled by an apparently impossible crime, they call on The Great Merlini, a retired stage magician who now runs a Times Square magic shop. In his first case, two occultists have been murdered in a room locked from the inside, their bodies positioned to form a pentagram. **Introduction by Otto Penzler.**

Craig Rice, *Eight Faces at Three*. Gin-soaked John J. Malone, defender of the guilty, is notorious for getting his culpable clients off. It's the innocent ones who are problems. Like Holly Inglehart, accused of piercing the black heart of her well-heeled aunt Alexandria with a lovely Florentine paper cutter. No one who knew the old battle-ax liked her, but Holly's prints were found on the murder weapon. **Introduction by Lisa Lutz.**

Craig Rice, *Home Sweet Homicide*. Known as the Dorothy Parker of mystery fiction for her memorable wit, Craig Rice was the first detective writer to appear on the cover of *Time* magazine. This comic mystery features two kids who are trying to find a husband for their widowed mother while she's engaged in sleuthing. Filmed with the same title in 1946 with Peggy Ann Garner and Randolph Scott. **Introduction by Otto Penzler.**

Mary Roberts Rinehart, *The Album*. Crescent Place is a quiet enclave of wealthy people in which nothing ever happens—until a bedridden old woman is attacked by an intruder with an ax. *The New York Times* stated: "All Mary Roberts Rinehart mystery stories are good, but this one is better." **Introduction by Otto Penzler.**

Mary Roberts Rinehart, *The Haunted Lady*. The arsenic in her sugar bowl was wealthy widow Eliza Fairbanks' first clue that somebody wanted her dead. Nightly visits of bats, birds, and rats, obviously aimed at scaring the dowager to death, was the second. Eliza calls the police, who send nurse Hilda Adams, the amateur sleuth they refer to as "Miss Pinkerton," to work undercover to discover the culprit. **Introduction by Otto Penzler.**

Mary Roberts Rinehart, *Miss Pinkerton*. Hilda Adams is a nurse, not a detective, but she is observant and smart and so it is common for Inspector Patton to call on her for help. Her success results in his calling her "Miss Pinkerton." *The New Republic* wrote: "From thousands of hearts and homes the cry will go up: Thank God for Mary Roberts Rinehart." **Introduction by Carolyn Hart.**

Mary Roberts Rinehart, *The Red Lamp*. Professor William Porter refuses to believe that the seaside manor he's just inherited is haunted but he has to convince his wife to move in. However, he soon sees evidence of the occult phenomena of which the townspeople speak. Whether it is a spirit or a human being, Porter accepts that there is a connection to the rash of murders that have terrorized the countryside. **Introduction by Otto Penzler.**

Mary Roberts Rinehart, *The Wall*. For two decades, Mary Roberts Rinehart was the second-best-selling author in America (only Sinclair Lewis outsold her) and was beloved for her tales of suspense. In a magnificent mansion, the ex-wife of one of the owners turns up making demands and is found dead the next day. And there are more dark secrets lying behind the walls of the estate. **Introduction by Otto Penzler.**

Joel Townsley Rogers, *The Red Right Hand*. This extraordinary whodunnit that is as puzzling as it is terrifying was identified by crime fiction scholar Jack Adrian as "one of the dozen or so finest mystery novels of the 20th century." A deranged killer sends a doctor on a quest for the truth—deep into the recesses of his own mind—when he and his bride-to-be elope but pick up a terrifying sharp-toothed hitch-hiker. **Introduction by Joe R. Lansdale.**

Roger Scarlett, *Cat's Paw*. The family of the wealthy old bachelor Martin Greenough cares far more about his money than they do about him. For his birthday, he invites all his potential heirs to his mansion to tell them what they hope to hear. Before he can disburse funds, however, he is murdered, and the Boston Police Department's big problem is that there are too many suspects. **Introduction by Curtis Evans**

Vincent Starrett, *Dead Man Inside*. 1930s Chicago is a tough town but some crimes are more bizarre than others. Customers arrive at a haberdasher to find a corpse in the window and a sign on the door: *Dead Man Inside! I am Dead. The store will not open today*. This is just one of a series of odd murders that terrorizes the city. Reluctant detective Walter Ghost leaps into action to learn what is behind the plague. **Introduction by Otto Penzler.**

Vincent Starrett, *The Great Hotel Murder*. Theater critic and amateur sleuth Riley Blackwood investigates a murder in a Chicago hotel where the dead man had changed rooms with a stranger who had registered under a fake name. *The New York Times* described it as "an ingenious plot with enough complications to keep the reader guessing." **Introduction by Lyndsay Faye.**

Vincent Starrett, *Murder on 'B' Deck*. Walter Ghost, a psychologist, scientist, explorer, and former intelligence officer, is on a cruise ship and his friend novelist Dunsten Mollock, a Nigel Bruce-like Watson whose role is to offer occasional comic relief, accommodates when he fails to leave the ship before it takes off. Although they make mistakes along the way, the amateur sleuths solve the shipboard murders. **Introduction by Ray Betzner.**

Phoebe Atwood Taylor, *The Cape Cod Mystery*. Vacationers have flocked to Cape Cod to avoid the heat wave that hit the Northeast and find their holiday unpleasant when the area is flooded with police trying to find the murderer of a muckraking journalist who took a cottage for the season. Finding a solution falls to Asey Mayo, "the Cape Cod Sherlock," known for his worldly wisdom, folksy humor, and common sense. **Introduction by Otto Penzler.**

S. S. Van Dine, *The Benson Murder Case.* The first of 12 novels to feature Philo Vance, the most popular and influential detective character of the early part of the 20th century. When wealthy stockbroker Alvin Benson is found shot to death in a locked room in his mansion, the police are baffled until the erudite flaneur and art collector arrives on the scene. Paramount filmed it in 1930 with William Powell as Vance. **Introduction by Ragnar Jónasson.**

Cornell Woolrich, *The Bride Wore Black.* The first suspense novel by one of the greatest of all noir authors opens with a bride and her new husband walking out of the church. A car speeds by, shots ring out, and he falls dead at her feet. Determined to avenge his death, she tracks down everyone in the car, concluding with a shocking surprise. It was filmed by Francois Truffaut in 1968, starring Jeanne Moreau. **Introduction by Eddie Muller.**

Cornell Woolrich, *Deadline at Dawn.* Quinn is overcome with guilt about having robbed a stranger's home. He meets Bricky, a dime-a-dance girl, and they fall for each other. When they return to the crime scene, they discover a dead body. Knowing Quinn will be accused of the crime, they race to find the true killer before he's arrested. A 1946 film starring Susan Hayward was loosely based on the plot. **Introduction by David Gordon.**

Cornell Woolrich, *Waltz into Darkness.* A New Orleans businessman successfully courts a woman through the mail but he is shocked to find when she arrives that she is not the plain brunette whose picture he'd received but a radiant blond beauty. She soon absconds with his fortune. Wracked with disappointment and loneliness, he vows to track her down. When he finds her, the real nightmare begins. **Introduction by Wallace Stroby.**